# Cruel Sister

# Cruel Sister

*A Haunted Ballad*

*Deborah Grabien*

THOMAS DUNNE BOOKS / ST. MARTIN'S MINOTAUR ≈ NEW YORK

FICTION

This is a work of fiction. All of the characters, organizations, and events portrayed in this novel are either products of the author's imagination or are used fictitiously.

THOMAS DUNNE BOOKS.
An imprint of St. Martin's Press.

www.thomasdunnebooks.com
www.minotaurbooks.com

Grabien, Deborah.
    Cruel sister : a haunted ballad / Deborah Grabien.
        p. cm.
    ISBN-13: 978-0-312-35757-3
    ISBN-10: 0-312-35757-5
    1. Musicians—Fiction. 2. Architectural historians—Fiction. I. Title.

PS3557.R1145C78 2006
813'.54—dc22

                                                          2006045489

First Edition: October 2006

10 9 8 7 6 5 4 3 2 1

*For the bands who keep the music alive*

# Acknowledgments

Thanks to the usual suspects: Beverly Leoczko, Juliana Egley, Anne Weber, and Rebekah Martin, plus my writer's-support cadre (Melissa Dodd, Bea Taumann, Ken Howard Wilan, Reen Bodo, and Stephanie Trelogan), Jennifer Jackson, Marina Drukman for the world's prettiest book jackets, Toni Plummer, and of course Ruth Cavin.

Special thanks are due my favourite Londoners, Roz Kaveney and Nick Wright, for sharing their memories of the Isle of Dogs. For help with Elizabethan research, thanks to Deena Fisher, Amy Parker, Alexandra Lynch, Connie Neil, Danielle, and Jon Black. I owe a debt of gratitude to both Beverly Williams of the Royal Engineers Museum and Steve Venus at the Royal Engineers Association, for providing crucial details about the vital, dangerous work done by Britain's postwar UXB units, as well as to Mat Andrews and the staff at the Bodleian Library at Oxford, both for information provided and for terrifying efficiency.

Saving my last thanks for Jacqui McShee and Pentangle, because it would be impossible to do a better version of the title song.

# Cruel Sister

# Prologue: January 1948

Under a choking black fog, in which the air itself seemed composed of ash from the winter coal fires, a battered ten-year-old Austin Tilley lorry rumbled and bounced along Westferry Road on the south-eastern edge of London's Isle of Dogs.

Two men, the older holding on to the door handle and the younger navigating the bumpy road with an urgency too fast for safety in the growing darkness of a January afternoon, had come across London from Ashley Gardens, Victoria. The older man, Maj. John Windle, made no comment about the speed; he'd given driving duty over to his promising nineteen-year-old recruit, Peter Cawling. If the boy was driving too quickly, he was also driving well.

Besides, the urgency was as real as the red-painted mudguard on the Austin's front, designating it as an emergency vehicle. Ten members of the Royal Engineers Bomb Disposal Unit's Company 33, under Windle's command, were already on site, building protective scaffolding in case the bomb required relocation, mounding earth, sandbagging a perimeter, establishing safe distances. . . .

"This bomb, sir—it wasn't one of the big ones, was it?" Cawling kept his eyes on the road, trying to anticipate turns where none could be seen. "Not a Herman, or one of the tricky buggers? I was down in Maintenance when the call came in."

"No—it's a basic SC, fifty kilos. Nothing unusual. And we've got lucky this time; it's on an empty patch of ground, right at the water-line. Only a small area to be evacuated by the local coppers, and of course, they'll have closed the road."

Windle peered ahead into the darkness. He had been born and raised in Sussex, and he thought he would never get used to the smell of those deadly smogs known as London particulars. He was not a fanciful man, but he could never convince himself that the reek of coal tar, the choke in the lungs, the red-shot blackness that settled on London like a stage magician's cloak, were not somehow images of hell. "Next to St. David's Square. The lads have worked with the local fire station—it's barely two minutes away. Bomb's fairly shallow, so they've been steaming the explosive out and setting up the rigging all day. We should be able to detonate the damned thing where it is, without any damage. Here's hoping, anyway."

Something, its form lost in the darkness, moved across the road in front of them. Cawling swerved the Austin slightly, swore under his breath, and steadied the vehicle. "Bloody dog," he said, and then, apologetically, "Sorry, sir. Scared me, that did. Wish people would keep their dogs tied up. I don't want to hit one, and it's hard to see in this muck."

"Never mind, Peter." Windle squinted, his eyes on the road ahead. "Slow down, will you? We're just passing Napier Avenue, and we should be just about there. You're going to want to stop a safe distance behind the barricades. That means a bit of a walk."

Cawling pulled over, and killed the engine. Together, they climbed out and began to walk eastward, along the periphery of Westferry, the main road on the the Isle of Dogs. Something roared past them, a lorry. Windle swore aloud, and blew out his breath as the heavy vehicle made a left turn and headed north.

"Blimey, sir! What's he doing out here, then?" Cawling was as startled as his superior officer. "Where's the local police? There shouldn't be any traffic out here—where's the barricade?"

"I don't know, but I'm going to find out," Windle said grimly.

"Someone's not done their job. Damnation! We can't afford any mistakes."

Windle's pace, already purposeful, quickened to urgency. The fuses in German bombs were tricky, and if the timer hadn't yet been removed, even the vibration of a passing lorry could set it off. The thought made Windle's blood run cold; he'd lost close to two dozen men in his long career as a bomb-disposal expert, and he was damned if he wanted to ever lose another one.

They rounded the curve of the street and saw, through the shifting curls of fog, that both of Company 33's Morris 8 CWT heavy cargo lorries were in place. Considerable work had clearly been done; scaffolding had been set up, and the company's experts in steaming and defusing were hard at work.

"Evening, sir." One of the company came up to meet them. "Oi, Pete. No trouble getting here? This is a proper muck, this fog."

"Mick, where in hell are the local coppers?" Windle, seriously disturbed, broke in. "There's not a single barricade across West-ferry. We were nearly run down by a lorry that came far too close to here—why aren't the local lads out there, diverting traffic? The entire area should have been closed off hours ago. What's going on here?"

"I don't know, sir." The subordinate, clearly startled by the news, stared at his commanding officer. "I went down to the local con-stabulary in Millwall myself, a good five hours ago. They said they'd see to it at once. We've not left the site—got most of the TNT steamed out, and should be ready to tackle the fuse fairly soon. I don't know why—"

"Accident." Another of the company had come panting up, his breath catching as he choked on the thick air. Behind them, to the south, the river Thames looked almost theatrically dirty and men-acing, melding with the streaky sky. "Sorry, sir—they've only just sent someone round to let us know. The Millwall captain and two of his officers ran head-on into another car—the entire shop's in chaos over it, everyone's been taken off to hospital, one of the lo-cal coppers is critical. With all the uproar, they never got the word out about the barricades. I've just sent two of our own blokes out to see to it." He wiped a hand over his face; the hand came away filthy with sweat and soot. "Bloody fog," he muttered.

Major Windle opened his mouth, but whatever he had intended to reply was lost. From Westferry Road, not twenty yards from the barricaded bomb, came a heavy rumble. The ground beneath their feet shook slightly. The lorry, a multiwheeler carrying supplies to the London docklands to the north, turned off, the growl of its engines dying out in the distance.

For a moment, the three men stood in frozen silence. Then the shouting began, as the men who had been working in proximity to the bomb erupted from the enclosure.

"It's live! The bloody timer's ticking—lorry set it off! It's live, take cover, everyone out, behind the barricades, hurry, get out, go!"

Windle stood his ground, shooing the men towards the safety of the perimeter. Thoughts ran through his mind, rapid-fire: *not residential damned good thing eight, nine, right that's everyone under cover maybe fifteen seconds how long before it goes, just enough time . . .*

He turned and sprinted for the shelter of the outer perimeter. A few feet from safety, he stopped. Something had caught the edge of his vision, something moving through the darkness and the ugly, swirling streams of fog.

There was someone here. A person, hurrying, not quite running, not away from the bomb, but directly towards it.

Windle strained his sight through the darkness. Was that a woman, what on earth was she wearing, what was she doing here? they'd said no residents, who could it be . . . ?

"Miss!" His voice rang out, urgent, stilling the excited chatter behind the sandbags into appalled silence. "Miss, no, that's a bomb! Get away from there!"

The nearest man to Company 33's commanding officer was Peter Cawling. He heard the shout, saw Windle turn and run, not for safety, but back towards the bomb, fifty kilograms of planted death left as a surprise package by Hitler's air force, ticking, live, about to go. . . .

4

"Sir!' Cawling, held hard by two of his mates, barely noticed the restraint. "Sir! No! Come back!"

"Miss! *Miss!* Get away get away get away . . ."

She ignored him. Windle had time, just before she disappeared into the bomb enclosure directly in front of him, moments before he reached the enclosure himself, to realise that the woman was just a girl, a teenager really, and that there was something very odd about her clothing, somebody's daughter had come out to the middle of this desolate dockside place in fancy dress, and now she was running, she must be mad, she was running straight into her own death, her arms were behind her and she was stumbling, oh no, no, there was no time left, no time, he couldn't help her, time was gone. . . .

The timer reached bottom, and clicked the fuse into place. The ticking stopped. There was a moment of silence.

The blast sent metal, and earth, and scraps of wooden scaffolding, forty feet into the air. The hollow that had held the bomb lifted, becoming a visible, positive mound of earth, and settled back to ground as a concave, a crater twenty feet wide, littered with the debris of a war now over, and with a new tragedy to report, back at the headquarters of the Royal Engineers, Bomb Disposal Unit, Ashley Gardens, Victoria.

# One

*There lived a lady by the North Sea Shore,*
*Two daughters were the babes she bore.*
*As one grew bright as did the sun,*
*So coal dark grew the other one.*

On a sun-washed April afternoon, Penny Wintercraft-Hawkes and Ringan Laine sat drinking cider on the grass behind Ringan's Somerset home, Lumbe's Cottage.

"Wasn't that a lovely wedding?" Penny's first action on arrival had been to kick off her shoes. She wriggled her bare toes in the grass. "I thought Char looked sensational. So did Julian, of course, but then, one expects that of him. What's the point in being a movie star if you can't look like Adonis at your own wedding?"

"Charlotte looked amazing. A definite change from the usual clothing of choice. I was half-expecting her to turn up at the door of St. Giles draped in purple and orange homespun burlap, but that wedding dress was brilliant on her. I noticed her hair still wasn't behaving, though; there were red-gold bits flying everywhere." Ringan, never comfortable in formal dress, had changed clothes entirely. He took a deep chug at his cider, and sighed. "I expect they'll be quite happy. They're weirdly well suited. And it was nice to be able to walk into Callowen House and not worry about ghosts. But how nice to be home again."

"Isn't it?" Penny agreed. "As much as I'd love to sit in this chair and get snockered on cider for the rest of the week, I have to head back to London tomorrow. And aren't the Broomfields coming here to rehearse for your new CD? Is that tomorrow as well? What time are they due to arrive? I'd love a few minutes with Jane before I head out. . . ."

The conversation continued, idle and pleasant: their notes on the wedding they'd just attended; Ringan's upcoming time in the studio recording a new CD with his band, Broomfield Hill; Penny's reluctant agreement to be interviewed for a television piece on the difficulties faced by women in theatre. Both of them were old enough to recognise and treasure these brief interludes of peace, and neither was inclined to break the moment, even for dinner. In the tall grass, the local cat, an orange Persian called Butterball, stalked butterflies and pounced on pillbugs. The afternoon sun touched the grass, the people, Glastonbury Tor in the near distance, with soft colour and vagrant warmth.

They had reached the point of Penny suggesting that scrounging for a scratch meal might be desirable, and Ringan bemoaning their lack of foresight in not stealing some of the sumptuous goodies Miles Leight-Arnold, Lord Callowen, had provided for his only daughter's nuptials, when they heard themselves hailed. Albert Wychsale, Baron Boult of Glastonbury, Ringan's landlord and Penny's business partner, strolled across the grass towards them.

"Hello, Ringan, Penny—I see you had the same idea I did, shedding the fancy plumage and pouring a good stiff drink." Albert, sixtyish and on the round side, settled carefully into a lawn chair. "Good to be back where it's quiet."

"Hello, Albert. What on earth are you doing back so soon? And do you want some cider?" Penny waved a languid hand towards the kitchen's Dutch doors. "There's lots. Only, I'm being a lazy cow and not getting up, so you'll have to fetch your own glass."

"Thank you, Penny, but no, I've already had some. It was the first thing I did when I got home, that and getting rid of the tie." Albert moved his fingers in the grass, and Butterball pounced. "Silly cat, are you glad to see everyone? Anyway, I'm home early because, having done my duty as a godparent and stood at Charlotte's side and supported the bride during her wedding, I consider that my responsibilities stop well short of watching a display of, er, well, foreplay."

Penny blinked. Ringan, quicker on the uptake, grinned. "Ah. I gather they'd reached the smooch-and-meaningful-glance stage?"

"Oh, no, that would have been tolerable, not to mention normal, and expected. But this is Char we're talking about, remember? No inhibitions at all? Julian was nibbling her ear and feeding her petits fours, and she was just beginning her announcement that she was glad everyone had come and now could we all get the hell out of it so that she and the groom could go upstairs and have a lovely slap-and-tickle?, thanks ever so, goodbye, and drive carefully. I heard the last of it as I joined a small throng of guests backing out as fast as our legs would carry us. Julian was grinning like a very handsome satyr." Albert shuddered. "She certainly does know how to empty a room."

On the lawn near Penny's chair, something suddenly buzzed furiously. Albert jumped. "What on earth was that?"

"My cell phone. Damn!" Penny scrabbled for the vibrating phone, and peered at the caller identification. Her jaw dropped as she registered the name. "Oh my God, it's my brother!"

She clicked the answer button. "Stephen! Is that really you? Right, sorry, it took me a minute. Where are you? Are you calling from Hong Kong? What?" She was silent for a long minute, listening, her face growing perceptibly slacker. "You're what—you did what? Are you joking? Do Mum and Daddy know?"

As she listened to the tinny rattle of her older brother's voice, Ringan and Albert watched her face, at all times mobile and reflective of her feelings, going through a remarkable variety of changes: pleasure, surprise, caution, bewilderment, and, at the end, something less easy to identify. The two men exchanged glances; Penny was not an easy woman to confound.

"Right," she said finally. She sounded stunned. "Well. Stephen, look, hang on a bit, would you? Just—give me a moment. This is a bit much to take in. I'll put you on to Ringan, but first of all, you can't really think I wouldn't be staggered. I mean, you're fifty-something, you've been gone for twenty years, and all of a sudden you're in London and you've got a wife? Who is she—no, not her name, you told me her name, and a very pretty name it is, too. So I've now got a sister-in-law called Tamsin. That's lovely. But where did you meet her?, what—?"

The rattle started up again, stopped. Penny shook her head, rather in the manner of a swimmer trying to clear water from her ears.

"All right," she told the phone. "Here. You talk to Ringan—yes, I'm aware you've never met, but really, as Scots go, he's very social. Not a hint of dour. And besides, if I understand you, this is his patch you want to be on, not mine. Here he is."

She handed the phone to Ringan, who, slightly slack jawed himself, was staring at her. "This is my brother Stephen on the phone," she told him, enunciating carefully and clearly. "He's back from living for donkey's years in Hong Kong, and he's got a new wife called Tamsin, and it seems that Tamsin is keen to build a house, and Stephen says you're what's needed for the purpose. Here. Cope with it, please."

Ringan, blinking in bewilderment at Penny, took the phone. "Hello? Ringan Laine here."

"Yes, I know." The voice was deep, and commandingly firm. "My sister told me she was giving you the phone. This is Stephen Wintercraft-Hawkes. I was wondering if you might be available to consult on an architectural project."

"Consult? What sort of project?" Ringan was beginning to understand Penny's reaction; there was something unexpected about Stephen, a kind of eccentricity. It was there in the very cadence of his voice. "Penny said something about building a house. I don't do anything in the way of modern architecture; I specialise in period restoration."

"Yes, I'm aware of that. But I believe you're just the person we need for this. Here's why. . . ."

It was now Penny and Albert's turn to watch Ringan's face go through a succession of rapid changes. Really, Albert thought,

Penny's brother Stephen seemed to have a peculiar effect on facial muscles.

"Yes, well, right. Of course." Ringan sounded as bemused as Penny had. "Okay, then. I'll give you my number—I'm busy rehearsing and recording for most of the next month, but I have got this weekend free. I could come up to London and have a look. Did I hear you say the building site is on the Isle of Dogs? Which bit—on the river itself? Bloody hell. No, nothing. Tell you what, does Saturday work for you? If it's all right with Penny, I can come up late Friday, and we can discuss this over lunch. Yes. Yes, of course. See you then. Yes."

He clicked the phone shut, and stared at Penny. There was a long silence.

"The Isle of Dogs?" Albert finally managed. "Did you say something about a building site on the Isle of Dogs? On the Thames?"

"He said that, yes. Land down there goes for, what? About two trillion quid per half cubic yard of dirt, or something?" Ringan looked at Penny. "Would you mind if I asked what your brother does for a living to make that kind of money? The only thing I can think of would be something like international arms merchant, or maybe official blackmailer of potentates."

"He's a banker and financial adviser for wealthy industrialists." Penny remembered her cider, and drained the glass. "But that land wasn't bought; I've just remembered about it. It was his coming-of-age gift from my uncle Stephen, and yes, that same uncle Stephen who was married to my eccentric French aunt. My brother was named for him. He's had that patch of ground for nearly thirty years. I remember that it wasn't worth much back then; it was really filthy. All polluted and whatnot—the Isle of Dogs used to be your basic mix of environmental disaster area and occasional bit of green parkland. But these days, I don't even want to think what a nice tidy patch of residential zoned building land on the Isle of Dogs, all cleaned up, is worth. However . . ." She looked meaningfully at Ringan. "Right now, I'm far more interested in this new wife and this consulting job they want to offer you. Since when are you willing to touch modern projects? Explain, please."

"The new wife—Tamsin? Right, Tamsin." Ringan was grinning now. "She apparently wants to build a Tudor-style manor house. And she wants it to be as exact a replica as possible, using as close to the original building materials as possible. Of course, even money on her also wanting central heating and a washer-dryer combo and double-glazed windows and all the rest of the mod cons. But there you are. I gather that either your brother or his wife has a direct pipeline to the Bank of England. And they're offering to pay me a hefty chunk of lolly—he said something about money not being an issue. So if you don't mind offering me houseroom, Pen, I'll sneak up to the City Friday afternoon, and we can meet up with your rich relations at Saturday lunch."


"Penny for them?"

Penny, at the wheel of her elderly Jaguar, spared Ringan a quick glance, and then brought her eyes back to the road. Driving in London on a pleasant Saturday morning, especially near an area as popular with tourists as the Tower, required as much concentration as possible.

"I was thinking about Tamsin, of course. Wondering what to expect." She muttered something rude under her breath as a taxi nearly clipped them. "My money's on a trophy wife. You know what I mean? Twenty years his junior, twee and spoiled, probably gorgeous. I'm envisioning blonde, skinny, legs up to her neck. I bet the wanting a Tudor repro house comes from reading too many historical romances. Trophy wife." She shook her head mournfully. "I thought my brother had some sense."

"So, you think a younger woman, latching on to a wealthy older banker, you mean?" Ringan considered it. "I don't know, Pen. Your brother sounded very crisp, very decided, and terrifyingly competent and sure of himself. And in any case, you don't get as successful as he seems to have got by being a fool, even about bed-room matters."

"Terrifyingly competent? Yes, that's Stephen to the life." She turned off towards the south. "But any man might make a fool of himself over a pretty girl. And Stephen's fifteen years my senior—he's well into midlife, and right at the age for that sort of thing." Her profile was unreadable. "I don't know—I suppose we'll find out soon enough."

"True." He glanced at her, and spoke gently. "You adore him, don't you?"

"Meaning, that's why I'm upset about the idea of him possibly being fool enough to get hooked by a harpy? Or do you mean, it's why I'm upset about the idea of him marrying at all?" She considered this, with some dismay. "Oh, damn, Ringan, now you've got me thinking about it, and truly? I don't know. I always did worship him when Candy and I were schoolgirls. Much-older brother—not to mention, only brother—and, what's more, mysterious. You know how it is, Ringan, or no, maybe you don't. You and Duncan and Roberta, you're all close in age. This is a rather different thing. He wasn't around much, but when he was, he seemed so splendid. He'd take us out for treats, and buy us things we weren't supposed to have, and always give us brilliant advice. I rarely saw him after I left for school, because he'd gone off to Hong Kong with the bank—an occasional phone call back then, an occasional email these days, strictly at holidays. So I suppose he is rather fixed in my head as my very own personal godlike older-brother-man-of-mystery figure, someone I don't want to share outside the family. Damn! I hope I'm not that petty. I don't want to be. Damned childhood remnants."

"You aren't petty, love, and those reactions are all perfectly natural. I was just wondering about it." Ringan patted her thigh, and changed the subject. "You know, I don't think I know anything at all about this bit of London. Why is it called an isle—it's not one, is it? And why dogs?"

"It's sort of an island—or really, more of a peninsula, now that I think about it." Penny kept her eyes on the road. "I'm not familiar with it either, except that it used to be the docklands; all the big shipping came here before container ships made it impossible to get to. Oh, and the Canada Tower is up nearer the north end of it—look, you can see it from here, it's the blinky pyramid thing. Tallest building in Europe, or something. As to the dogs, I haven't got a clue."

"Right." Ringan peered ahead, seeing the Pyramid coming nearer. This, he thought, was awfully flat ground. "Where are we meeting? On this patch of pricey turf he owns?"

"No, we're having lunch first. Some restaurant at the Canary Wharf, on Churchill Place, right near the Canada Tower, actually— a restaurant called Galliard. Sounds very trendy. It's probably some overpriced mix of bad fusion. You know, Thai meets Algerian, athletic chunks of overcooked lamb, sprinkled with turmeric and garnished with wilted parsley, or something." She slowed the car, and peered sideways. "Ah—there it is."

They parked the car as, somewhere nearby, church bells lightly chimed the hour. The restaurant, in an old warehouse that had been refurbished and restored within an inch of its life, boasted lofty ceilings, cool smooth tables and chairs, and a sense of roominess. Penny gave her name to a cheerful waiter and was told that her party had already arrived and been seated and was led to a corner table, Ringan following in her wake. He was surprised to realise how curious he was about this unknown member of Penny's family.

The man who stood at their approach was immediately recognisable as Penny's sibling. Here was her dark cloud of hair, though his was faded at the temples; here, too, were her generous mobile mouth and dark eyes, her sharp cheekbones, a more warlike version of her straight nose.

Ringan, who had known Penny for a dozen years, got his first look at her in the guise of exuberant baby sister; before this, he had only seen her as the careful older sister to the family's skittish youngest, Candida. This was a side of Penny he hadn't known existed. She flung herself into Stephen's arms, babbling with delight. Since she was actually a bit taller than he was, this manoeuvre left him staggering.

"Hello, little one. Do you realise I've not seen you in the flesh since you were at school?" Stephen, looking faintly amused, managed to disentangle himself from her enthusiastic grip. "The one time I know of that your theatre troupe did Hong Kong, I was away in Singapore on business. And you're not so little, now I look at you; you're all grown-up. I'm betting you lace up your own shoes, and everything."

"Shut your face, you." This was clearly an old Wintercraft-Hawkes family form of conversation. Ringan, weirdly charmed, watched in fascination. Lightly, affectionately, she punched Stephen on the arm. "So, you're really back to stay, then?"

"Yes, indeed. And if you've bubbled yourself out, perhaps I can introduce you to Tamsin?" He spoke over his shoulder to the woman in the booth behind him, who had been sitting and watching the family byplay with interest. "Here's Penny. We weren't actually raised by wolves; I'm sure her manners will come back to her in a moment. Training, and all that. Or maybe genetics; I'm never sure which covers what."

"Oh, my God, I'm sorry!" Penny was laughing, her face alight. "He's right, my manners went straight down the loo, but honestly, it's been decades since I've seen him, and he *is* my only brother, after all. I'm Penny. So, you're my new sister-in-law?"

"Indeed I am. Let me out, Stephen, do." Tamsin Wintercraft-Hawkes stood up, and edged her way out of the corner, past her husband. As she did so, Penny caught Ringan's eye in a tacit acknowledgement that every preconception they'd come up with between them had been completely, and ludicrously, wrong.

Tamsin, five feet tall at the most and ten stone in weight at the least, fit no known description of a trophy wife that Ringan had ever come across. Her smooth round face could have been any age between thirty-five and fifty; her brown eyes were enormous and bright behind a pair of thick glasses. Pale wavy hair showed silver streaks, which Tamsin made no attempt to disguise. She reminded Ringan of a very distinguished bird, small yet vital, perhaps a sparrow, or a robin, or even a . . .

". . . Finch," she said cheerfully, and Ringan jumped. It took him a moment to realise that she was responding to a question or comment of Penny's. "Much easier to sign when grading papers than 'Wintercraft-Hawkes,' so it's probably for the best I've retired from teaching. Excuse me? Oh, history—I taught Renaissance sociology for a few years, and then decided to specialise in the Tudor period. Such fun!"

Her voice was beautiful—musical and well educated. Ringan, trying to reconcile the preconception of the woman with the woman herself, took a second look and saw something in her face that made him wonder. It might have been a kind of ruthlessness, or simple detachment. Whatever it was, it took a tiny round woman with a mild voice and added an edge to her. Tamsin Wintercraft-Hawkes, née Finch, was somehow formidable.

"Tamsin's not just a teacher—she's also a writer." There was a fond pride in the look Stephen threw his wife. "Three enormous volumes about the social infrastructure of England during the Tudor years, for a university press." He thought for a moment. "At least, I think that's what they're about. I'm still trying to read them. I don't do the scholarly thing very well, I'm afraid, although I do read thrillers. Shall we get on with it? Let's order."

They had a very nice lunch, eating Galliard's beautifully cooked traditional English food and discussing a wide range of subjects, none of which included the main topic on Ringan's mind. Stephen, after leaving an impressive pile of bills on the table, led everyone out into the Saturday sunshine, and finally got to the point.

"Ah. The valet's brought our car around. Excellent." He gestured at a gleaming silver Mercedes. "If everyone's ready, shall we go have a look at the site we want to build on? Penny, I'll wait for you, and you can follow us down. Take Westferry Road, southwest. It'll be just beyond St. David's Square—you can't miss it, really. Big open patch of ground, with nothing on it. South side of the road, right by the water."

The drive down took less than fifteen minutes, even with Saturday traffic, and was done in near-silence. Penny was busy readjusting her thoughts about the newest member of her family, and Ringan was taking as much of a look as he could at the neighbourhood that would likely be his immediate surroundings for stretches of the next several months.

He was completely unfamiliar with the Isle of Dogs. Despite having lived in London for some years before settling down near Glastonbury, he couldn't remember ever having so much as set foot in this area before.

The immediate impression he got from it was one of absolute flatness. London has few hills of any note, but even by London standards the Isle of Dogs felt completely level. Ringan reflected that it would be impossible to get lost on this patch of ground—all you'd have to do would be to orient yourself to the blinking pyramid atop the Canada Tower, at least until something taller blocked your view. Of course, it might not have been so simple during the days before the Canary Wharf project.

He tried to mentally gather the bits he knew about the area. The Isle of Dogs, immediately recognisable on a map of London because of the huge curve dipping into the profile of the Thames, had been mostly industrial for a good long time. Ringan found himself wondering, what with the London Docks, whether the structures in those days, the cranes and gantries and whatnots, had been tall enough to provide a central visual reference point. And before the docks, before the original East India Pier had been built, what then? Had anyone lived here? Of course, people must have lived here; there was all of the borough of Millwall, on the western side of this deep spit of land. How . . . ?

"Wake up, darling. We're here."

Stephen had swung the Mercedes off the road, with half its bulk and two of its wheels up on the kerb. Penny gingerly followed suit, holding her breath as she eased the Jag's wheels up onto the bumpy kerb. As she did so, a lorry, overweighted and swaying and nearly as wide as the road, rumbled past, missing the side of the car by inches. Penny let her breath out, said something unprintable, and got out of the car. Ringan was already out.

"This was a bog at some point, wasn't it?" he asked. "Or a marsh, or something? Some kind of wetlands, anyway." He bounced in place a few times letting the balls of his feet take his weight. "Has the ground been checked for building-code suitability? It's so flat, and feels so wet, and there's a sensation that the ground's moving underfoot."

"Really?" Tamsin, her hair lifting a bit in a soft light breeze blowing inland off the Thames, had come up behind him. She bounced a bit, experimentally. "It feels quite firm and dry to me, which is a good thing since we want to put our house on it. Yes, to both your questions; we've had the borough people out, and we're good to go on the house. And yes, this was actually Stepney Marsh—they began a massive drainage project back around the time the Children's' Crusade was going on, early thirteenth century. For a while, this was actually some lovely land for growing veggies."

Penny, having made certain that her beloved car was well out of the path of any oversized vehicles, joined the others. "How long did it stay drained?" she asked curiously. "I mean, water has a way of reclaiming any land it wants. Not just the river, either—you see that out in the fen country."

"About two centuries. Really, it was a very successful experiment, considering the technology that was available to them at the time." Tamsin turned to Stephen, who was standing a few feet away, surveying an empty and sizeable patch of land. "Stephen, darling, you're looking pensive. What's wrong?"

"Nothing. Just the opposite, actually: I'm inwardly beaming with pride of ownership. This is a much-larger patch than I'd remembered its being after so many years away."

He was right about the size. Ringan, eyeballing the area, estimated the better part of an acre. The ground was scrubby, with very short grasses and a few oddly stunted trees that looked like small, unhealthy cousins of lime trees. Near the road, on the north-western edge of the property, was a kind of crater, a depression about twenty feet across. Other than that, the land was flat.

"Dear God." Penny, her eyes elsewhere, sounded almost reverent. "Would you look at that view? You can see the masts of the *Cutty Sark,* clear across the Thames!"

The aged uncle for whom Penny's brother had been named had done his namesake proud. The vista was postcard quality, absolutely staggering: this land ran all the way down to the river, offering a completely unimpeded look at the Thames, the boats, the borough of Deptford, and the inlet to Deptford Creek, southward across the water.

"Fabulous, isn't it? And the drop-off to the water is perfect—just steep-enough pitch to minimise flooding risks. I'd be willing to wrestle the powers in charge for the privilege of building our own dock if either of us had the slightest interest in sailing." Tamsin began picking her way towards the southern edge of the property. "Come along," she called over her shoulder. "If you stand at the far bit here, you can see the Millennium Dome and most of Green-wich, across the river."

"It's absolutely incredible." Penny sounded enraptured. "If I lived with that view, I'd never get any work done. Honestly, I don't think I'd ever even leave the house—I'd just spend my entire life staring out the windows, and have all my meals sent in. I may have to ditch my Muswell Hill flat and set up a squatter's camp under your front windows, Tamsin."

"Yes, well, we're going to have to discuss windows." Tamsin was grinning now. "Earlier Tudor houses had very little in the way of them, actually—Hardwick Hall, Bess of Hardwick's house, was the talk of the town when she put all those bizarre bits of glass in the walls. Shock! Horror! It simply wasn't done. However, I'm planning to buck tradition on that, and going post-gothic with it. As Stephen has pointed out to me, what's the point of having a view like this if you don't take advantage of it? Besides, I hate dark houses."

"True." Ringan looked a bit troubled. "You know, just looking at this, I'd love to take it on. But honesty compels me to point out that I've always consulted on existing structures. I'm no sort of designer. There are a few firms, right here in London, that do this sort of thing from the ground up, period blueprints and all. I can name at least two that specialise in period-reproduction properties—they're very good, as well, and they do the research, everything from woods available at the time to door hinges. It seems wasteful to pay me as well. Are you sure you wouldn't rather be dealing with them?"

"We are dealing with them, and so will you be, if you take this on." Stephen sounded mildly amused. "We've been on to BIDA, and they've hooked us up. That part is taken care of. They're dealing with the zoning, water feed, electrical, all that. Also, we've got some brilliant architects. You don't have to worry about the plans. That's already in hand."

"I feel as if I'm listening to a language I don't know," Penny said plaintively. "BIDA? What's that, please?"

"British Interior Design Association," Ringan told her. "A superb organisation, one of the best resources anywhere for this sort of project. I've worked with them before, many times. The thing is . . ." He took a breath. "Look, Stephen, Tamsin, I want to make damned sure I understand you before I commit to anything, even verbally. Just what is it, precisely, that you want to hire me to do?"

"It's about the feel." Tamsin spoke up at once. "As Stephen says, we have a firm of architects lined up and ready to go. The house is going to be a classic Elizabethan floor plan, in the shape of an E: central reception, wings, staircase at the back. Two bedrooms, two offices, two full baths, and a downstairs loo for guests. All that, and windows, of course. We'll have a greatroom overlooking the river. All that's just basic design work. I trust them to do that for us. But the—the honesty of it, that's going to be beyond them. Because a designer, a researcher, an interior decorator—they're not what's needed for the feel of it. For that, well . . ."

Her voice trailed away. Penny suddenly understood.

"You want a folklorist, don't you?" She saw that Ringan's beard, which had been jutting slightly, had relaxed; he'd got where she was heading. "You want someone who can stand under your not–Tudor windows, presumably all double-glazed, in the middle of all that half-timbering and period furniture, and sing a nice juicy ballad from the period, and see if it clashes with its surroundings. That's it, isn't it?"

Tamsin was silent a moment. Stephen was looking at his sister, surprise and dawning respect in his eyes. Tamsin smiled suddenly, an extraordinarily open and beautiful smile.

"Well, yes. That's exactly right." She leaned forward unexpectedly, stood on tiptoe, and planted a light kiss on Penny's cheek.

"You were quite right, Stephen," she said. "I do like your family."

# Two

*A knight came riding to the lady's door;*
*He travelled far to be their wooer.*
*He courted one with gloves and rings,*
*But he loved the other above all things.*

The following week, after three intensive days in rehearsal with Broomfield Hill, Ringan locked up Lumbe's Cottage and headed for a week's stay in London.

He was surprised to find himself nervous. There were several things contributing to his sense of uncertainty. The major cause was obvious enough: he was about to take on a job doing something he'd never really tried his hand at before. There was also the timing of the Isle of Dogs project; since it came when it did, he was going to have to juggle the schedules of his two livelihoods with pinpoint precision. Lastly, he was going to be staying at Penny's flat without Penny for the first time in their long relationship.

Still, the cramp of nerves in his stomach was as unexpected as it was disturbing. It had been there, he realised, since he'd agreed to take on Stephen and Tamsin's project or, more accurately, since he'd stepped out of the car onto that barren acre of land on the Isle of Dogs.

He considered it, heading northeast towards London. Something about the situation, whether the job offer or the people involved or something else entirely, had planted an edgy little barb in him. It would be wise, he decided, to track it down to its source and confront it.

He turned his battered Alfa onto the A303, and headed for the main highway into town. As the car covered the distance, his mind was teasing at the question, busily taking each possibility and examining it.

One possible source he could, and did, eliminate at once. It wasn't the people. He had liked both Stephen and Tamsin right off—there was nothing there to induce this level of nerves. Nor was it his own agreement to take on the responsibility of authenticating the feel of their house as it went up around him. He had been very clear with them about this being a first for him, and they'd understood and accepted the fact. Anticipatory nervousness at doing something new was only to be expected.

So what had set up this small alarm, which refused to be shut off? Not the people, not the job itself. The schedule surely wasn't it either, he thought. He kept one eye on the road signs, looking for Staines and the entry to the M3. For most of his adult life, he'd been juggling studio time that had already been booked and paid for with sudden demands for his restoration expertise. He felt his own beard bristle with concentration and some frustration. What in hell was causing this?

*The location.*

The answer came simply, with the certainty of truth behind it. Ringan looked up ahead, saw an exit for a roadside cafe, and abruptly pulled off the highway and into the carpark, killing the Alfa's engine.

That was it, of course. It wasn't the project or the people or the fine line he was going to have to walk to balance the music with the architecture; it was the land itself. There had been something about the Isle of Dogs that had worried him from the moment Penny had turned onto Westferry Road. There was no reason for it at all that he could find, but the fact remained: something about this ancient, once polluted, and now expensively residential corner of the Tower Hamlets had got under his skin, and not in a good way.

*A crater, twenty feet across, too big for a grave . . .*

"Oh, put a sock in it." Enough was enough; he was spooking

himself. His memory told him that he was exaggerating the extent of the reaction he'd had at the time. Suddenly claustrophobic, he got out of the Alfa, stretching his legs, thinking. A sandwich, he decided, wouldn't come amiss, nor would something cold to drink. The day was warm, and his throat was dry with what he insisted to himself was road dust.

*Stunted little lime trees, but none anywhere near that crater. What is that about, then?*

"Right," he said aloud, "that's enough of that." He shut his thoughts off and walked into the café, grabbing a week-old newspaper on the way in. He spent the next forty minutes munching a ham-and-cheese sandwich and drinking lemonade, distracting himself with football scores and half-naked Page Three girls and the mind-boggling stupidity of, it seemed, every leader of every nation on earth.

By the time he'd reached the outskirts of London, he'd come to a decision. He was due to meet some friends for dinner that night, and have a few beers at a North London pub afterward. Penny was already on her way to a three-week-long engagement on the Continent with her acting troupe, the Tamburlaine Players. He had his keys to her flat in his pocket, and no other commitments. There were hours of daylight left, and no reason not to go and have a second look. Instead of turning north towards Muswell Hill, Ringan skirted Central London entirely and drove straight east, heading for the Isle of Dogs.

It was still warm and sunny when he passed the cluster of buildings just to the west of Stephen and Tamsin's land. The air was light and soft, and tasted of spring. As he climbed out of the Alfa and walked over to the building site, Ringan thought he smelled the faintest tang of Thames water on the breeze. In the medium distance the masts of the China tea clipper *Cutty Sark,* moored at the Greenwich Pier across the river, swayed against the southern sky.

*Miss no get away*

Ringan's steps slowed, then stopped entirely. One foot rested on the pavement, the other on the scrubby short-grass cover of the

Wintercraft-Hawkes property. He lifted a hand to his brow. It came away wet with clammy moisture. Out of nowhere, he was dizzy.

*You'll not have him, not now, not ever, all you have now I'll have tomorrow, he's mine, mine*

"What . . . ?" It was suddenly intolerable, vertigo, cold sweat, his eyes wouldn't focus. The masts of the *Cutty Sark,* those weren't masts, they were gibbets or spikes, places where the heads of criminals and their rotting bodies could serve as a warning and a brutal display of power to those who could claim no power at all. . . .

*get away get away get away*

The soft blue sky and scudding white clouds seemed to freeze, coalesce, reshape. Ringan took one faltering step forward, and felt his knees give out under him.

He sat down hard, landing with an audible thump on a patch of turf that would, some months down the road, probably be covered by a stone balustrade, or perhaps a welter of roses. Swallowing hard on an uprush of nausea, he leaned forward and tucked his head between his knees, closing his eyes and wrapping his hands around his shins. He stayed that way until the sickness and dizziness passed. He was aware of a vague hope that no one would pass by and notice him, but he was far too dizzy to really care.

Eventually, he relaxed his hands and forced himself to open his eyes. Above him, the sky was once more simply the sky, and at the periphery of his vision, the *Cutty Sark*'s rigging swayed and settled as the tide moved beneath its hull. He got shakily to his feet and stood, breathing deeply, feeling his heartbeat even itself out.

Directly in front of him was the crater he had wondered about. He stared at it, at its smooth edges, at its depth of perhaps four inches below the surrounding ground, at the scrubby grass and black-eyed Susan dotting its surface.

*Miss no get away*—had he heard that? What *had* he actually heard before that attack of vertigo?

He circled the crater. *Crater,* he decided, was too grand and formal a word for it; *depression* would be more accurate. Oddly, he could not shake the feeling that this hole in the ground had a history of its own. He wondered if Stephen knew anything about it. *It must,* Ringan thought, *be more than a simple sinkhole;* the edges were too defined for that, and the height difference between the depression and its surrounding earth was too small.

*too big for a grave . . .*

He walked around it, searching for something, anything, to mark this place, to tell him how it had come to be there, and when, and what it might be. It looked, in some way he couldn't really define, as if it might be a tiny caldera of sorts: the remnant of a volcano, something that had blown fire and earth into the sky in some sort of eruption, settling back, leaving this hole behind.

But there was nothing to be seen—no plaques, no markers, nothing at all.

Ringan went back to the car, and lowered all the windows. He felt badly in need of a good stiff breeze. As he was fastening his seat belt, he stopped for a moment, listening to what sounded like someone's dogs barking off in the distance.


Three days later, having signed a precisely worded contract whose language bore the clear imprint of Stephen's legal and corporate training, Ringan met with the representative of the architectural firm that had been hired to design Tamsin's Elizabethan manor.

He'd had to push away his reluctance to go anywhere near the Isle of Dogs, and the task of doing so had been difficult enough to surprise him. What had happened to him—voices, weakness, dizziness, the sense of the past blurring with the present—was all too familiar. It reminded him of another soft, balmy day, his first as owner of Lumbe's Cottage, when he was hit by weakness and cold and the feeling of someone standing unseen, at his back, in an empty house. That someone had turned out to be a girl called Betsy Roper, dead nearly two centuries, tied to the place that had been the only home she'd known in life, the place where she had drawn her last breath.

Since then, he and Penny had dealt with other ghosts. Yet Ringan had come to believe himself largely immune to murmurs from the world beyond the perimeters of human vision or understanding. Every time, it had been Penny's sensitivity to it, her inability to shut out the past, that had allowed these remnants of times now gone to clear the dust of age from the road to the present.

Ringan too had been touched by those remnants, but he felt he had never been completely open to them or engaged by them. And this was despite the fact that the story of every ghost they had been forced to confront had been kept alive in the very songs Ringan himself played for a living.

What had happened three days earlier had shaken Ringan free of his comfort zone. Something had wakened or moved, or perhaps just lifted an as-yet-invisible head, and had stared straight at him. This time Penny could not be held accountable for triggering it; at that very moment she was probably somewhere in Italy, lacing herself into the first costume of the Tamburlaines' tour. Whatever this was, it was his entirely his problem.

He pulled the Alfa half onto the pavement, behind an innocuous Volvo. The architect, it seemed, had got here before him. Ringan walked across, aware of a strong disinclination to set foot on that patch of earth that felt so wet and shaky to him and yet perfectly solid to its owners, and found himself confronting a pleasant-looking man in his forties.

"Mr. Laine? A pleasure to meet you—I've seen some of your work. I'm Marcus Childe, with Sutliffe and Rhoades. I'm the lead architect for this project. Please, do feel free to call me Marcus." He held out a hand. Behind a pair of elegant gold-framed glasses, his eyes were a clear hazel.

"Thanks, Marcus, I will. And it's just Ringan, here." As he shook the man's hand, Ringan wondered for a moment what Childe meant by the reference to having seen some of Ringan's work. Restoration work? Musical shows? "This is a first for me, consulting on something that doesn't exist yet."

Marcus grinned. "It's a first for me, as well. Not the nonexistent bit, I specialise in those, but working with clients like the Wintercraft-Hawkeses. They're remarkable people."

He paused, clearly curious, but visibly uncertain as to how to ask questions without risking offence. Ringan, who found him congenial enough, decided to break any potential ice straight away, and offered information.

"Aren't they, though?" he agreed. "Stephen's sister Penny is my significant other—has been for the best part of a dozen years. She's a good bit younger than her brother, and I hadn't met him before—he'd been off working in Hong Kong since she left school, or so I gather. He's—interesting. Awe-inspiring."

"He's all of that. Very smart and reasonable, though. And his wife, of course, is a leading authority on the period. Most of our clients have some idea as to what they want, but they tend to only know the surface details. It's all pretty vague. Professor Finch—Mrs. Wintercraft-Hawkes, I should say—knows her stuff."

"It doesn't surprise me to hear that, not at all." Ringan had suddenly remembered the sense of detachment, of something that might be ruthlessness, he had felt from Tamsin. Maybe, he thought, it was simply that she was a scholar; heaven knew, scholars, especially period specialists, were an odd and formidable breed. . . .

Marcus had obviously relaxed. His voice held an overtone of rueful amusement. "When she talks about dividing the storeys with classical entablatures, or says she's considering Flemish curved gables for the northern façade, I know I've got the client of my fondest dreams to work with. It makes a pleasant change."

"You mean, because most of your clients will ask for some of those pretty curvy bits, you know, the ones that are all made of wood, and get hung over windows and things?" Ringan was grinning. "I feel your pain. Where it gets really miserable is when half the members of a local so-called preservation society ask for the pretty curvy bits. And when they're asking for them on a church from the eleventh century, nothing but straight lines from top to bottom, it gets really tricky, being polite. There are the days I just want to yell at the top of my lungs."

"I can imagine." Marcus nodded towards the Volvo, a few yards away. "If you have a few minutes to spare, I'd love to show you some of the early sketches. Mrs. Wintercraft-Hawkes is leaning towards using Montacute House as a sort of prime example of what she wants for basic E-style architecture, and I must say, it's a classic choice, with a few alterations, of course. Shall we? There's virtually no wind, and it's quite dry out here, so we can spread them out, and you can have a look. Unless you'd rather come back to the office? We're just up the road, at Canary Wharf."

"Actually, all things being equal, I'd much prefer to look at them right here. *In situ,* so to speak—I can get a much-better sense of things, standing on the actual build site."

To Ringan, who loved the look of a well-executed blueprint, the plans were objects of beauty. They were clear, delicately done, and very easy to read. Marcus unrolled the first, found a handful of small stones, and weighted down the corners.

"Ground floor first." Mindful of his trousers, which were gabardine and expensive, he carefully levered himself down to his knees. Ringan, in jeans, had no such concerns. "Front entry will face due north—nice clear view of the Canada Tower from the front stairs and windows. That's going to provide some very interesting contrasts, which may have been in her mind." He ran one fingertip horizontally, just above the actual drawing. "A long greatroom— it's rather the equivalent to the Clifton Maybank corridor at Montacute House, which of course was added a good two centuries after Montacute was built. Here, it won't be a corridor, it'll be the entire central rear of the house, ground floor with a gallery above it, facing the river."

"My God, what a lot of windows! Tamsin told us she was going to buck the early Tudor tradition when it came to the windows, and run rampant with them. She wasn't kidding, was she? This entire wall is mostly glass. What a view they're going to have!" Ringan raised his head, framing the south bank of the Thames with the classic rectangular gesture of both hands. "She's broken up the glass with—what are these thin dividing columns going to be made of? Not wood, surely?"

"Stone. This close to the water, we want something that's as damp-resistant as possible. And stonework is a good Elizabethan conceit, after all." Marcus pointed to the drawing. "Now we get down to the nitty-gritty. Wings, of course, that being one of the definitions of the E-style. We agreed that because she's going for larger rooms in smaller quantity, the slender wings with only four rooms per wing would be the most pleasing aesthetically. What do you think?"

"Me? I think it's Tamsin's house. I think she's got the know-how and the details in her head. I also think she's got the cheque-book." Ringan bounced a bit, shaking off a cramp. "But even if I had no connection with them on a family basis, I'd be applauding. If I'm reading this thing properly, it looks to be a piece of rare good sense on display here: modern details like room size and access, melding with the period details she wants and understands. Beautiful. What are the four rooms per wing? She mentioned something about guest bedrooms and offices, as in computer rooms or studies. Is that still the idea?"

"Mostly, but that's on the first floor. The ground floor wings are more service-oriented: kitchen and dining areas in the east wing, with a spare loo and a laundry room, and two guest bedrooms and a connecting full bath in the west wing. Upstairs, the wings are more symmetrical. Here, I'll show you."

He unrolled a second drawing, this one a semi-transparency, and overlaid the first drawing with it. Suddenly, with a kind of alchemy, the two sections came together, and right before Ringan's eyes, there was the house: windows, a drive-up to the front façade, a broad central section with two slender wings. A vagrant wind, tasting faintly of the river, riffled the edges of the drawings.

"And of course," Marcus said cheerfully, "there will be gardens. With all this land, they'd be mad not to."

"True." Ringan straightened up. His gaze had fallen on the

crater. "What were you planning to do about that crater over there? Fill it in, to even it out?"

"Crater?" Marcus, who was rolling his plans together with expert speed, paused, and followed Ringan's pointing finger. "Oh, you mean the bomb cavity? I don't know yet. I haven't discussed that with our clients. We're a long way off from dealing with the gardens, and that's far from the house itself, of course."

*Get away get away get away. . . .* "Bomb cavity?" Ringan kept his voice casual. "You mean, what, something like an IRA bomb went off here? Or are we talking about wartime?"

"Wartime." Marcus tucked the plans under one arm and turned towards his Volvo, Ringan falling into step beside him. "Second World War, I believe, or, actually, rather after. There was some tragedy associated with it—bloke in charge of the bomb squad was killed trying to rescue a child who'd wandered onto the bomb site, or some such thing. I don't know the details, but I am fairly sure it was a few years after the war, and that it was one of those unexploded bomb stories, where something went wrong and the bomb went off before they could muck all the explosives out of it and clear the area. This was just an empty field, of course—it's not as if there was a house here, or anything."

Ringan was conscious of a deep sense of relief. "No house here? Marcus, can I ask you question? Has there ever been a house here? So far as you know, I mean?"

"No, there hasn't." There was a faint puzzled line between Marcus Childe's brows; something in Ringan's voice, a kind of intensity, had caught his attention. "I had a look at the records for this patch before I began to rough out the plans. There hasn't been anything here for at least four hundred years, and probably there was no one living here before that, either. Why?"

"No reason. Curious, that's all." They'd reached the parked cars. Ringan shook hands with his new associate. "So, what's the timeframe on getting started here? Plan approval, code approval, all that?"

"Soon. We're probably about a week away from actually breaking ground for the foundation and plumbing work—Stephen has a lot of influence, and the zoning people, light and electric and whatnot, have been moving very fast on this one."

"Excellent." Ringan opened his car door. "Can you ring me up when you know? I'll stay in London for about two weeks—I live in Somerset, just outside Glastonbury—but I can always come up when needed. I'll want to block the time out, since my band has studio time booked, and I don't imagine I'm going to be needed much here during the very early stages. Let me give you my numbers, and also the number at Penny's flat. She's on tour, but I'll be staying at her place for the next little while."

They drove off in opposite directions, Ringan heading northwest. The relief he felt was so intense, it was making him giddy.

There had been no house on that patch of ground. If Marcus was right, there had never been a house there. And whatever tragedy had left its mark and its echo in that bomb cavity, it was purely modern and had nothing whatsoever to do with music.


Alone in Penny's bed for the first time, Ringan found himself unable to sleep.

Despite the familiarity and comfort of his surroundings, his mind would simply not shut down. His eyes were open in the darkness as the internal pictures kept cycling in a continual dance: the house that would soon begin to take on shape and substance on the Isle of Dogs, his own conversation with Marcus Childe and the information about the Wintercraft-Hawkes land, the choice and placement of tunes for Broomfield Hill's upcoming CD.

Ringan shifted, decided the new position was no more comfortable than the first, and shifted again. This, he told himself was ridiculous. There was nothing in the varied threads of thought, however tangled they might be, to keep him awake. He wasn't even taking advantage of having the entire bed to himself; habit had planted him on his usual side, and he found himself inclined to stay there. So why the wakefulness?

*There was some tragedy associated with it—bloke in charge of the bomb squad was killed trying to rescue a child who'd wandered onto the bomb site, or some such thing.*

He rolled onto his back, staring at the ceiling. The memory of Marcus Childe's words was exact; it was his own memory that was proving dodgy. What had he heard, what had those odd chopped fragments of voices said, and what had it been about those voices that had kicked his legs out from under him? *Get away miss,* or something like that? That would certainly fit Childe's story of the bomb squad tragedy. . . .

*You'll not have him, not now, not ever, all you have now I'll have tomorrow, he's mine, mine*

Ringan sat up, the light summer duvet falling away from him. A damp, chilly sweat had broken out along his hairline.

That was it. A woman's voice, that had been, surely? He remembered that much, and remembered it clearly. Not a child's voice, a woman's: high, vicious, passionate, implacable. There was something else about it, too, something he ought to be able to touch, identify, place, but it kept teasing away from him, maddening, just out of reach. . . .

"Oh, bollocks." With some surprise, he heard his own voice spiral out into the night. He took a deep breath. "Right. Knock it off. Don't be an idiot. You're embroidering. You couldn't possibly remember all that." *You'll not have him, not now, not ever. . . .* "Oh, hell!"

The night offered no response, and Ringan, suddenly dizzy, reached for the duvet and curled back up into bed. *Right,* he thought, *that's enough of that. Focus. Think about something else. Order of songs to be recorded, that should do it.*

After a while, his breathing steadied. With snippets of song choices easing him into rest, Ringan finally slept.

*You'll not have him, not now, not ever*

Suddenly, shockingly, he was wide awake. Something seemed to have taken him from Penny's bed and put him entirely elsewhere, dropping him into the middle of some bizarre alternate reality.

He was on his feet and standing, dressed in his usual street cloth‑
ing. How had he got here? And where in hell was he? Why
couldn't he remember?

A cold wind blew across his face, riffling his beard. The sky
above him was grim, bleak, shot through with the shadows and
sharp edges that mean an English winter. Off in the distance, birds
called out harshly, and dogs were barking, baying, on the hunt.
Touching his tongue experimentally to his lips, he caught the harsh
tang of Thames salt. He looked around him, but there was nothing
to see, just empty flatland, with water close by. There were no
structures anywhere on the horizon. This land, wherever it was,
was empty.

Completely disoriented, he strained his senses, trying to find
something, anything, to tell him what was happening. From just
behind him, down at the water‑line, a voice came, gasping, uneven,
choking: *No Margaret please please I'll stand away I'll give him up he'll
be as nothing to me no Sister please oh please*

The voice faltered, stopped, died. There was a horrible gurgle,
the sound of a human throat trying to clear itself of water, the
voice of a woman trying vainly, desperately, to protect her lungs.

It came to Ringan that he was standing there listening to some‑
one being forcibly and deliberately drowned.

He turned. *South,* he thought, *turn south towards the river, how do
you know it's the river?, never mind, doesn't matter, get off your arse and
do something, there's murder being done, a girl's being killed and you've got
to stop it, turn south.*

His head felt enormous, heavy, slow to move as it fought his
every neural demand. The sheer effort threatened to break him in
half. Yet he was moving; more and more of this unfamiliar envi‑
ronment began to solidify, taking shape, becoming visible. He saw
the Thames, then a familiar curve of land, seen recently—the infor‑
mation, when or where he had seen it, danced maddeningly just
out of his memory's reach. A few small shapes, bobbing in the tide
on both banks, near and far. Across the river, to the east, atop an
enormous palace of creamy stone, brightly coloured pennons

streamed out in the winter wind, jarringly gay and inviting against a grim dark sky.

He heard a harsh gurgle of sound, a final cry of water-choked begging, the last whisper of a woman's name—*Margaret please*—a rattle of breath. He brought his gaze downward, closer, too close.

Not twenty yards away, a dreadful tableau presented itself. There was a woman standing there, but was she a woman? She seemed hardly more than a girl, a mere teenager. Her long, full-skirted gown, what Ringan could see of it, was a vivid peacock blue; the bottom half, exquisitely and ornately embroidered, was soaked through and torn at the hem, the rest splashed with Thames mud, the dress likely ruined, impossible to clean or repair. Her hair, a cascade of flaming ginger, hung down her back. Her shoulders were heaving, perhaps with emotion, perhaps with exhaustion, perhaps with simple cold; her pale skin seemed blue with the winter chill. Her hands, with their thick short fingers, were partially clenched at her side.

At her feet was something he could only partly see. What he could see was unspeakable: a sodden shoe fabric, full skirts rucked halfway up to reveal a limp leg, twisted at an angle its owner could not have borne in life.

Ringan's throat was closed to speech—there were no words available to him. He was aware of several things, feelings jostling for supremacy, fighting their way through the unnatural moment: urgency, nausea, fear, helplessness, outrage. As he tried to lift one foot, to make a move towards the horror at the river-bank, the standing figure turned and saw him.

For a moment, their eyes locked: Ringan frantic and disoriented, the girl shocked into immobility. He saw her face, small dark eyes in a round freckled face, sandy lashes, something around her neck that looked to be pearls. Something had happened to those gauds of hers, the strand had broken, pearls dropping one after another into the soaked earth.

Slowly, horribly, the girl opened her mouth. He saw her plump shoulders tighten; really, that dress was much too tight at the waist.

She moved one shoulder, the other, and he understood that she was moving towards him, at him.

Then the entire scene imploded, collapsing in on itself, buried under the weight of bells, there were bells ringing, bells slamming into his skull, coming from nowhere in this flat, empty landscape, she was opening her mouth, she was talking to him, she knew his name oh Jesus how did she know his . . . ?

"Ringan? Ringan! Pick up, for God's sake, please pick up! Ringan?"

His name, in a different voice. This time, he knew it. One hand moved, the motion breaking whatever oddity had held him as a witness to murder. It reached out and found the telephone on the night table beside him.

"Ringan Ringan pick up are you there . . . ?"

"I'm here." His eyes were wide open. It came to him that, whatever had just happened, he had not once closed his eyes. "Penny, my love, my lamb, my life, I'm here. Where are you?"

"Arezzo, near Florence. We had a show at the festival this evening." Her voice was shaking. "Ringan, are you all right? Look, love, I know this sounds as if I've gone totally barking mad, but I've just had the oddest dream, at least I think it was a dream, and I had to ring you, I know it's late, but it scared me so badly I couldn't not—"

"Drowning," he said, stilling her. He was awake, completely awake; he thought he'd never been so awake in his life. "A murderess. Someone called Margaret. Ginger-haired girl in a sort of vaguely Elizabethan blue dress. She drowned someone. That's it, isn't it?"

"Yes." Her voice was shaking. "You were there. I could sort of see you. It woke me up. Oh God, God, what just happened? I was asleep, and it was happening, and you were there, but you weren't—you were a ghost, or something. Darling Ringan, are you all right? Really all right?"

"I think so, lamb, yes." He sat up and flipped on the bedside lamp, dispelling the shadows, the echoes of the dying girl's voice

37

pleading for mercy, the horror of that death rattle, the taste of odd-ness in the air. "Where . . . ?"

"The Isle of Dogs." It was ridiculous, he thought. They were finishing each other's thoughts over an impossible distance. "Didn't you recognise it? That was Stephen's patch of land. The one where you're helping with the house. I recognised the curve of the shoreline."

Of course, he thought, that was it—the Isle of Dogs, but not now, not today—it had been too empty, and besides, there were the girl and her dress to consider. Tudor? Elizabethan?

"Ringan?" Penny's voice had calmed considerably, but there was still the flavour of disorientation behind it. "Hello?"

"I'm just getting up. Give me a second, will you? Ta." He swung his legs and, planting both feet, pulled himself upright. "Good—I was a bit dizzy, but that's gone. Penny, have you got any idea what just happened? And what did you mean when you said I was a ghost? Talk to me, sweetheart—I need help. This is new to me, and the thing is, I had the feeling something was going to happen. Be-cause of the voices I heard at the site."

"Voices! What voices, for heaven's sake?" Her voice slid upward again, towards the higher registers of worry. "You mean you had a premonition, or a dream, or something?"

"No. Voices in my head. Listen." He told her about his initial unspoken unease, about his meeting with Marcus Childe and the information he'd been given about the bomb tragedy. Aware of a peculiar reluctance, he told her about the two voices, male and fe-male superimposed against each other, that had knocked his legs out from under him. When he'd finished, he was surprised at how relieved he felt; sharing the burden had lessened the weight.

"Welcome to my world," she said wryly. "Believe me, I know just what you're talking about. But what we saw—and I can't even begin to fathom how we both saw it—that wasn't postwar or any-thing like it. That girl was wearing a dress that would qualify for a Best Costume award if the production happened to be about

Henry VIII. It was pure Tudor, I think, not Elizabethan—too early for that. The shape of the dresses got radically different when Elizabeth got the crown. And did you catch the accent? That girl was a Scot."

"My God, so she was. Bless you, Pen—I'd been trying to catch hold of something about her voice that I couldn't pin down, and that was it: her accent." *Margaret,* he thought, *Margaret. Scots, Elizabethan or Tudor dress.* "About her dress, that's what I thought as well, and I haven't got half your expertise on this stuff. She looked as if she'd stepped straight out of a Holbein painting. . . ." His voice trailed away. Penny understood why.

"Earlier than the painting of Lady Susannah Leight-Arnold, definitely." She was fighting to keep her voice as matter-of-fact as possible. "At least half a century earlier, maybe more. What is it?"

"Nothing. I was swallowing a yawn. The hour caught up with me—it's just gone four here. Penny, what do you think we should do?"

"I don't know." Exhaustion had hit her as well, or perhaps it was the tide of adrenaline that had wakened her, ebbing away. "I don't think there's a damned thing we *can* do, not at the moment. I mean, I don't know what time it is, but it's late. You said you heard two voices, male and female. Maybe find out more about the bomb incident?"

"Good call." He climbed back into bed, the springs whispering as it took his weight. "This bed feels absolutely enormous without you in it, you know. I'll ring up the army and see what I can find out. About that girl we saw . . ."

"I don't know, Ringan. I think we need to confab a bit more on that. And at this distance, I can hardly do anything. And I'm not getting back home for, what? Nearly two weeks? So for now, do what you can, but don't—don't take any risks."

"Right." He turned out the light. There was something he ought to remember, something he'd heard, or seen, something he had to tell her. Whatever it was, it wasn't coming. "Pen, I'm about to be fathoms deep. Call my cell later today, will you, if you aren't on-stage?"

"I will." She hesitated. "Ringan?"

"What, lamb?" He was already beginning to drowse.

"Be careful," she said quietly, and rang off.

# Three

*"Oh Sister, Sister, will you go with me*
*To watch the ships sail on the sea?"*
*She's ta'en her sister by the hand*
*And led her down to the north sea strand.*

Three days later, after the first of what would be many afternoons spent in the studio with his fellow members of Broomfield Hill, Ringan found himself pushing the doorbell of a small flat near Wimbledon.

As he'd promised Penny, he'd begun what he suspected might prove a long, futile attempt to track down the history of that bomb cavity on the Isle of Dogs. His first call, to the Royal Engineers, had been the product of memory only; he vaguely recalled watching a television programme about unexploded bombs, and the idea that the Royal Engineers were responsible for disarming and removing them had stuck in his memory. As it happened, he was right—a fact he found gratifying.

Almost as gratifying was the ease with which the Royal Engineers had been able to direct him to exactly the person, and place, that were needed. There was something very reassuring about that level of competence in a military organisation. One phone call, a wait of less than half an hour, and he had a name, an address, and a promise that the person in question was expecting him.

The door was opened by an elderly man. "Mr. Laine? The woman at the Royal Engineers rang me up and said you were coming. I'm Pete Cawling. Come in, do."

The flat was small, and very tidy. It was also very sunny, with an air of comfort and quiet good cheer about it. Cawling ushered Ringan into a pleasant sitting-room, offered tea and biscuits, and got them both settled.

"Well, now." He sounded curious. "Headquarters didn't give me any details—they just said you had a few questions, but they didn't say about what. How can I help you?"

"It's about a specific incident, I think a couple of years after the war ended—on the Isle of Dogs." Ringan saw Cawling's face change. "Damn. Looks like I hit a sore spot, there. I'm very sorry."

"The Isle of Dogs . . ." Cawling let the words trail and die. He got to his feet abruptly, his mouth oddly tight. "If you don't mind, if you mean what I think you're meaning, I'll need a bit more than tea. Can I get you a beer? I'm having one."

"I wouldn't say no. Thanks." Ringan hesitated. "I wouldn't ask you about this if I didn't really need to know. But I do."

"It's all right." The polite lie was completely unconvincing. As if sensing it, Cawling grimaced. "Well, no, it's not all right, but really it's just a bad memory. And you know, I've never once spoken about this, not since the day it happened, not since I made my report. Let me get those beers, and you can ask me whatever you need."

Once Cawling had settled back down, taken a pull of his beer, and begun to speak, it was clear just how heavily the events of that day in 1948 had affected him. The words, at first taut and careful, opened out and became a stream of clear, lucid memory, as vivid as it was disturbing. At first, Ringan asked no questions and offered no interruptions; Cawling's need to speak was palpable.

"It was right after the new year," he told Ringan. "Cold as hell, and wet with it, but the worst was the smog. You're likely too young to remember those London particulars, and from the sound of it, you grew up in the north anyway, but London used to be buried under the damned things. They called it fog, but there was no fog there; it was black soot and ash from the coal fires everyone used for heating back then. Proper lung-chokers, they were—like being in hell's front parlour."

Ringan, listening intently, found the description both vivid and familiar. He knew about London's clean-up after the health authorities had put two and two together and come up with pollution, specifically the tar-laden residue left in the city's air by those coal fires, as the reason London's population had shown so little resistance to the crippling flu epidemics after the war. "Go on."

"We got a call at headquarters, over in Ashley Gardens, in Victoria, that the local coppers at Millwall had come across an unexploded bomb on a patch of empty land, south end of the Isle of Dogs. Not one of the cluster bombs, and not one of the big buggers, either—we were still finding some of them years later. This was a standard SC, a fifty kilo. They were common in the early days of the war, and the Nazis got fancier later on, but these could do plenty of damage. So our major, a bloke called John Windle, sent the Company 33 crews in there, to steam out the explosive and defuse the damned thing."

He paused for another mouthful of beer, raising an eyebrow at Ringan in an obvious invitation for questions. Ringan, who was getting a nice clear picture in his head, leaned forward.

"You said the bomb was on an empty patch of ground. Was there nothing there at all? No derelict house, or foundations of any old buildings?"

"There wasn't so much as a beaten path," Cawling told him. "It was just a patch of land. Nothing on it at all, and no sign there had ever been anything on it—just scrub, and stones. Boggy ground, too; it felt wet to me. I remember I said something about it to one of the unit's drivers, when our major was finding out why there were no barricades up across Westferry Road, and he said it felt nice and dry to him."

The memory of a casual back-and-forth with Tamsin came back to Ringan in full clarity: himself bouncing lightly on the balls of his feet as he stood a yard or so from that bomb cavity, the feel of wet earth, sucking at him, moving unsteadily beneath him, Tamsin feeling nothing at all.

He took a hard swallow of his own beer. Looking over the edge of his glass, he saw Cawling watching him, comprehension on his face.

"Right, then." Cawling spoke slowly. "You felt it as well, didn't you? How—I don't have the word for it, but, well, how *hungry* that ground felt?"

"I felt it," Ringan said grimly. "Go on, please? I really want to hear all of this."

"Well—you have to understand what the procedure was when one of those bombs got spotted. About the traffic control, one of the first things we always did was to have the local police set up barricades. Those bombs could be sensitive, and the longer the war went on, the smarter the Jerries got about how to do the most damage with them. Even a heavy vehicle passing by could set one off if it hadn't been steamed out and defused. So the local coppers were supposed to make sure the area was free and clear of all vehicular and underground traffic. That was their responsibility; it was standard. But that day . . ."

He stopped. His eyes were wide, unseeing; he seemed to have forgotten that he spoke to a listener. His concentration was fully fixed on the memory of what he had never before discussed.

"Bloody choker," he said quietly. "You couldn't see more than a hand span in front of you, and it was hard to breathe. There was an accident, a car full of the local coppers, including the Millwall captain, ran head-on into another car—injuries, the lot. Everyone was taken off to hospital, and in the middle of all that upset, no one saw to the barricades. They'd forgot about it. And our people didn't know—they'd parked their own transports and set up their own barricades, and had steamed most of the explosive out, but they didn't know that no one had seen to making sure the roads were kept clear. And they hadn't got all the explosive out, and the fuse hadn't been touched yet. They'd done everything they needed—

dug a good deep pit, put rigging up to hold the bomb steady, set up a frame and the covering. It was all in place."

Ringan, with the memory of the Wintercraft-Hawkes property clear in his mind, found the scene all too easy to envision. He could place the men in his mind's eye, cover the ground and the air with dirty darkness, hear the babble of conversation and the footfalls of the UXB squad as they squelched across the boggy patch that felt so wet to some, so dry to others.

"So we're standing about, talking this over," Cawling continued. "A couple of our blokes went off to deal with setting barricades. And all of a sudden, close enough to read the plates and the tags, here comes a lorry, sodding huge thing, all weighted down with heavy supplies, bouncing down Westferry Road. It was probably stuff for the docklands to the north. And I hear the boys down with the bomb start yelling, 'Look lively, everyone out, the damned thing's gone hot!' The lorry going past—the vibration, you see, it set the timer in action, and the fuse engaged, and there was still some explosive left inside the casing—not a lot, but you didn't need a lot to do damage."

Ringan had his teeth sunk into his lower lip. He knew what was coming. Knowing didn't seem to lessen the apprehension, or the sense of helpless dread.

"So we all run for the outer barricades, and right in the middle, there's Major Windle, standing his ground, counting us as we bolted, like a shepherd counting his flock." Cawling stopped. His hands were unsteady, and his eyes damp. Ringan waited, keeping silent.

Cawling took a deep breath. "I was nearest the edge of the barricade—we were a good thirty feet away, to the southeast. I'm safe behind the barricade when all of a sudden I hear the major, and he's yelling at someone, telling them, 'No, stop, don't go there, that's a live bomb, are you mad?, don't do that, get the hell out of it.' And I look out, and there's something—someone—running, heading straight for the bomb enclosure, fading in and out of the choker."

"A girl." Ringan had forgotten his beer. He was tensed and waiting, seeing her, the girl in blue, the ginger-haired murderess called Margaret with the ring of Scotland in her voice, standing at the river's edge. *Miss no get away.* . . . "A girl with long ginger hair. A blue dress, looking like a movie costume. Right?"

"I don't really remember what colour her dress was," Cawling told him. "I was just gobsmacked by her being there at all. That movie costume, yeah, that would be it. I remember it looked like fancy dress, long and full, not the sort of thing girls wear usually. And I do remember red hair, a lot of it, flying out behind her. She was running as if someone was chasing her, but you know, it made no sense. Where in hell did she come from? There was no house, nothing at all. It was as if she'd just been dropped out of all that muck in the air from another world or another time or something—just, all of a sudden, she was *there.*"

He met Ringan's gaze, and Ringan saw remembered horror in his eyes. "She went straight at the bomb. She had her hands behind her, stumbling a bit, and she went straight at it. And the major went after her, shouting at her, telling her to get back."

Cawling stopped. There was a brief silence.

"Two of my mates were hanging on to me." Cawling shook his head, as if the weight of memory was too much to hold. "I was screaming at him to get back, it was going to go, and my mates had me and they had me hard, they weren't letting me go after him. I saw her—that red hair, you couldn't miss it—just as she went into the enclosure, and the major was right behind her. I wasn't close enough to hear the bomb making any noise, so I know I couldn't have heard what I remember hearing, that steady ugly tick-tick of the timer winding down. And then—"

Cawling stopped, his lips hard together. In the brief silence that followed, he lifted one hand to his eyes and rubbed them.

"The bomb went up, I'd guess. Damn. I'm sorry." That shallow depression made a lot more sense now, Ringan thought. "I'm going to be consulting on a house built on that patch of land—I don't think I mentioned that? But that crater worried me. It made me very uneasy. Maybe not quite so much, now that I know where it came from."

"I go by every year, every January, on the anniversary. I leave a wreath on that spot. I wonder if the new owners will let me go on with that? I hope so."

"I'm pretty sure they will. But I'll ask them, to be certain." Ringan got to his feet. "Thanks, Mr. Cawling, for the beer and for the information, too. I'll let you know what the new owners say about that memorial. But I suspect there won't be a problem. They aren't the sort of people who'd mind."

They shook hands, and Ringan headed towards the stairs. Before he reached them, he was arrested by Cawling's voice.

"Mr. Laine, if you don't mind—I've got a question of my own to ask."

Ringan turned back. "Tit for tat? Of course."

"You knew about the girl. Well—I'm fairly sure that girl wasn't alive. And you said you had the same wet feeling about the ground, and you said you felt disturbed by the bomb cavity." Cawling's voice was steady. "I've heard about people who can sense things like that. Are you a sensitive, then?"

"No." Ringan, bright sunlight touching his shoulders from the warmth of the day outside, shivered suddenly. "God, I hope not," he said, and went.


A few days later, right around the time the foundations for Stephen and Tamsin's house were being dug, Ringan sat down to a pub lunch with Dr. Richard Halligan, secular archivist emeritus of St. Paul's Cathedral.

They'd arranged to meet at the Beldame in Ashes, the ancient pub at the end of the tiny street that also housed Penny's theatre. Ringan had got there first, and snagged a table near the window; over the past year, the pub had become the local for Penny's theatre group, and the owner, Mike Dallow, had become a friend.

The excellent weather had held, and outside, London was summery and warm. It had also stayed dry, which meant that the work on the Isle of Dogs could continue without the ground becoming a swamp. It wouldn't last, of course, Ringan thought. At some point the weather would remember what it was supposed to do during England's summer months. There'd be a pressure build-up, a couple of days of increasing humidity and discomfort. Trying to breathe would be like filling your lungs with wet cotton wool; those unfortunate enough to suffer from migraines or sinus problems would curse the weather and wait helplessly. Then the sky would go purple and black, there would be a noisy, spectacular storm, the streets would run with water from the downpour, and they'd start the whole process over again. He didn't envy the workmen who'd have to deal with the building site once that happened.

"Gorgeous weather, isn't it? It's a pity it can't possibly last." Richard had a plate of shepherd's pie in front of him, and a half-pint of beer. "Thanks for the invite. I haven't seen you in— goodness, has it really been nearly a year? What have you been up to, and is Penny well? No more problems with the theatre, I hope?"

"No more problems. The theatre is just a theatre, which of course is a damned good thing. Penny's fine—the Tamburlaines are in Italy right now. They're doing a short run at some festival in Tuscany." Ringan took a mouthful of steak-and-kidney pie. "Her older brother's just come back from Hong Kong with a superb wife and a terrifying building project, over on the Isle of Dogs. Yes, I've got an ulterior motive, I'm afraid. If you don't mind, I want to fill you in on the story, and see what you can suggest."

Richard grinned. "Ask away—I've got my handy little notebook to write jumbled notes in. So long as you're keeping the beer flowing . . . no, I'm joking about the beer. Of course, I'll help if I can. What's been going on, then? What's terrifying about it, and did you say the Isle of Dogs?"

"I did. Here's the thing: unless I'm losing my mind completely, we've got a haunting on our hands—a double haunting in fact. Of course, if I'm losing my mind, then Penny's gone nuts as well, because—oh, hell. I think I'd better just tell you the whole story."

Ringan took a deep breath. "And let me say, ahead of time, that not having to try to get you to believe in the weirdness factor? A very good thing and a time-saver, too. Here goes . . ."

He gave Richard the entire story, beginning with Stephen's initial phone call and finishing up with his conversation with Peter Cawling. When he finally stopped talking, both their lunches had cooled, forgotten on their plates, and both their glasses were empty. Richard had been scrawling notes, never looking down as he did so.

"That's quite a story." Richard's brows had contracted; he reached for his glass without looking, realised it was empty, and set it back down. "So this gentleman—you said his name is Cawling? His feeling is that his superior officer went to his death trying to save a ghost? That the girl they saw running into the bomb enclosure was already dead?"

"That's right. And there's the fact that I kept hearing those two separate strains of thought, two voices. They're really distinct from each other. But what really got it for me was what happened the night I had that—dream, or whatever it was. And Penny had it too. And she's in Italy." Ringan got up. "I need more beer. It's my round. Another?"

"Yes, please. I need to think about what we're looking at here, and I can do that best with a pint of beer." Richard Halligan's eyebrows had stayed contracted in thought. He accepted a refill, and regarded Ringan over the lip of the glass.

"I want to make sure I've understood what you're looking for. First of all, this should go without saying, but I'll say it anyway: I'm always happy to do the looking-up bits for you. It's what I enjoy the most. But let's be clear: we're looking at antiquity, yes? It's not the incident in 1948 that's got you worried, is it? It's the earlier incident—the drowning."

Ringan nodded. "Exactly. Because if Marcus Childe, the bloke from Stephen and Tamsin's architects, is right, then we've got a haunting where there's never been anything standing to haunt. He said he couldn't find any record of anything having been there during the last four hundred years, and he thought it was a good bet there hadn't ever been a house there. And if there wasn't ever a house there, then a teenaged girl with a Scots accent had no business being on the isle at all, much less murdering someone there. It doesn't make any sense. What do you know about the history of the Isle of Dogs, Richard? Because the area's new to me."

"Well—I don't know a lot of detail, but I can give you a few basic facts. The name, for instance—do you know where it supposedly comes from? No? The story is that Henry VIII, he of the headless wives and the syphillis and the taste for throwing game hens over one shoulder while yelling for more ale, used to keep his hunting pack kennelled on the southern tip of the isle. There are some historians who argue it—I've heard one theory that says the name is supposed to be the Isle of Docks or the Isle of Ducks—but really, there's a lot to support the story. Henry lived right across the river, for one thing, at Placentia—that was the palace across the river at Greenwich. Henry was actually born there. And for another thing, Henry is well documented as having been addicted to the hunt, and the isle would have been a perfect spot for game birds. It was marshland for miles, and not much else. What is it? You're looking at me as if you'd seen a—" Richard stopped.

"Placentia. The Palace of Placentia." Something was moving at the back of Ringan's memory. What was it—what had he seen? The river, the south bank, sparse, different, and something else, a building, creamy stone, gaily coloured banners fluttering in the breeze from the river, like something out of a film . . . "On the south bank. Richard, I think that may have been the building I saw. Placentia. Is that any help in tracking things down? Or not?"

"Not really, Ringan. It's confirmation, of course; you said the girl's dress—Margaret, was it?—looked Tudor. Placentia was where the Royal Naval College is today. It was built back when the Plantagenets were still around—Henry V or VI, I think. It's got its deepest connection with Henry VIII and his family. Not only was he born there, so were both of his daughters; I'm not sure about the boy, Edward. There's a tree in Greenwich Park that's called Queen Elizabeth's Oak."

"Did she plant it, or something?" *Henry VIII,* Ringan thought. *A ginger-haired girl who was willing to hold her sister's head down in Thames water. The palace, flags flying, across the river Thames.* "Richard . . ."

"Plant it? No, probably not. I suspect she used to play under it, or dance around it, or something. What is it?"

"There were banners, up above the palace—I'm going to call it Placentia, because, well, why not? I've got a strong feeling that's what it was. Those banners—there really seemed to be a lot of the damned things. I mean, an absolute forest of them, with different banners—what are they called, pennons?—shoved all together. Would that have been normal, to have that many flying at one time?"

"I don't know, but I can find out." Richard's attention was fully caught. "What are you thinking, Ringan? That there was some sort of event, something going on at the palace at the time of whatever it was you and Penny both saw?"

"That's it. And another question for you. Assuming that what I saw was real, that it happened, that Penny and I haven't got locked up into some sort of bizarre mutual psychic acid flashback, or something, what in hell were those two girls doing there, anyway?" Ringan's beard was bristling. "It seems pretty clear, between Marcus Childe's information and your recap of the place, that there was never anything there. I know I've already asked the question, but I get the feeling the answer may cut the amount of research in half: if the only thing over there was a bunch of dog kennels and some wild geese, what in hell would bring two young girls across the river on their own? Because it really doesn't sound likely, does it? Especially during those times?"

"No, it doesn't. That's a damned good point." Richard was quiet a moment. "Let me get started on this. I'm looking for some mention of a murder, possibly during a major event of some sort, held sometime during the reign of Henry VIII. And if I can find any reference to a girl called Margaret, from Scotland, being involved in anything, that's also on the list. Right?"

"Sounds right to me. Richard—I really appreciate this. I'm just sorry it's so vague. I'm going to have to spend a lot of time at that site, and everything I've felt about it, seen about it, sensed about it, makes me jumpy. What's funny?"

"Nothing, really, except your definition of 'vague.' Do you happen to remember the last bit of research I did for you?"

"You mean, where all you had to go on was a location and a fire?" Ringan grinned, and got up. "Point taken. This definitely gives you more information than that. I need to get moving—I'm due in the studio in half an hour."

"More to the point, when are you due back on the Isle of Dogs? Should I hurry?"

"Day after tomorrow." Ringan's smile had faded. "And while I wouldn't want to hurry a man who's doing me a favour, I'll tell you this much: I'd like to go into this with some solid information."


"Okay, people, ready to play? Take one, 'May Morning Dew.' On three: One, two . . ."

"How sweet 'tis in summer to sit by the hob, Listening to the growls and the bark of a dog. . . . As you wander through the green fields where the wild daisies grew For to pluck the wild-flowers in the May morning dew."

Jane Castle's voice, rested and ready, sounded as bright and clear as the sky she sang about. She was separated from the rest of the band, enclosed in a vocal booth, to prevent her voice from bleeding through the microphones set up to record the instruments. To anyone unfamiliar with the process of sound recording, the contrast of the song's lyric with the high-tech environment, including the set of headphones each band member wore, might have seemed jarring.

"Oh, summer is coming, oh summer is near, With the trees growing green and the skies bright and clear. . . . The birds they are singing, their loved ones are winging, And the wildflowers are springing in the May morning dew."

Liam McCall, out in the studio's main room with the rest of the group, had his fiddle ready on his shoulder. He gave her an appreciative glance, tensed his bow hand, and waited for his cue.

"God be with the old folks who are now dead and gone, Likewise my two brothers, young Dennis and John . . . As they trip through the heather, the wild heron pursue And the wild hare they hunted in the May morning dew."

Liam drew the bow across the strings. A plaintive note, in a minor key, laced Jane's vocal, curling up, supporting it.

". . . The house I was raised in is a stone on a stone, And all 'round the garden wild thistles have grown . . ."

"Nice." Matt Curran, hearing the perfect blend of vocal and fiddle coming together in his own headphones, mouthed the word rather than saying it. Jane really was in superb voice today. Matt's concertina followed the fiddle in, adding a third level to the layers of the song.

". . . And all the fine neighbours I once ever knew . . ."

The fourth instrumental voice, the guitar, was mournful and somehow regretful. Ringan adjusted his headphones slightly and finger-picked the grand guitar he called Lord Randall, letting the bass strings hold the flavour, stitching a melody through the midrange, counterpointing Jane's clear soprano vocal line.

". . . Like the red rose have vanished in the May morning dew."

The three instruments moved twice through the melody, slowing as the song wound down. Liam sustained his final note, Matt held it, and Ringan hit a perfect fifth, ending the song on an echoing fade of harmony. There was a moment of quiet.

Jane, done with singing, took off her phones and emerged from the booth. She found bottled water and a chair, and relaxed. There was still her flute to add to the mix, but that would be done on a separate track. It was time for a break.

"Gorgeous." Jimmy, the recording engineer Broomfield Hill had been working with for several years, gave them the classic signal of a job well-done, one thumb straight up. "Absolutely gorgeous. Great job, mates, I think you got this one on the first try. We'll do the overdub for Jane's flute in a bit. For now, take a break. Ringan? You want me to bring that up on the monitors and you can give it a listen, mate?"

"Yes, please. We'll need to give it a once-over, but my feeling is that you're right—I think we got it first time around. It sounded damned near perfect to me. Jane's got some sort of extra sparkle to her voice today, a bit of jewellery draped around the top end. And we all hit the timing."

"Right. You guys want to go get something to eat? It's after two. I can give this a listen myself and have it ready when you get back here."

"Good call." Ringan realised, with some surprise, that his stomach was making sour complaining noises. He tried to remember when he'd last eaten, and couldn't. Dinner last night, maybe? "I'm half-starved. Let's head over to the café and get some food, and then I think back here for some more work. Jane's in such amazing voice today, it would be silly not to take advantage. Is everyone all right with that? Matt, did you and Molly have anything planned for tonight? Because we can always add your bits later."

The café, a popular lunch spot for both the City workers and the musicians making use of the cluster of studios in the area, was open. At this point in the afternoon, during the lull between the lunch crowds and those wanting their afternoon tea, it was also mostly empty. The waiter got them settled at their usual round table in the corner, took their orders, and left them alone.

While they waited for plates of sausages and chips and salad, the conversation was general, a kind of catching up that, with their deep immersion into the recording process, there hadn't yet been time for. Jane had been asked to contribute backup vocals on two songs for a well-known band's new CD, and couldn't make up her mind whether or not to do it. She wanted advice, and got it. Liam had a new girlfriend, and was waxing lyrical about how he thought he had finally found the right woman. He didn't notice the others biting back grins; Liam had a habit of falling madly in love—or, as Jane liked to put it, falling madly in lust. He'd then decide she was the moon and the stars and everything he'd ever wanted, and start quoting dead poets in Gaelic no one got but him. That phase usually lasted a month or two; his mates all knew when the first flush had died, because, as Ringan had noted, he began to sigh a lot. The affair always ended when the girl in question tried to pitch a tent in his life, after which Liam would talk about his heart being broken, quote a few more lines of poetry in Gaelic, and move on to the next girl, starting the process all over again.

Matt and his wife, Molly, had booked themselves a holiday in Italy. They'd found a farmhouse in the Tuscan hills, and were planning on a cooking tour in and around Florence. That led to a discussion of what Penny was up to with the Tamburlaines.

The food arrived, smelling wonderful, and all conversation was suspended in favour of sustenance. Jane finished first, sighed with contentment, and turned to Ringan.

"You know, we haven't heard what you've been up to. How are you holding up in Penny's flat, without Penny there? Didn't you say you were going to be involved in some house-building thing with her family? How's that coming along?"

"Damn." Ringan set his fork down. "Do you know, I'd actually managed to put it out of my head for a few hours? So much for that. Right. Damn."

"Good grief." Jane exchanged a startled glance with Matt. "That doesn't sound like any reaction I've ever heard from you on a restoration project—worst I've ever heard from you was choice language for incompetent preservation societies. What on earth is going on, then?"

"Would you believe ghosts? Two of them, at least?" He saw their dropped jaws, and shook his head. "Very much not what I needed. Yes, indeed, two ghosts. A double haunting. On ground that, so far as anyone can tell, has never had so much as an outhouse built on it."

His bandmates exchanged glances. "Bizarre," Liam said briefly. "Double bogles. How'd you find out they were there?"

Ringan gave them the story, waving at the waitress, getting their teacups refilled. When he was finished, Matt spoke up.

"That's a hell of a situation you've got there, Ringan. All right. Here's the thing—leaving out the scariness factor of having you and Penny seeing what you saw at the same time, with her not even being here—there's the basic song issue."

"What song issue?" Ringan blinked. "I'm not sure I get you, Matt. Could you explain?"

"Isn't it obvious?" Matt sounded surprised. "Look, you're pretty sure you know who one of those voices in your head was. This bomb-disposal officer, right? So you don't really have to worry about that one, do you? Because if you're right, and if this Cawling bloke is right about the officer chasing a ghost in the first place, then it seems to me he's really just sort of an overlay. So should we be looking at the girl, finding out about her? The one in the song, I mean."

"What song?" Ringan's brows had come together. "I think I may be getting dim in my old age. I haven't heard any music out there, just those voices. And believe me, the voices are more than enough—they keep knocking me down. Where are you going with this? What song are you talking about?"

"Oh, my God." Jane sucked in her breath. "Ringan—he's right. Every one of these miserable things has had its own little sound-track. Think about it for a moment. Two girls, sisters, one drowns the other—from the sound of it, a fight between two hormonal teenagers over the same bloke. It's staring at you. Hell, it's not staring, it's jumping up and down and waving. Go over the set list for this CD. What's the eighth song of ten? Second to last, due to be recorded in a couple of days?"

They watched the realisation hit him. Liam, shaking his head slightly, suddenly sang: "And as they walked along the shore, Lay the bent to the bonny broom, The dark girl threw her sister o'er . . ."

Across the room, the proprietor and waitress lifted their heads from getting plates loaded up, and stared appreciatively. Liam looked around the table. "'Cruel Sister' it is, or were we doing the English version, the 'Bows of London' version? What's the next bit? 'Oh, Sister, Sister, let me live, And all that's mine I'll surely give'?"

"Damn it. Oh, damn it!" *Two girls,* Ringan thought. His mind, having been forced into gear, was now catching up at high speed. *Sisters. Scots.* Margaret, the red-haired killer, what had she said? *You'll not have him, not now, not ever, all you have now I'll have tomorrow, he's mine, mine. . . .* And the dying girl, pleading, what had she said? *No Margaret please please I'll stand away I'll give him up he'll be as nothing to me no Sister please oh please.*

"But it doesn't fit." He had the sense of fighting a rearguard action. "The version we're doing, it takes place in Scotland, not here. It's completely specific: mentions the North Sea. And the other one, the London setting? Those girls are English. It doesn't fit. Someone tell me it doesn't fit?"

They were quiet. He looked from one face to another, and buried his head in his hands. "Bloody hell. And we're going to be recording this, when? Tonight? Tomorrow? Lovely. Just lovely."

"You're not really surprised, are you?" Matt patted him lightly on the shoulder. "I mean, it's not as if you haven't got the precedent right there staring you in the face. And it's not as if you're sitting on your hands, waiting to see what's going to happen. Tell me something—you said you had this friend of yours doing some research?"

"Richard Halligan, yes. Why?" *Another damned song,* he thought grimly. He was going to have to tell Penny. She wasn't going to be happy about it. He already wasn't happy about it.

"Well, you said the lady of the new house, the woman who commissioned all this building in the first place, was a Tudor-period scholar." Matt cocked an eyebrow. "Have you mentioned this to her? Because she might at least have some ideas about where to begin looking. Besides, it's her house, her patch of swamp, not to mention her cheque-book. She probably ought to be told anyway, don't you think?"

"How right you are." Ringan was aware of a sense of relief, and of a sudden surge in awareness, the need to be up and doing. It was becoming a feature of his life, and, at the moment, it felt damned good, a harbinger, a signal of action to come. "I'll ring her up in the morning. And now, if everyone's finished, let's head back to the studio and finish up the flute on 'The May Morning Dew.' Because when we get down to tackling 'Cruel Sister' in the morning, I don't want anything to get in my way."

# Four

*And as they stood on the windy shore,*
*The dark girl threw her sister o'er.*
*Sometimes she sank, sometimes she swam,*
*Crying, "Sister, reach to me your hand!"*

"Do I believe in *what*? Did you say ghosts?"

Tamsin Wintercraft-Hawkes, stopped in the act of raising one of Penny's cherished china teacups for a sip, stared across the table at Ringan. At her side, Stephen had his head tilted and his eyes narrowed. He looked, Ringan thought bitterly, as if he were moments away from ringing up someone to come with restraints and a wagon. . . .

"Ghosts. Yes." With Penny's permission, he'd chosen the Muswell Hill flat for this meeting. There were good reasons for his choice, which he wasn't quite ready to acknowledge to himself just yet. They were both cheerfully curious to see where Penny lived, and, as Tamsin had pointed out when Ringan rang her to request a sit-down, there weren't any chairs yet at the Isle of Dogs; in fact, there wasn't any roof, or any walls, either. On Ringan's end, atop the list of as-yet-unacknowledged points in its favour, was the sense that Penny's flat was more his territory than theirs. The conversation, from his point of view, promised to be tricky; he had the feeling that any advantage he could muster would be useful.

They'd accepted Ringan's invitation with enthusiasm, bringing along some fancy pastries. Ringan had shown them around the area, listening to Tamsin reminisce about how the last time she'd been in this part of the world was so long ago, Alexandra Palace had still been standing. Tour over, they'd accompanied him back to Penny's digs. Over a pot of tea, Ringan had blurted out his question, and then silently called himself several rude names. That had certainly not been the way he'd planned to bring the subject up.

"Interesting question." Stephen, at least, was actually considering it seriously. "Yes, I probably do. Never had any reason to think about it, at least not for a good long time. But I'm damned if I'm arrogant enough to assume that, just because something doesn't happen to me, it doesn't happen to anyone. I'll go with a yes answer on this one, pending proof one way or the other. Why?"

Ringan opened his mouth, but was promptly interrupted by Tamsin.

"Well, I must say, Stephen, that's a superb answer." She was nodding vigorously. "Very sensible. As a matter of fact, it's my answer as well. I knew we were well matched. I've known a few people, not particularly imaginative and very unwilling to believe anything they couldn't carbon-date or measure with a calculator, who've had odd things happen that they couldn't or wouldn't explain. As to ghosts, well, I don't know. I mean, my own inclination is to say no, that's ridiculous. But when it comes to it, I've got no right or reason to say there aren't any such things. Why would you want to know that, Ringan?"

"Well." He took a deep breath. Had either of them answered with derision, incredulity, disbelief, he would have moved on. As it was, he'd lobbed his grenade, and they'd given it right back to him. Nothing to do now but tell them. And Matt had been right: it was their land, their house, their haunting, and in the end, it was going to be their problem. "I'll tell you. But there's a bit of history you both need to hear first. Let's go into the lounge and get comfortable. I'm afraid this is going to take me a bit."

Settled on Penny's sofa, Ringan launched into a detailed account of the ghostly encounters he and Penny had had to deal with over the past two years. If his listeners were sceptical, they were too well mannered to show it; all he saw was interest and attention. In fact,

Ringan surprised himself. For all that the three hauntings he'd faced were well behind him, he found his voice wanting to dance up and down the scale. When he finished the story of the explosive exorcism that had been the finale of Broomfield Hill's stay at the Callowen House Arts Festival, he lifted a hand to his brow and felt his fingertips come away damp with chilly sweat.

"You say Penny was there for all of these." Stephen's voice was unrevealing; he was watching Ringan closely. "So, you think she's some sort of, what? Medium?"

"No. At least, I don't think so. I've read up a bit on some of the famous mediums since that first haunting, at my cottage, and Penny doesn't really fit the profile. She just seems to be vulnerable to it, somehow." If Stephen was unconvinced, Ringan thought, he could hardly blame the man. The story sounded completely daft. "She's home at the end of next week, you know. She'll tell you herself if you don't believe me."

"Oh, I believe you." Stephen sounded mildly surprised. "Especially since she had an experience at our parish church when she was barely old enough to put whole sentences together. Stampeded the entire congregation into the churchyard, right out into the middle of a December sleet storm. After that little lot, nothing would surprise me."

"She had—what?" Ringan's jaw dropped. "She's never said a word about anything like that. Hell, this entire experience has left her gobsmacked, since day one. Are you saying she's always been a sensitive? Why in hell didn't she tell me?"

"I doubt she remembers it, Ringan. I was home from school— Christmas, it would have been—home for the school holiday. She wasn't quite five, I think. That has to be right, because I remember my mother had Candy still in her infant gear, just a few months old. She was wrapped up a bit too warm, and my mother had to take her out in the vestry and peel off a few layers of blanket to stop her fussing. As to Penny knowing, I doubt anyone's ever brought it up. It's not really what you'd call a family 'Do you remember?' moment, is it?"

"Can you tell me what happened?" It was amazing, Ringan thought. Could she honestly know nothing about this? "I'd love to know."

"So would I." Tamsin exchanged a glance with Ringan. "Considering what we've just heard, it sounds as if you're talking about the initial spark catching, or something."

"Not a lot to tell, really." Stephen furrowed his brows, clearly looking back, trying to recapture something thirty-five years in the past. "I know we'd gone off for Boxing Day services to St. Nicholas—that's the parish local for Whistler's Croft, gorgeous, thirteenth century."

"I know the church." Ringan was mentally setting the scene. "You're right, it's mostly thirteenth century."

"Well. Had to be Boxing Day, because except for Easter, those were the only times we ever went, and this was winter. The rector—damn it, I've long since forgotten the man's name—did the usual celebratory bits, and got everyone into singing happy hymns. He was big on hymns, I seem to recall."

Ringan grinned. "So am I, but then, I'm a musician and a musical folklorist. Go on, will you?"

"Right, well, he led us into a hymn. 'Angels, from the Realms of Glory'—do you know that one? Very popish, which he seemed to prefer. Even the High Anglicans in the congregation got sniffy over some of his musical choices. It's got a line in there, something about 'yonder shines the Infant Light,' and then something about 'angels, at the altar bending.'"

Tamsin made a face. "Sounds like one of those High Church things from right around George III. And half the congregation droning on, off-key and uncomfortable. Go on, Stephen, do. What happened? What did Penny do?"

"Well, everyone was bellowing along with the rector—you know how English congregations do it, sort of droning on the way you said, Tamsin, everyone wondering when they can get home for some lunch, wanting to kick off the shoes that keep pinching. No one noticed Penny slipping off the end of the pew until she was right up in front of the altar. She was all dressed up, holiday best, pale pink and shoes properly shined, hair nicely brushed. Everyone stopped singing, but people were smiling, you know? Looked to be one of those moments where everyone except the parents coos over how adorable the child was, and later the unfortunate child catches hell for being disruptive in church."

It was very clear in Ringan's mind. He'd seen a lot of baby pictures of Penny, one way and another; until he'd come into Lumbe's Cottage, he and Penny had spent every Christmas with Penny's family at Whistler's Croft. He could see the brushed black hair, put up in ribbons for the holiday, the long dimples in the child's face, Penny walking up to the rector. And then, suddenly chilled, he was hit with a memory: Penny in the churchyard of St. Giles in the Green, Callowen's ancient church, seeing and hearing and feeling the naked savages who had lived there in the days before there was a Christ to dedicate a church to, curled together against the plague that had come to take them, her eyes wide as she saw beyond the now and into history. . . .

"She saw something, didn't she?" He swallowed hard. *Not fair,* he thought. Watching an adult go through it was nasty enough; the idea of a small child having to cope with it made his stomach move unpleasantly. "And said something?"

"She certainly did. One of the more bizarre incidents in my life. The rector looked down at her, opened his mouth to send her back to our pew. She said, clear as a bell, 'Look, Mummy, the angel's praying that she'll stop bleeding, will you give her a chocolate?' And she reached out one hand, and touched nothing. Air. But she looked so focused . . . her hand seemed to stop, as if she'd found something solid, and was letting her fingers rest on it. You could have heard the deathwatch beetles chomping in the woodwork, it was so quiet in there."

"My God." Tamsin's eyes had stretched wide. "Stephen, how frightening for her, poor child. What happened?"

"Frightening for *her?* She wasn't even nervous. We, on the other hand? Terrified. Spooked like a bunch of horses. We got up, and we ran. I mean, literally—there was something about it—we just emptied the building. Stood around in the churchyard and in the vestry, no one saying anything, and out she came, pretty as pie, my baby sister, and she said, perfectly normal and matter-of-fact, 'Angel all gone now, but she was crying, and Mummy needs to clean up the floor, it's dirty, mind you don't slip and fall.' I have no idea what she'd seen or what she meant, but services were officially over as of that moment. People couldn't move out fast enough. You'd have thought the place was infected with the Black Death. We had half the village cowering out of doors, with the sleet simply pissing down."

"Oh, lord," Tamsin said quietly. "That poor girl, how terrifying, and how unnecessary. It's a mercy she was too young to remember."

"You know something?" Ringan got up, a bit too carefully. "I'm going to tell you the second half of what I wanted to tell you, the bit that actually directly concerns you both. But first, I think I need a beer."


After hearing that bit of Penny's history, Ringan found talking to Stephen and Tamsin about what he'd seen and heard on their property easy enough. They heard him out, getting through rather a lot of beer while they listened.

"This former bomb-disposal man." Tamsin patted her lips. "Would it be possible for me to talk to him, do you think? If not, please do tell him that yes, of course he can continue to come lay a wreath whenever he likes. But honestly, I'm far more curious about these girls you say you saw. I'd like to pinpoint the dates as closely as possible. Does Penny have a computer here, Ringan? Because if you can remember any details about your murderess's frock, I think we can get within a few years either side of the actual event."

"She certainly does." They followed him into Penny's bedroom. One of the flat's original selling points had been the small adjacent dressing-room; Penny had seen its possibilities as a home office, and converted it into a functional workspace. "Can I say how glad I am that you're willing to help? Even if you don't believe a word of it, Tamsin, it's a relief. These past couple of years I've got really tired of having to convince people we aren't mad as a sack of frogs."

"Our land, our house," Stephen told him. "Of course we'll help. Tamsin, what's the starting point?"

"Fashion, of course." Tamsin settled herself into Penny's computer chair, and turned the monitor on. Ringan, whose relationship with the world of the internet bordered on avoidance, watched in fascination as her fingers moved from keyboard to mouse and back again, nearly too fast for him to follow. "There are a few websites—ah. Sketches and modern reproductions. Excellent! This is just what we need."

She highlighted something, and clicked the mouse. Suddenly, the monitor was vivid and alive with the Tudor period, in full fancy dress.

It was astonishing. As Tamsin scrolled, a march of tiny sketched people seemed to run up the screen and disappear. A dainty lady, flat faced as a nun and just as ageless, folded her hands over a stomacher and looked demurely at her own feet; below her, a man who somehow made Ringan think of Sir Walter Raleigh jutted an aggressive beard over an ornate ruff of lace. Ringan, peering over Tamsin's left shoulder, was irresistibly reminded of a kinetoscope, or the kind of book designed to amuse small children of an earlier age, in which each page had a single movement, and the rapid flicking of the pages could produce the illusion of a galloping horse or a dancing girl, leaving the child wide-eyed at the magic.

"Early Tudor," Tamsin said cheerfully, and the dancing figures stopped as the mouse paused on a pair of images. "I don't know how clear a look you got at the girl, Ringan. And you haven't mentioned whether you saw the front of her gown. It was blue, you said—a rich dye, or a pale one?"

"Rich." He was surprised at how clearly he remembered the scene, how many of the details seemed to jump out at him. "Almost shiny, but dusky, as well. It was the sort of blue I think of as peacock, but probably darker and shinier."

"I'm assuming that's important." Stephen was regarding his bride with respect. "Would you mind telling us why?"

"Because the poorer classes didn't have access to the richer dyes." Something had happened to Tamsin's voice; a note of authority, the cadence of the lecture hall, had crept in. She was suddenly professorial. "The cheaper vegetable dyes were weaker, more muted. If this girl was wearing a frock done in that sort of colour, she wasn't a servant, and she wasn't from a poor family. Ringan said it was dusky—I'm not an expert on dyes, but it was likely something like a logwood base. Those dyes weren't available to the average citizen. They cost a lot of money, and, in any case, there were very strict laws about the use of dyes, who could use them at all, and when, and where."

The two men regarded her with respect, and waited. She tapped her fingers gently. "Damn. It could have been a woad-based dye, I suppose. Those were available—but the richer the colour, the more times the cloth would have been dipped. Very pricey process. I think it's a safe inference: the girl was well-to-do."

"Right." Stephen had caught up with his wife. "So, if we follow that out, we're looking at—what? Rich Scots girl, not afraid to wear her Sunday best? But would she wear it out to go kill someone in a swamp?"

"As a starting point, yes, at least the Sunday best bit. As to the swamp, isn't that what we have to find out?" Tamsin leaned back, and looked up at Ringan. "Tell me, can you remember any other details of what she had on? I mean, besides the colour? What I'm after are details, her jewellery for instance, a head-dress or hood, or any embroidery on the dress itself. The sleeves—can you remember anything specific about them? Full, straight, slashed?"

Ringan closed his eyes. It was odd, he thought, odd and unsettling and really damned nasty, how immediately and how vividly the ginger-haired murderess came up in his mind's eye, with her round freckled face, her sandy brows, her small dark eyes, her short fingers. . . .

"Pearls." Little gems, polished and with the soft lustrous sheen of the genuine article, dropping off the strand around her neck, falling unnoticed into the mud beneath her feet churned up by her sister's struggles as she begged for her life, the mud and the shoes and pearls all slippery with death. . . . "Broken. She had a strand of them on—the real thing, I'd say."

"Good. A family with money, then—it doesn't really tell us anything we hadn't guessed, but every little bit of confirmation adds to building a picture. Anything else? The bodice of her dress, for instance; the collar if there was one; the sleeves. . . ."

"She had—there was something white." Ringan, unaware, was swaying on his feet. "White, with a lot of what looked like embroidery all over it. Intricate. The dress was blue—I know it was. But . . ."

His voice died away. She was there, in his head. White sleeves, bits of white elsewhere, dirty and fouled. Too close . . .

Tamsin's voice, prosaic and carrying no emotion beyond interest, jerked him back to reality.

"Blackwork." She clicked the mouse a few times. "Here—a very famous portrait, Jane Seymour, in fact. Henry's third wife, who died a few days after childbirth. See the detail at her wrists? Along the collar as well. That kind of fancy embroidery is called blackwork. And while I've got the portrait up here, Ringan, take a look at Jane's head-dress. Do you remember if your murderess was wearing anything over her hair?"

"She wasn't. In fact, her hair was loose—it was coming down at the back. Although it may not have started out that way. She'd been—struggling. And you asked about shoes, but the one I saw was only the sole, on the dead girl. I think . . ." He closed his eyes again, placing, remembering. "Flat leather sole. You could see stitches. Not very informative—sorry, Tamsin."

"All right." Tamsin drew in a good long sigh. "So far, we're fairly clear that it's Tudor, but that's a very long span of time in terms of narrowing things down. One last question, and then I'll stop, I promise. Did you get a good look at the front of her dress? And if you did, do you think you might recognise the style? Because Elizabethan dresses, later on in the Tudor period, were really radically different in the way they were constructed."

"I can try," he told her, but he sounded dubious. She lifted an eyebrow at him. "Truth is, Tamsin, I barely notice fashion now. Not my thing at all—it irritates hell out of Penny. But I'll have a whack at it. Have you got stuff for me to look at? Bring it up, and I'll do the sort of line-up thing they do on American telly, and eliminate if I can."

The first pictures Tamsin brought up were all of a very familiar face. Ringan tilted his head.

"Good Queen Bess, isn't that?" He grinned suddenly. "Of course, being a Scotsman, I grew up with a few other names for her. Am I supposed to be looking at her dress? What about it do you want me to look at?"

"The front." Tamsin touched the screen with the tip of her finger. "Do you see how long the bodice is? My heavens, it must have made them look to be all torso. Very distinctive, very sculpted; see the deep V shape to it? This one's from after she actually became queen—it's Hilliard's 'Ermine' portrait, from about 1585. Was the dress this kind of shape, Ringan?"

"No." He didn't know why he was so certain, but there was no arguing with it. Nothing about what Elizabeth Tudor had worn in 1585 rang the slightest echo. "Nothing like it. It's more ornate, but that's not why—the shape's all wrong."

"Good. Let's move backward—what is it?"

"That's it." Ringan was staring. The cursor had flickered, blinked, brought something up: a girl, red haired, round faced, but not the same girl. What had caught him was the dress, hitting him like a sense memory, the short fingers freckled and clenched, her eyes on him, identifying him over time and space, the girl she'd killed in the cold Thames mud at her feet. Those hands, those fingers . . .

"The sleeves—they're very similar. Hers were blue, not so fussy as these, but they were slashed like these, and the white bits with the embroidery poked out at the bottom." His voice was concentrated, dark, fierce. *Got you, lady.* "And the front, the shape, the sort of inverted V, with that overskirt effect on top of it. And the square cut at the top—it sort of flattened her out across the chest, but her shoulders were plump." Another detail, sharp and ugly, jumped out from behind the veil of waking memory. "I'd almost forgotten, it was definitely winter. The sky was that colour—midwinter bleak. And she was patchy with cold. Her skin was mottled with it. Does that help?"

"Very much. In fact, I'd say it's perfect." Tamsin moved the mouse, clicked, and suddenly there was the image at three times its previous size. "This is from a fantasy painted by some unknown court painter in the early or mid-1540s. That's Princess Elizabeth, as she was then—I say fantasy because the lady seated next to Henry is Jane Seymour, and she was long dead by then. The boy at Henry's other elbow is supposed to be Edward, and he was a week old when Jane died. So we can say that, based on your homicidal teenager's dress, whatever happened happened roughly between 1535 and 1545. Call it 1540 as a nice median date—1540, for a midwinter event noteworthy enough to get not only all those extra banners flying over the Palace of Placentia, but also to get a gently bred pair of sisters all the way down from the north."

Her eyes were gleaming, her mouth was curled up. She looked very smug.

"Fifteen-forty?" Stephen, who'd been quiet throughout the search, spoke up. "Come on, Tamsin, don't be a tease. You're the expert. What happened in 1540? Anything?"

"Oh, yes. Yes indeed." Tamsin smiled up at the two men. "Would you accept a royal wedding?"


Richard Halligan, rather to his own surprise, had begun his research into Ringan's problem by ringing up Dr. Madeleine Holt at the British Library. Even more surprisingly, she'd invited him over at once.

They'd met the previous year, during Penny's quest to learn the identity of the violent ghost infesting her newly inherited London theatre. Richard, retired from the secular archives at St. Paul's Cathedral, had been the one to first put a name to Agnés de Belleville; Maddy, in her thirties and in charge of an arcane section of the enormous archive known as the King's Collection, had been hunting for anything to do with Agnés de Belleville since her university days at Goldsmith's. Somehow or other, during the course of the cataclysm that had ended in a spectacular exorcism, a minor rivalry had sprung up between them: civilised, cordial, urbane, but with an edge to it.

But Maddy, on a soft day with the taste of late summer rain on the morning breeze, seemed pleased to see him. She ushered him into her comfortable office, offered him an espresso from the machine she kept near the window, and got him settled in the visitor's chair across her desk.

"Now then." She cocked her head at him. "You said this was a professional thing, for Ringan and Penny. What's going on? Not a problem with the Bellefield, I hope? Because I was pretty sure we'd got rid of Agnés for good. Hang on, coffee's ready. Plain, or do you tart yours up?"

"Just cream, thank you. No sugar." He accepted the cup, and set a small notebook on her desk. "It's not the theatre—so far as I know, everything there's just as quiet as it should be. Actually, this has to do with a piece of land in Penny's family."

He gave her the story just as Ringan had told it to him, omitting nothing, adding nothing. She listened carefully, her brows drawing together. It was an odd story, she thought, odd in more ways than one.

". . . and Ringan rang me up last night, to fill me in," he finished. "It seems that the musical pattern is holding. His group is recording a new CD even as we speak, and it seems that one of the songs they're covering fits what we know of the haunting so far."

"Which haunting? The man who stepped on the bomb, or the redhead with the fancy dress?"

"The redhead." He set his cup down. "Thank you, Maddy—I may have to get one these machines for my flat. Damned good coffee. You know, that question—I'm not sure we're actually talking about two hauntings here. Ringan didn't see anything to do with the modern bloke, did he? The bomb-disposal officer was purely voices in his head. Almost a sense echo, there."

Maddy nodded. "Yes, that was my thought as well. Whereas what you've told me happened to him when he saw the girl—was her name Margaret?"

"Margaret, red-headed, Scots. And here's where I think it gets interesting: Tamsin Wintercraft-Hawkes is a Tudor specialist. She's written about life during the period for a few university presses. What's wrong?"

"Wait a minute." Her eyes had gone wide. "Are you telling me that Penny's new sister-in-law, not to mention my beloved Candy's new sister-in-law, is Tamsin Finch?"

"Yes, I believe so. Or was, anyway. You look stunned."

"Gobsmacked." She grinned at him suddenly. "Finch is a bit of a deity in the field. Top-of-the-line expert. Why in the world are they bothering with us if they've got Tamsin Finch on tap for questions?"

"No idea. But she seems to have narrowed down the period we're looking for, rather drastically, too. She says we're looking at the court of Henry VIII, the year almost certainly being 1540. And yes, I asked Ringan why she was so certain; it seems she got him to remember every possible detail of what that girl was wearing, right down to the colour of her gown and the amount of embroidery on her sleeves. She popped up a classic portrait from the period, and Bob, as they say, is your uncle. So we're to look in early 1540."

"Why 1540?" Maddy was up and pacing, her restlessness a sure sign her interest was engaged, as if her body couldn't bear being left behind while her mind was moving at full speed. "This is fascinating stuff. The Tudors are after my period, Richard. I'm a Plantagenet woman to my boot heels. But even I know enough about the fashion of the period to understand that narrowing it down to a single year on that basis is beyond tricky. Ten years as a span maybe, but a single year? Why . . . ?"

71

"Something else he saw—the palace across the river, on the south bank, at Greenwich. He said it was flying what he called a forest of pennons."

"Placentia?" Her eyes were alight. "He saw Placentia? Damn. I wish I could close my eyes and see something out of the period like that, although I must admit, I'd rather just see the palace, and leave the homicidal dolly-bird out of it. She doesn't appeal at all. But the thing about the extra pennons—that would mean a state occasion of some sort if he's right. What happened in winter of 1540? Or are you going to make me do my homework like a good child, and look it up?"

"Heaven forbid." He grinned at her. "Especially since Ringan didn't make *me* look it up. What happened, according to Tamsin, was Henry tying the knot with the only one of his wives he apparently wouldn't have touched with a barge pole."

"Oh, my. Are we talking about Anne of Cleves?"

"That's the one. He called her a Flanders mare and said he was so put off, he couldn't, er, perform. Which, considering that he was one of the most oversexed human males in history, is really saying something."

"He was a bit high on the testosterone count, wasn't he? Hang on a bit—I want to think about this, and I process best when I'm chewing something." She pushed a tin of biscuits across the desk towards him. "Right. Which end of 1540 was this? Early in the new year, or late? I don't know enough about this bit of Tudor history, apparently. They've always bored me a bit."

"Six January. I looked it up—hang on, I've got notes. Nothing special, just the basic stuff my generation was made to memorise and then spew back out at school." He flipped open the notebook, and got his reading glasses on. "Right. Marriage took place at Placentia on 6 January. Already well-known that Henry wanted a way out of it—legend says he'd visited her in disguise before they were formally introduced, and he came away cross enough about it that Holbein was lucky to have kept his head, let alone his job. He'd painted the picture of Anne that convinced Henry to propose in the first place."

"Ugh." She twitched her shoulders. "He wasn't exactly the Dish of the Day himself, what with the syphilis and the extra five stone in weight. I suppose that if you can drag anyone who doesn't fancy you off to Tower Green and separate them from their head, you're going to get lied to a lot. Henry's chances of hearing 'Nice legs, shame about the face' were pretty slim."

"Actually, Thomas Cromwell—who pushed for the marriage, for political alliance reasons—did lose his head over it, a few weeks after Anne cheerfully allowed herself to be divorced and became the 'King's Sister,' instead of his wife. Charges of treason, and goodbye to Cromwell."

"Anne survived him, didn't she?"

"Indeed she did—two of the six wives did. Katherine Parr was the other. As I say, most of this is schoolroom stuff. What I'm curious about is where we're supposed to start looking for the Scots visitors to the festivities. Because we need to identify them. And Ringan says the song is very mythical and magical, along the same lines as 'Famous Flower of Serving Men': that one had magical talking animals; this one apparently has a musician making an instrument out of a bit of the murdered girl, and the instrument accuses the killer."

"Oh, wow." Maddy was pacing again. "Are we talking about 'The Bows of London,' by any chance?"

He shook his head. "I don't think so—Ringan told me the title, and I've forgotten it, but it has the word 'sister' in it."

" 'Cruel Sister.' " She rubbed her hands. "The one I mentioned is basically the same song, same story—it's just set in London instead of Scotland. I had a boyfriend back at university who had a tape of Pentangle doing it—'Cruel Sister,' I mean. Brilliant version—I heard it a lot. That one, though, the sisters aren't just Scots, it actually takes place in Scotland. One sister murders the other over a bloke, drowns her—"

73

She stopped abruptly. Richard was nodding.

"Yes," he told her. "I hunted up the song last night, when Ringan told me about it. If we ignore the whole 'fee fi fo fum' bit about instruments playing by themselves to out a murderess, I'd say we've got an exact match."

"And a date, and an event, and an exact location." She settled down into her chair, and waved Richard around to join her. "Are you busy for the next few hours? No? Good. Let's get this started."

# Five

*"Oh Sister, Sister, let me live!*
*And all that's mine I'll surely give."*
*"It's your own true love that I'll have and more,*
*But thou shalt never come ashore."*

It was long past the normal time for Broomfield Hill to be taking a dinner break. The band had been together a very long time; each member was old and experienced enough to pay attention to his or her personal interior clock. Skipping dinner, even when things were on a roll in the studio, tended to lead to cranky musicians, headaches, and general irritation all around.

Tonight, however, the instinct seemed to have deserted all of them. They had gone back to work after the late lunch, laying down flute and second and third vocal harmony tracks to "The May Morning Dew." Headphones in place, listening to Jane's vocal work, Ringan found himself staring at her. She was a wonderful singer even on her off days, but today was something special. Some magic, a kind of high-end sparkle, had found its way into her voice.

"Brilliant." Jimmy, the recording engineer, had caught that extra kick as well. "Jane, that was just perfect. I don't think I've ever heard you sound better. Matt, were you still planning to add some keyboard to this? Or is it better as is?"

"Leave it as is, I think." Matt looked at Ringan; he'd been listening to the three-part vocal harmony on his own headphones, and his lips had pursed into a silent whistle of appreciation. "My God, this is perfect. Jane, did you take extra vitamins this morning, or what? What's going on with your voice?"

"No clue. Hang on—I want to hear it again and see if it sounds as good as I think it does." She took her headphones off. "Jimmy, can we hear that on the monitors, please? Just the vocal tracks first?"

"Sure." He punched a button and suddenly, curling out into the room, there was Jane's voice, three exquisite individual lines blending into a perfect meld. She sounded remote, chilly, pure; the song, with its lyrical echoes of regret, sadness, time passing with no hope of human remedy, seemed to beat like a pulse, given its own life by the sheer beauty of the vocal.

"Right." Ringan looked at his bandmates. "Let's have a vote, shall we? I vote we're here, Jane sounds like a goddess tonight, Jimmy's here, we've got the studio, let's use it. I say we keep going."

"I was hoping you'd say that." Jimmy consulted his own recording set list. "I show 'Cruel Sister' up next. Are we still on for that? Did I say something wrong?"

"No. 'Cruel Sister' it is." Ringan was aware of something, it might have been reluctance, moving down his back. He picked up Lord Randall, his guitar, and slung the strap over his shoulder. "Let's get going. A run-through first. Anyone have any issues they want to deal with before we start, or are we all fairly comfortable with it? No? Good. Let's go. Jimmy, count us down."

"Okay—ready? Take one, warm-up only, 'Cruel Sister.' On four. One—two—"

Ringan, who hadn't played the song in a couple of years, found that his fingers seemed to retain a sense memory of where they needed to be, from simple chord progressions into trickier movements down through the scales. Matt played his concertina, frowned, and put it down again; Liam stayed out entirely on the first try, listening, marking where the fiddle ought to come in, and what it ought to counterpoint.

And Jane's voice, if anything, was sounding even better. She took the opening verse—"There lived a lady by the North Sea shore,

Lay the bent to the bonny broom, Two daughters were the babes she bore, Fa lalala lala lala"—and did something extraordinary with it. Ringan, whose guitar was the sole instrument behind her, jerked his head to watch her; she sang it, he thought, as if she was God's own recording angel, chilly, austere, offering no judgement. This was the presentation of Everyman, or in this instance, of Every-woman: she observed, she recorded, she spoke. The listener was left alone to judge.

They finished the first run-through. Jane, who had been singing with her eyes closed, opened them. She focused, shook her head a bit, and exhaled in a long sigh.

"Well," she said. "How was that? Good enough to get on with? What are you all staring at?"

After that, there was no question of breaking for dinner, or for anything else. Matt set his concertina aside, and opened the case that held his custom-made hurdy-gurdy, a beautiful thing made of spalted maple and ebony. Ringan looked at it, felt his fingers tingle with the lust of a player for a lovely instrument, and listened to Matt explain why he felt the odd medieval voice of the hurdy-gurdy would work best with the song. He played the line that would normally have come on his concertina, heard his bandmates suck in their breath, and stopped. It was a perfect accompaniment, eerie and somehow speaking of antiquity.

"Oh, God, Matt, that's gorgeous." Jane took a mouthful of water. "Let's go with it. Anyone ready for take two?"

The second run-through, with full band, was staggering. Liam seemed to know instinctively when the dark acrid voice of the hurdy-gurdy needed the fiddle to lift it; his lines were sharp and clear, giving a sweet edge to the hurdy-gurdy's tartness. Ringan, whose guitar would normally be the most present of the instruments, had little to do; the version they were doing seemed to have taken on its own life, chosen its own direction, developed its own attitude. It was demanding something indefinable, something he would personally never have thought to give it. Whatever that was, it worked.

"Right. Wow." Jimmy, who had worked with Broomfield Hill on their last four CDs, was sounding dazed and a bit punch drunk. "You guys are really on tonight. Jane, do you want to head into the booth? And Ringan, you do the backup harmonies right after. We can try a hot version, get rid of the bleed, and see if we can get a final out of it. If it works out that way, we can play with the overdubs—the flute, for instance. I can hardly wait to hear it against the hurdy-gurdy. Good. Everyone ready? Take one, live, 'Cruel Sister.' Counting down, on four. One—two—"

"As one grew bright as did the sun, Lay the bent to the bonny broom, So coal dark grew the other one, Fa lalala lala lala. . . ."

Ringan, playing and listening, heard the words in his headphones. *Odd,* he thought. The girl he'd seen, Maggie, she hadn't been dark. She'd had bright carrot-coloured hair, hanging loose to her waist. Maybe "dark" was a metaphor, as it so often seemed to be in songs? Light and dark as good and evil, Snow White and Rose Red . . . ?

"A knight came riding to the lady's door, Lay the bent to the bonny broom, He travelled far to be their wooer, fa lalala lala lala. . . ."

*Sisters,* he thought, *two girls fighting over the same bloke. An old story, sibling rivalry.* But this one had ended in murder. The question was, was the song accurate in its basics? Was it enough to give him a starting place in which to look for the truth?

"He courted one with gloves and rings, Lay the bent to the bonny broom, But he loved the other above all things, Fa lalala lala lala. . . ."

Right. So he'd set the two girls up, that nameless young knight, flirting with both of them, whispering sweet nothings in both their ears. Apparently, he'd ended up actually falling in love with one of them. The girl he'd loved, the other one, Margaret's sister—what had her name been? All Ringan had seen of her was one leg at an unnatural angle, a Thames-soaked hem, the sole of a shoe.

And her voice, of course—he shuddered, playing, hearing the archaic drone of the hurdy-gurdy, concentrating on Lord Randall's midrange and treble range to counterpoint it. Oh, yes, he'd heard her voice. He'd heard her last breath, her death rattle. It wasn't likely to loosen its grip on his nightmares any time soon.

The song moved on, the story spooling into murder and inevitability. The dark sister taking the fair one by the hand, off to the seaside to watch the ships, pushing her sister into the water, holding her down, weakening her, taunting her as the drowning girl's clothes soaked through, becoming a lethal sponge, heavy, pulling her down into the current as she begged for her life, being denied by her sister. This, in essence, was what Ringan had heard, and seen.

"And there she floated like a swan, Lay the bent to the bonny broom, The salt sea bore her body on, Two minstrels walked along the strand and saw the maiden float to land, Fa lalala lala lala. . . ."

The lyrics, all of them, were there in Ringan's mind. This, he thought, was where the song and the true story had to have parted company. A pair of travelling musicians out on the Isle of Dogs, where there were nothing but dog packs and wild birds, was unlikely enough. Add to it what happened next, and you'd have to go well beyond reality into some kind of particularly nightmarish necrophilia. Besides, hadn't mutilating a corpse always been a criminal offence? No, this had to be a metaphor. The trick was finding out for what.

"They made a harp of her breastbone Whose sound would melt a heart of stone, They took three locks of her yellow hair, And with them strung the harp so rare, Fa lalala lala lala. . . ."

*Ridiculous,* Ringan thought, and felt his lips curve up into a spontaneous grin of appreciation as Liam's fiddle suddenly undercut the other stringed instruments, dancing high and sustaining. Impossible. Here it was again: a song telling part of the truth, but maddeningly incomplete.

No one had made a harp out of anyone's breastbone. That was total pants. There was a musician in there, probably; Ringan was fairly sure about that much at least. Three previous efforts at having to determine where the song took a hard left, leaving him grasping at the kernel of truth while cursing over what stayed hidden, had given Ringan something approaching a nose for where the shift occurred.

Something had happened, obviously. But what?

"They went into her father's hall To play the harp before them all. But when they laid it on a stone, The harp began to play alone, Fa lalala lala lala. . . ."

A Scots family, down in London for a significant event: Bluff King Harry's unwilling marriage to the complete *naïf* he'd got a good look at and promptly called a "Flanders mare." Tamsin had filled Ringan in on a few facts; there had been political reasons why Henry would have thought twice about getting on the wrong side of Anne's father. And with his reputation for being the last husband on earth any woman would want, he couldn't simply trump something up and bang her head off. He'd been stuck.

"The first string sang a doleful sound: 'The bride her younger sister drowned.' "

What else had Tamsin said? Something about Henry not being on the best of terms with the border lords? Certainly the Percys, that solidly Catholic family, would be furious with him. So if a Scots family had been invited—or summoned—to the wedding, there had to have been a damned good reason for it.

"The second string as that they tried, 'In terror sits the dark-haired bride. . . .' "

It seemed as if the search for the girls' identity might not be too tricky this time—the luck looked to be running with him. Richard Halligan was a superb researcher, and Tamsin was apparently one of the leading lights in her field. There was also Maddy Holt; the Tudors weren't her thing, but she'd probably be delighted to open whatever bits of the King's Collection might prove useful.

If Tamsin was right, they had not just the year but the exact date, to within a few weeks in either direction. They had an event. They knew the location. Discovering the names of those two girls, how they'd come to be victim and predator on the Isle of Dogs on a winter's day, ought to be easy enough.

There was a small voice at the back of Ringan's mind, nagging and persistent. He'd done his best to block it out, but in the end, he'd accepted it: he didn't really give a damn what they were doing there, or what had happened to them, not for their own sake. What he wanted was the answer to the bigger question, the question haunting him as surely as the girls themselves haunted the mud and scrub of the river's edge.

Why had he heard what he'd heard, seen what he'd seen, in the first place? What had happened to leave him susceptible to this degree?

"The third string sang beneath their bow, 'And surely now her tears will flow.' "

The hurdy-gurdy sang, a drone with a perfect fifth at its heart, bringing to the song a picture of minstrels, of travelling *jongleurs,* of the Courts of Love and open-air markets and fairs in the days when the streets of Europe ran with filth and sewage and ladies wore conical hats and the Renaissance was still centuries away. Guitar and fiddle came together, swelled the midrange as the hurdy-gurdy went deep into the bass and Jane's voice, clear as a Highland stream, took the high end.

"Right," Jimmy told them, and got up to stretch. "It's gone ten. Would anyone else like some dinner? Or should we do the last bit first, Ringan's vocal?"

"Let's get it done. If I eat now, I won't want to come back and sing." Ringan headed into the booth. "Besides, it's only the verse refrains, the 'Lay the bent to the bonny broom' and 'Fa la la' bits. Here, headphones on—cue me up, Jimmy. On three."

Jane's voice, the instruments, the lyric, pure and clean. Ringan sang, his vocal adding a deeper tone to the filler bits. One refrain, two, three. He listened. He sang. He closed his eyes, lost in the music, seeing the girl with the ginger hair, hearing that pure chilly note, was that a voice, his voice or Jane's voice?, and there was music, warmth, dancing. . . .

The music pouring from the headphones clicked off, in mid-note. Ringan opened his eyes.

Outside the glass booth, four pairs of eyes were fixed on him. Jane opened her mouth, and shut it again.

"What in hell was that?" Liam was not so reticent. "Ringan? Did you just scarper off for a wee bit of dance on another planet? What were you singing?"

"I don't understand." Something unpleasant moved along Ringan's nervous system. "I was singing the refrain. Why are you all staring at me?"

"Listen." Jimmy moved a hand and pressed a playback switch. And suddenly the room, the glass booth, the headphones, were filled with Ringan's voice.

"Pastime with good company, I love and shall unto I die— Grudge whoso will, but none deny, so God be pleased, this live will I."

Ringan swallowed. It was his voice, certainly. He'd been singing. That was him, no mistake.

"What *was* that?" Jane was staring at him. "Ringan?"

"I—I don't know." Dancers, warmth, music. What in hell had just happened? "I didn't know I was singing it. I don't know what it is. I've never sung that song before in my life."


As it turned out, it was actually Maddy Holt who found the first mention of Alison MacLaine.

While it was doubtful she'd have admitted it even to herself, Richard Halligan's visit had triggered a competitive streak that she usually kept well buried. She was honest enough, had she looked at it, to understand that there was a bit of pique at the root of it; after all, when Penny had wanted help in dealing with Agnés de Belleville, she'd rung Maddy. And when she'd wanted information about the Leight-Arnolds of 1629, she'd done the same. Yet Ringan had rung up Richard Halligan, and that was despite the far-greater resources immediately available to Maddy's hand. It was galling; it rankled a bit.

After Richard had left, she began, not with the library sources, but with the internet. She rang home, got her husband, and let him know she might be working into the night. Then she made herself another cup of espresso, settled down, and brought up her favourite historian's search engine. The cursor sat there blinking, awaiting the entry of search parameters, awaiting her pleasure.

"Right." Alone in her office, Maddy had a habit of speaking aloud to no one. "We're off."

She started with the most basic of requests, the linking of "Henry VIII" and "Anne of Cleves." The result would have daunted a lesser researcher; there were over twenty thousand entries listed. Maddy, an old hand at manipulating the internet, had expected that. She thought about it, tapping her fingers in a light, sharp rhythm on the mouse pad. Time to narrow it down.

"Henry VIII," she told the empty room. "Anne of Cleves. What else? Okay."

She added a single word—"Scotland"—to the search string, and pressed "Enter." It came back with just over five thousand hits. *Better,* she thought, *definitely better. Still unworkable, though.*

She tried a series of additions. She typed in "guests," and came back with a message telling her the search had resulted in no hits. She changed "guests" to "wedding guests"; this apparently confused the database so much that the computer decided to temporarily put it out of its misery, and locked up entirely. During the five minutes of powering down and rebooting her system, Maddy paced. While she paced, she thought.

The problem, she decided, was that she was being forced to come at a research requirement from behind instead of before.

Had she known the girls' identities and needed to know what in hell they'd been doing at Henry and Anne's wedding, that would have been a relative piece of cake; she'd simply have entered a name—Mary Seton, for instance—and in less than two seconds a mass of facts would have been there onscreen for her use. She could then have cherry-picked the bits of information she wanted, entered those in as her new search parameters, winnowed down further.

As it was, though, she was stuck. All she could do, it seemed, was to keep trying various combinations of the parameters she already had, and hope that one of them didn't knock her system offline again.

The machine beeped at her, letting her know it had fully rebooted. Maddy glared at it for a moment, put her coat on, and headed across the street to the off-license for some cheese and bread. She was determined to find something Ringan could use, even if he hadn't had the sense to ask her first. If her efforts so far were anything to go by, she might be in for a long night.

As she went through the library's courtyard, a few drops of rain spattered the stones at her feet, sending up dust and grime. She glanced up, and saw the evening sky tinted purple and vermillion. The lazy warmth of the past few days was about to give way to a drenching summer downpour, and not only was her brolly at home, she was wearing open-toed shoes. That pretty much settled it: unless the weather either held off or passed quickly, she wasn't leaving her office. Apparently, she was meant to be working tonight.

Thunder rumbled, and the sky lit up with gold behind the clouds. Maddy sprinted, outrunning the cloudburst by a matter of moments, and got indoors just as the world outside the building turned to a huge thundering wash of rainwater. She stood where she was, watching it for a few minutes. There was something purifying, soul-cleansing, about a good summer storm; it was as if the atmosphere had decided to throw a tantrum, a few minutes of meteorological foot-stamping, followed by calm. But this wasn't a storm, after all. It settled down and became an even, steady rain, light but inexorable.

She headed upstairs, made herself yet another cup of coffee, and ate some of her makeshift dinner. Then she settled down in front of the computer and went to work.

"Okay. Think, Maddy." She mumbled the words around a mouthful of sharp cheddar cheese. "Let's work this out. We've tried two obvious combinations, and we have sod-all to show for it. Obvious, in this case, doesn't look likely to work out. Now what to do next?"

She ate some more cheese, and considered it. What did she actually have?

An event, for one thing. She had a royal wedding, a historical event. She had the date: 6 January 1540. She had two locations, the Palace of Placentia for the wedding and the Isle of Dogs for the crime itself. She had names: Henry VIII, Anne of Cleves. . . .

*Margaret, you fool. One more name, remember? Margaret.*

She straightened up in her pricey office chair, her eyes wide and staring. That was right—she had another name. The girl, the murderess—her name had been Margaret.

And, it suddenly occurred to Maddy, she had something else. She had a murder. Why assume the murder hadn't been documented? For a moment, feeling herself flushing, she was glad she was alone, with no one to observe her making an error so elementary, a novice would have been ashamed to admit it; she'd been so busy fixating on the wedding, she'd ignored the event that had spurred her to hunt in the first place.

She brought up the historical search engine, positioned the cursor, and began to type.

"Fifteen-forty." She thought for a moment. "Isle of Dogs. Margaret."

She hit the "Enter" key, and waited.

"Your search returned one hit."

Maddy peered at the screen. Not for the first time, she thought she really ought to go in and see about getting glasses, or contact lenses. The older she got, the smaller and harder to read the typeface on the screen seemed to get.

*Hever . . . 1540 . . . word from my poor sister . . . still in the grief and pain of her loss . . . grievous indeed to lose both Margaret and Catriona in such fashion. . . .*

Maddy cracked her knuckles, and knew she was smiling. There it was, the historian's favourite payback, the reward for using her mind, puzzling out the logic behind the hunt, knowing what questions to ask.

She hit "Enter." The screen flickered, captured. The pixels resolved. She read the text:

*Journal fragment. Excerpted from a series of journals kept by Mistress Alison MacLaine, lady-in-waiting and companion to Anne of Cleves, from her arrival in London from Mull by way of Edinburgh in December 1539 until June 1547, when the journals stop.*

"Damn it!" Maddy, alone in the office, listened to the words spiral and die. Outside, the rain was still coming down, streaking the windows, leaving the patterned stonework of the library's enormous plaza glimmering under the lamps.

A fragment? Well, it was a beginning. And who in hell was Mistress Alison MacLaine, anyway? From the excerpt, she seemed to have been aunt to Margaret and her sister, on the maternal side. Maddy settled down in her chair, pulled closer, and began to read.

*Hever Castle, Kent, 12 September 1540—Tho I did not think enough that I might expect it, after suffering these long months in deepest anxiety, word hath today by God's grace come from my poor sister. My mind is relieved thereby of such weight of care as might have rendered me incapable of my duty of companionship to my gracious Lady Anne that the King did summon me to provide and that, indeed, I am most inclined to offer.*

*Elspeth hath in no wise recovered from the deep sorrow of her affliction. So overset was she by that horror, in such grief for what befell my nieces, that her very faith was sore oppressed. May God in his mercy and wisdom be thanked, that she hath taken no course of action that might rebound upon her, to her eternal cost.*

*I spoke a while with the messenger, and bade him rest himself, the journey from Edinburgh being long and arduous, and he hath been many days on the road, in weeping weather. Tho he thanked me for my kindness, he protested that he must not bide, as he bore messages to the King. I saw him provisioned and sent on his way, therefore, and I returned to the Lady Anne, who waited in her apartments, with a tankard of that English ale of which she hath grown so fond.*

*She did enquire, in her halting way, after my health, and asked me how had I been keeping. How deep into our affairs she sees I could not say, for she speaks most times the language of her own country, finding little to commend the English tongue to her favour.*

*As for my poor sister, my God have her in his keeping. 'Twas a grievous thing, indeed, to lose both Margaret and Catriona in such a fashion. What ending comes to Margaret is not yet known and, indeed, may never be known to any but God.*

Maddy downloaded the page, and printed it. She looked out the window, thinking, wondering. After a few minutes, she hunted around in her desk drawer and found Richard Halligan's business card. It had his number on it.

"Hello?"

"Richard? Sorry to ring you up so late—this is Maddy Holt, at the British Library."

"Maddy! Good evening to you. It's not late—barely nine o'clock. I was just hoping this rain would let up, so I could go for my usual walk."

"Well, I'm in open-toed shoes, so I feel your pain. But I was ringing because I found something for you. Listen."

She read off the fragment, beginning to end. Halligan's reaction was immediate and jubilant.

"But that's brilliant! This has got to be them, surely? How many more pairs of sisters could possibly have had something nasty happen to them on the Isle of Dogs in the middle of January in 1540? Congratulations, Dr. Holt—this is a superb bit of work."

"Ta." She was amazed to feel warmth in her face; the praise had hit home in a spot in her self-esteem she hadn't realised she possessed. "But I have a question for you, or rather, for Ringan. I was thinking I'd like to ask it, but really you should be there as well. Would you mind if I rang up his cell, and put this on my conference call function?"

Ringan answered his cell phone on the second ring. "Hello?"

"Ringan? Listen, it's Maddy Holt and Richard Halligan here. I've got us on three-way conferencing. I need to ask you about something, and I hope you don't mind; Dr. Halligan told me what had been going on at the Isle of Dogs, that dream you and Penny both had, the bomb thing, all of it. And I found something that may lead us straight to where we need to go. Have you got a minute? I want to run this by you."

"Hell, yes. As a matter of fact, I've got all evening; we were in the studio very late last night, and tonight both Jane and Matt have things they need to do. I'm just eating take-away and looking out Penny's kitchen window. It's pissing down rain out here. I was going to pull you in, but I wanted to wait for Penny before I did— damned if I know why, but, well, there you are. I'm glad Richard had the sense to get you in on this. What did you find?"

She explained about the fragment. Ringan let out a whoop.

"Maddy, you superstar, you! That's perfect. It's them—it has to be them. Catriona was the victim, then, and Margaret the murderess—their mum was called Elspeth, you said?"

"Elspeth, yes. And the aunt, the woman responsible for the tidbit, was Alison." Maddy hesitated, and took a breath. "Ringan, listen. There's a lot of factual stuff here we still need to find out—we don't know how it happened, or why. But there's something. . . ."

Her voice died away. Ringan, a few miles north of her, felt his beard bristling.

"Go on," he told her. "You're not usually shy about getting answers. Hit me with it. What's this something?"

"It's about the family. Richard told me—I sort of got the impression that you seemed hypersensitive to whatever was going on out on the Isle of Dogs. And that's not your usual thing at all, is it? I mean, it's generally Penny, right?"

"Well, she's only been out to Stephen and Tamsin's site once." Where was she going with this? he wondered. "And she did have the same dream I did, only worse, because she could see me, even though all I saw was the murder. But yes, I do seem a bit more susceptible than usual. Come on, Maddy. Get on with it."

"Right. Here's the thing—the aunt, I'm assuming she was a blood aunt to those girls—her name was Alison MacLaine. I don't know much about Scots families, how they break down, things like that. But MacLaine—it's probably nothing, but—"

"Ringan, is it possible?" Richard, silent until now, had caught up. "Could there be a blood connection?"

"Oh, hell yes." Ringan looked around, and sat down on the nearest chair. "Yes, indeed. I'm pretty sure my father's family is a side-shoot of the Clan MacLaine—same root family as the MacLeans, but a spur, from Mull. My mother—who is just a skosh on the theatrical side of Scots nationalism—would be delighted to tell you all about it, I'm sure. In fact, she'd tie you to a chair and bore you to death with the doings of the noble Clan MacLaine, which is one reason I can't tell you any definitive details—I got into the habit of mentally tuning out whenever she'd go on about it. What you're asking is whether I could be related to, descended from, the same bit of family as those girls, or their mum, or their aunty. And if that's what's happening here, if that could possibly be why I'm susceptible. Right?"

"Right."

"I don't know." The rain was easing up, finally. Ringan wondered for a moment if it was raining in Italy; it was amazing, how much he was missing Penny, considering they spent most of their professional lives apart. "But I'll find out. I'll ask my mother—whose name is Maggie, but don't get excited, it's probably the most common girl's name north of the river Tweed. I'll ring her in the morning."

The next morning, before heading off to the Isle of Dogs and from there to the recording studio, Ringan took a deep breath, offered up a silent plea to anyone who might be listening for the ability to keep his patience, and rang up his mother in Edinburgh.

His plan, going in, was simple enough, and came from nearly four decades' experience of handling his mother: drop a few leading questions, let her ramble, take notes, try to mentally filter out the extra noise, and ring off. That plan, however, was jettisoned from the moment she picked up the phone.

"Mam? It's Ringan."

"Rupert." There was a moment of silence, and Ringan's heart sank. If she was calling him Rupert, and in that high piercing tone of voice, he had a pretty good idea of what was coming next. She proceeded to fulfil his forebodings, and greeted him in Gaelic: *"Ciamar a tha thu?"*

*Lovely,* he thought bitterly. *Just wonderful.* Maggie Laine was having one of what her three children liked to call her "for I *am* Scotland" days. Any time she greeted Ringan in the language of the hills, dragging her back to reality was likely to take time, and he simply didn't have any to spare at the moment. That left him with one option: deliberately annoying her. Luckily, there was an easy way to do it.

He took a deep breath, and tried to remember some of the broad Scots of his youth. "Hauld your whisht a wee moment," he told her, "and gie yer awnie sin nae scauldin'."

As he'd expected, that did the trick. Since she was in her High Scots persona, his use of Lallans, the Lowlands dialect, snapped her immediately from a bad modern impression of Mary of Scotland into outrage, and then into furious silence. *Good,* he thought, *very good.* If she was seething but quiet, maybe he could ask his question, get an answer, and get the hell out of the conversation with his head and his own temper intact. At no time did he find keeping his temper with his mother easy.

Maggie Laine, histrionic and slightly unbalanced though she might be, was a storehouse of knowledge about her family, and especially about her husband's family. Over the next twenty minutes Ringan, having begun by asking her to shut up and let him ask his question without scolding him over it, found himself asking her to slow down so that he could write down what she was telling him. Whether because the subject matter left her in her element or because she wasn't daft enough to turn down a rare invitation to talk to any of her children at any length about family history, Maggie pulled out all the stops.

When he finally got her off the phone—after enduring a short, sharp snarl in Gaelic that seemed to indicate Maggie was wondering if her own son had been exchanged with a mannerless, rude changeling—Ringan spent a minute reminding himself that it was far too early in the day to legitimately satisfy the craving for a tall glass of cider that was the inevitable result of dealing with his mother. He glanced at the notes he'd jotted down, and then at the clock. He had about ten minutes before he needed to leave— enough time to call Richard Halligan and Maddy, not enough to really go over his notes.

His first call, to Maddy at the library, dumped him straight into her voicemail; her voice informed him that she was unavailable, and it asked him to leave a name, a number, the date and time of his call, and a brief message.

Richard picked up on the third ring, and Ringan let his breath out. Until he heard Richard's voice, he hadn't realised quite how badly he wanted someone else to know about information before he again went near the Isle of Dogs.

"Richard? Ringan here. Listen, I have to leave in about ten minutes, but I'm glad you're there. I've just got off the phone with my mother, up in Edinburgh, and I've got some history to share. It's going to be a long day—I'm meeting with Tamsin's architect in about forty minutes at the site, and after that I'm off to the studio. It's a schedule from hell today, but can we have dinner, or maybe a quick pint? I've got a break right around six. And can you see if Maddy's up for it? Leave me a message on my cell, and we can hook up."

"Absolutely." Richard hesitated. "Ringan—can I make a suggestion? I don't want to pry, but whatever it is you found out, I have a strong feeling you ought to share it with Penny."

"I'm going to, as soon as I ring off. In fact, I'm off now. Let me know about dinner. And Richard—thanks."

Another look at the clock on Penny's kitchen wall. What was the time difference to Italy—an hour? As far as he remembered from the festival schedule, the Tamburlaines had only evening performances, except for Saturdays. She might be rehearsing, but she wouldn't be on-stage right now.

"Ringan! Is that really you? Is everything all right?"

"Penny, lamb, love, hello, yes of course it's me." It was amazing, he thought, that he could have forgotten how much he loved the sound of her voice. A wave of something passed through his system, leaving him a bit weak; it might have been longing. When she got home, he thought, he wasn't letting her out of bed for a few days. "Look, love, I'm off to the Isle of Dogs to meet with the architect and get a look at the progress they've been making with the foundations, and then we're recording all day. I've got about five minutes before I have to run, and I want to tell you something. Got a moment?"

"Of course." She must have picked up something in his mood; her voice had sharpened. "Ringan, what is it?"

"I just spent half an hour listening to my barmy mother, that's what. She was loading me up with information about the history of our family, or rather, my father's family. Listen, love, the whole thing with our murderess, and our victim? About me being susceptible, hell, damned near telepathic on this one? I roped Richard Halligan in for research, and he got hold of Maddy Holt, and she got busy."

"Oh, excellent!" He could almost see her nodding. "Someone found something, did they?"

"Got it in one—Maddy did. Turns out the family, Margaret and her sister Catriona? They were MacLaines, the original clan, from the Isle of Mull. There was a sort of split, back in the late seventeenth century—I'll need to decipher some of the notes I took, but my mother said there was an outbreak of plague on Mull, and some sort of family schism over property rights, which of the survivors got what. One of the branches was apparently illegitimate. That was my father's line."

"Wait a minute." She sounded stunned. "Have I got this right? Are you saying you're descended from one of those girls?"

"Looks like it—well, not from one of those two girls, Margaret or Catriona I mean, since they both died before bearing children. But their mother, Elspeth, is listed on the family tree as an ancestress. I'm giving my insane mum a day or two to recover from the shock of her 'awnie sin' cheeking her, and then I'm going to get drunk as a rat's nightmare, ring her back, and ask her to send me copies of that family tree."

"Oh, lord, you talked low Scots to her?" Penny was biting back giggles. "What did she do, go Gaelic at your first? I like the 'awnie sin' touch—calling yourself her 'bearded boy' must have royally ticked her off. Ringan, look, I'm off to block a stage set in a minute, and you said you had to go to work. I'll be home next week, thank goodness, but keep me posted if anything goes on, all right?"

"Will do. Penny?"

"What?"

"Be warned, lamb. I have plans for you when you get home, and they involve neither of us getting out of bed for a day or two. Just thought I'd warn you ahead of time."

"I can hardly wait. Damn, I'm late! I'm off—see you next week." She blew him a kiss, and he heard the click of her phone disconnecting.

He got to the Isle of Dogs just as Marcus Childe pulled up. Ringan parked the Alfa out of the way of the Westferry Road traffic, and stepped gingerly onto the Wintercraft-Hawkes land.

"Ringan! Good morning, or is it afternoon yet?"

"No, still morning by about ten minutes." Ringan let his breath out; he hadn't known he'd been holding it. *Nothing,* he thought, *not a damned thing, no echoes, no whispers, no nauseating vertigo-inducing voices in my head.* Maybe they were taking the day off? He had a moment of giddiness, and realized it was relief. "Hello, Marcus. Good God, look at that! The builders have been busy."

This was an understatement. Ringan had last driven past the site a week earlier, just to get a fast look at the foundations, and an impression of the general footprint of the house. A week ago, the trenching for the plumbing had been laid, but little else; Ringan, driving by at dusk on his way to a night session with Broomfield Hill, had seen stakes in place, builders' lines, plumbs, chalked lines on the ground. They'd been too amorphous to give him any visual sense of what was to come; the best he could do had been to try and match them with what he remembered of the architectural blueprints Marcus had shown him. What he chiefly recalled was looking past them, wondering for a cold moment if his eyes would do the odd little turning back of time, bringing up two girls down at the water's edge.

But there had been nothing, only the flat ground and the *Cutty Sark* swaying in the light evening air. Now, back on site in the daylight, Ringan found himself staring at fully poured foundations, at framing, at distinct interior lines that, if he squared them between his hands as individual views, showed where walls would be, windows, lintels, and passages. If he stood back and looked at the work in its entirety, he saw the letter E, just as Tamsin had intended. In the space of a week, while Broomfield Hill were recording six of the eleven songs on their new CD, Tamsin's house had sunk its roots into the Isle of Dogs.

"Isn't this amazing?" Marcus had the look of a man who could scarcely believe his luck. "You know, this the ninth project I've been lead architect for. Four of them have been period reproductions—this is the fifth. The usual time for getting this far is about six weeks. This? Nine days." He shook his head. "I've never seen anything like it. And so far, they've got it right, spot on. The builders haven't missed a trick. Every specification's been met. Considering some of the issues I've run into with the actual builders on other projects, I keep thinking I may wake up and find this has all been a very pleasant hallucination."

"I hope not. This is incredible. It's—"

*Help me someone help me Godamercy the dogs no don't leave me please you cannae be so cruel please give him back to me give him back I must have him please oh please sir*

"Ringan?"

*. . . writ by the King's own hand, this sentence, carried out in the sight of God Almighty, and no more shall you see the world . . .*

"Ringan!" Marcus sounded horrified. "Are you all right?"

He shook his head. "What—" His knees were sagging, the sky was in the wrong place, it was wheeling and blue, but it was beside him and before and behind, his hands, he couldn't move them, he must get upright, run, get out, go . . . "I—no—"

Marcus had him by the arm; that grip, Ringan realised dizzily, was the only thing keeping him upright. "You should sit. Here— my car's right there." Marcus led him over to the Volvo. He got the door open, and watched Ringan sink limply against the upholstery. "Any better?"

"I think so. Half a minute, okay?" *A new voice,* Ringan thought. His stomach was in an uproar, and a cold prickle of sweat had erupted across his brow, just under the hairline.

A man's voice, as cold and nasty and inexorable as anything he'd ever heard in his life. That voice had sounded like that of a hanging judge; all that had been missing was the customary "and may God have mercy on your soul."

"Would you mind very much if I asked you what just happened?" Marcus was squatting beside the car door; behind his glasses, his eyes had a bright, interested look. "You looked as if you'd just seen a ghost, or something. What—did I say something funny?"

"Yes, a bit. Ironic, anyway." He had a sudden driving need to get the hell off the Isle of Dogs, to get safely into the studio, where there would be no voices to slap him unexpectedly, no shaking earth beneath his feet, no need for help from a relative stranger in staying on his feet. "I'll tell you about it another time, if you don't mind, Marcus. Right now, I need to get going. Is there anything at all we need to go over on this project? Because if there is, I can come to your office. . . ."

"No, no, that's fine—I really just wanted to give you a look at what's been done, and how quickly, and to see if you spotted anything in the roughing-in that needed changing—if you have—there's still time for alterations."

"No, nothing that I can see. Let me take another look."

He got to his feet, bracing for dizziness, or weakness in his legs. Nothing. It seemed to have passed. He looked at the house again, the lines, the layout.

"From here, it looks fine—but really, Marcus, that's not my area of expertise. I think you'll want my input when we're farther down the road, but for now, honestly, it's you and the builders. I'm off—my band's recording, and we've got a block of time booked for today."

Ringan, his legs completely steady and the ground once again firm beneath his feet, headed back to his own car and drove away. As he rounded the curve, westbound on Westferry Road, he was aware of Marcus Childe, standing on the curb, staring after him.

# Six

*And there she floated like a swan,*
*The salt sea bore her body on.*
*She floated up and she floated down*
*Until she came to the miller's dam.*

The upstairs room at the Quarry and Crow, less than three minutes' walk from Broomfield's recording studio of choice, was generally used for public events or private functions. On any given day, it might host a political meeting, a drunken fête for a terrified bridegroom, or a folk concert. Tonight, at Ringan's request, the members of Broomfield Hill, along with Maddy Holt and Richard Halligan, had taken it over.

The barmaid was kept busy; with everyone agreeing that seven would be a good time to meet up, the choice to get pub food and a few pints for dinner, and combine them with the conversation Ringan wanted to have, was an easy one. Since the room was free that night, the publican had offered it up, and provided them all with plates of hot food as well. He also had the wit to keep the barmaid checking on their alcohol, an arrangement appreciated all around. As Ringan pointed out to Maddy, it didn't hurt that this place was Broomfield's local whenever they were in the studio. And this wasn't the sort of conversation he wanted to have down in the public.

Ringan waited until the plates of sausage and chips and kidney pie had been emptied, and wiped with torn-off chunks of dense bread smeared with butter, and everyone had taken at least a solid pull at his or her glass. Then he pushed his own plate aside and pulled out the notes he'd made that morning.

"I've got a problem." *Understatement of the day,* he thought grimly. While everyone knew the basics, the Broomfields hadn't heard about the blood connection to the MacLaine girls, and no one had heard about what had hit him at the Isle of Dogs that morning. That something had happened the band probably guessed, but no one had pressed him, beyond Jane's comment that he looked as pale as French yogurt.

Ringan himself had offered no information. Thinking about it, remembering the calm cold finality in that unknown masculine voice, made his stomach jump unpleasantly. The last thing he wanted to do was to tell the story more than once. It was bad enough that Penny was going to have to hear it.

He took a deep breath, and a mouthful of cider, and proceeded to bring them all up to date. Both Richard and Maddy, who knew about the blood connection, had been casting interested looks at the short stack of notes at Ringan's elbow. He kept his voice calm and matter-of-fact. When he reached the events of that morning's visit to the Isle of Dogs, however, he got as far as hearing his long-dead relative's voice pleading for her life, and stopped abruptly; to his own irritation, his voice had begun to shake. His beard was bristling in a way Penny would have recognised as meaning annoyance with himself.

"Right." Liam, who'd emptied his beer, wiped his lips. "Ringan, there's something about these ladies that's getting you down. You've had bogles to deal with before—hell, you've had them prancing up and down your stairs and perched on your loo, damned near. Even if these are kin, family, what is it has you so worked up?"

"Something else happened." Jane, who knew Ringan very well indeed, had heard that vocal tremor, seen that movement of his jaw under the black beard, and drawn her own conclusions. The last time she'd seen him this tight, this concentrated and edgy, had been because something had used him, used his body, to damage Penny.

Whatever had got to him, it had to be major. "Ringan—can you tell us?"

He did. He kept it as straightforward and unemotional as possible, but there didn't seem to be any hiding the effect that voice had had on him. Margaret's begging had been bad enough, but the horror that had taken the stiffener out of him had come from the man who, judging by the words spoken and her reaction to them, looked to have been her executioner.

His account, bare and unembroidered as it was, seemed to have had a similar effect on the others. Maddy swallowed audibly and reached for her glass.

"Damn," she said. "Nasty. I think I want more beer. Ringan, I'm so sorry. That sounds—well. I hope it wasn't half as bad as it sounds, but I suspect it was probably much worse."

"It was that bad, and way the hell worse." He looked around the table at his friends. "I thought listening to Catriona MacLaine begging her own sister not to drown her was bad enough, but at least there was passion in that—rage, hate, love, human feelings, for heaven's sake. This—I swear, I know this sounds over the top, but it might have been the voice of Death himself, or whichever archangel is supposed to be responsible for ushering the dead into heaven or sending them off to hell. Or maybe the voice of God, you know? No way to argue with it, and whoever it was wasn't open to anything."

There was a brief silence. Muted sounds eddied up from the public one floor below: laughter, conversation, the thump of footsteps, music.

"Well." Richard nodded in the general direction of Ringan's elbow. "Are those the notes about your father's family? Because if so, I propose another round of booze for everyone, assuming musicians can function on a lot of beer—what are you all smiling at? Anyway, I know you have to get back to your recording session when we've finished here, so my vote is for more beer, or more cider if that's what you're drinking, and a quick listen if Ringan feels like sharing. Maybe we'll get some insights from the genealogy. And unless I'm mistaken, here comes the nice lady, wanting to know if we want a topping-up."

When he first reached the studio, Ringan had taken a few minutes to look over what he'd written down, and to get his thoughts about his mother's information as clear as possible. The story, stripped of the bulk of Maggie Laine's histrionic embellishments, was actually simple enough. What he was likely to need his notes for, Ringan thought, was to keep track of the names. In his opinion, genealogy as a study bore an uncanny resemblance to the draggiest, most tedious bits in the Old Testament: So-and-So begat Such-and-Such by Whomever, daughter of Whatever. It was enough to drive him bonkers.

"Okay." He looked around the table; everyone was watching him. "I'll try to keep this simple, but I'm not big on reading genealogies—in fact, they make me want to kick something, usually. And there's a gap in the list my mother reeled off at me this morning—it's incomplete in at least one vital spot. But in a nutshell? This is about my father's family. The Laines are a side-spur of the Clan MacLaine. Of course, the MacLaines are a side-spur, as well—the original family, back when dinosaurs still roamed the earth, was the MacLeans."

"MacLean, MacLaine, Laine." Matt took a mouthful of beer, and drummed his fingers against the table. "Makes you long for a Wilson or a Jones, doesn't it? Right. So, how does this work in with those two girls? And more to the point, where does it work in with you, and how all this is affecting you?"

"That's what I'm trying to sort out—hang on, I've forgotten a couple of dates, and most of the names." Ringan shuffled his notes. "Okay, here we go. The original split, Maclean to MacLaine, isn't important here. Hell, I'm not even sure the dust-up that led to the Laines is important. Thing is, if my mother was right, the branch of the family that ended up producing my father actually got started in 1660 or thereabouts, with some sort of inheritance dispute between half-brothers. Some bloke called Murdoch MacLaine was the heir, the legitimate only son of the house, but he died of plague; there was an outbreak on Mull between 1659 and 1660. His only child was an illegitimate son. It got iffy because his half-brother, Iain, was illegitimate as well. Same dad, different mum—was wrong side of the blanket. And there's a straight line going back from him to Elspeth MacLaine. But there's a missing piece."

"So, Elspeth was the mother of the two sisters?" Jane sounded fascinated. She interpreted the look Ringan shot her, and laughed. "I know, I know, you don't like genealogy. My mother does it as a profitable little hobby, remember? I grew up steeped in it. So we have, what—outbreak of plague on Mull leaves the local branch of the clan without a legitimate heir. And that means the 'Who's the next head of the clan?' issue came down to a dispute between an illegitimate son and the legitimate son's illegitimate son? Good grief. Sounds like night-time telly at its most convoluted."

"Ringan, you said a straight line back to Elspeth MacLaine, didn't you?" Richard had pulled out his own small notebook and was jotting down notes. "Where does that gap occur, the missing piece you mentioned?"

"Need you ask?" Ringan said bitterly. "Right at Elspeth, of course. Where else? Sod's law, in action. We have Elspeth—hang on, let me check the dates. Right—Elspeth MacLaine, parentage not shown. Born 1505, died 1547. It lists two daughters, twins from the look of it. Makes it worse somehow, doesn't it, knowing they were twins? Sadder, I mean. Anyway, it's our sisters, all right: Catriona and Margaret, born 1524, died 1540."

"And?" Richard's pencil was poised. "Other children?"

"None listed. That's the problem. That's the gap."

"Damn!" Maddy Holt bit her lip. "So much for any hope that this would be straightforward. Ringan, I can't pretend to expertise on the subject of—lord, I don't even know what to call it. Let's just say that I can't imagine anything except a blood connection that would produce the kind of vulnerability you're being subjected to on this one."

"No more can I." Liam gave her an approving look. "That's

sense, if you can use sense when you're dealing with bogles." He was quiet a moment. "And a damned good thing we all saw the bogles, back in Ringan's barn," he added. "We'd think you were ready to be carted off to the rubber room, otherwise."

"We have a couple of problems to sort out here." Richard was by far the senior member of the party, and his voice had taken on a subtle undertone; Ringan thought that he sounded a bit like a professor handing out the assignments to the students. Maddy shot him an odd look, partly respectful, partly irritated. "In the first place, there's the matter of Ringan's connection to these people. I agree with Maddy entirely about it having the ring of a blood connection, but right now we can't verify that, can we? If those two girls died on the Isle of Dogs—and after hearing what Ringan heard today, I think it's a safe assumption that Margaret was executed there—then we have a missing family member somewhere. So there's some genealogy research to be done. I'm willing to take that on."

"Would you?" Ringan asked gratefully. "Because I haven't got the time or the interest. But we need to know."

"Yes, I will. But the second question is rather more pressing, I think. It's the cornerstone of all this. What actually happened to those two girls? What drove Margaret to murder her sister, and why was she not tried and executed at Tyburn, or maybe at Tower Hill? From the sound of it, she died there, on the Isle of Dogs, by the King's order. Something was going on there. When you consider just how nasty a death she'd have got at Tyburn, this had to be extra-special."

"Wouldn't she have been hanged at Tyburn?" Matt was listening, but he was keeping an eye on his watch as well. "We should think about heading back soon. Anyway, I don't know that I'd call hanging all that nasty. I mean, yes, barbaric, but—"

"She wouldn't have been hanged until she died, not at Tyburn during Henry's reign." Maddy had finished her beer, and got to her feet. "The practice was to hang the condemned until they weren't quite dead. Then they'd be cut down, disembowelled while they were still alive, and finally quartered. The Tudors were nothing if not thorough."

Chilled, they were all silent. She picked up her purse. "If Henry went to the trouble of issuing a personal sentence against this girl, with a specific method of execution, then something extraordinary had happened. You can take that one to the bank. He went to extraordinary lengths to make sure he was rid of Anne Boleyn: Mark Smeaton, Sir Henry Norris, even her own brother George, all arrested, pushed into trials for treason, executed. When it came to big broad sweeps of anything that narked him, he was the original master of the scorched-earth policy."

"Maddy's right." Richard had laid some money on the table. "Henry had a taste for wholesale indictments, but he never went to any of the executions he ordered; he was big on sobbing in his chambers while it was going on, and then, as soon as the bodies had cooled off, he'd dry his tears, change his shoes, and chase after the next skirt who might give him a male heir. This had to have hit him personally in some way, or offended him personally. We should let you get back to work."

"Before you go . . ." It was Jane, sounding very thoughtful. "Can I ask a favour? Or at least make a suggestion?"

The two academics paused, and looked back at her. She spoke slowly, carefully.

"Can I suggest you two look for a mention of a musician? Because we have a song, and there's a musician in there."

"What's on your mind?" Ringan was watching her.

"I'm not sure. It's just that, in what we've seen before, there's always been a sort of nugget of truth in the song—but it doesn't get the details right. This particular song is sort of casually gruesome: about a musician finding the drowned girl—that would be Catriona—and making a musical instrument out of her bits of bone and hair."

"Bollocks to that," Liam said rudely. "He'd have been tossed in prison and ripped apart. There's never been a time that sort of thing wouldn't get you in trouble."

"I think that's Jane's point, Liam." Ringan's beard was at full jut. He'd caught up with her. "The song's got a musician in it, but what he does in the song can't have happened in the real world. It's that nugget-of-truth thing. My guess is, there was probably a musician mixed up in the whole mess somewhere, but not where the song places him. Richard, Maddy—Jane's right. If you come across any mention of a musician, prick up your ears."

A week later, dragging her luggage, Penny Wintercraft-Hawkes climbed out of a taxi and up the shallow front steps to her London flat.

It was just short of the dinner hour, and she was very hungry. She was also bone-tired; the weather in northern Italy for the past few days had suddenly gone from perfect and balmy to hot and humid, and her body, for whatever reason, had refused to adapt. She'd done the final three performances with a sinus headache. It was very good to be home again.

"Penny!" Ringan had the front door open before she'd even had time to fumble for her keys. He got his arms around her and held on for a minute. "Lamb, it's good to see you, you can't even imagine. Welcome home."

He kissed her, long and deep. Penny, who had spent the past few weeks in a state of professional concentration, relaxed into it. It felt good. She pulled back slightly, took a deep breath, and realised the air tasted, not of the Florence of Lorenzo de Medici, but of the London of Ken Livingstone. She was home.

"Hello, love. What a nice way to meet me at the front door—I'm assuming you saved that one for me. I'd be really cross if I thought you'd been answering the door that way to the postman. Care to help me drag the suitcases indoors?" She hadn't really needed to ask; he'd already got one in each hand, and was holding the front door open with a knee. She gathered up the smaller pieces and dropped them in the front room of the flat; behind her, Ringan moved his leg, and the front door swung closed behind them.

They sent out for Afghani take-away. Over plates of savoury food, Penny did most of the talking; it had been a busy summer tour, the reviews were good, and there were incidents to share. Ringan himself stayed quiet, listening and eating, dishing out second helpings of *mantu* and *qabili pilau*.

After a while, Penny pushed her empty plate away and regarded him across the kitchen table.

"All right," she told him. "Now that you've heard all my bits and bobs, it's time for you to dish. You haven't said a word for the last half hour, and the very fact that you're being this quiet tells me you've got something on your mind, and you think I probably won't want to hear it. Well, whatever it is, I do want to hear it. So let's get on with it. What's been going on? Is something not going well with the new CD? Or has something new happened on the Isle of Dogs?"

"The CD is fine, thanks—we're almost done. Two songs left to do, and then the mix-down and the mastering for our record label." She was watching him, and very closely, too. He blew a short breath out, and met her look. "Yes, things have been happening to do with the Isle of Dogs. I want a glass of cider for this, though—it's going to take a while, and it's not going to be fun."

He gave her the story. She listened quietly, and without interruption.

". . . and that was nearly a week ago," he finished. "Nothing back yet from anyone poking around for historical information. Not one damned word, and I haven't rung anyone to see why. I had a tentative date to have a meal with your brother and his wife, but it hasn't happened—Stephen's got something going on with his company, and Tamsin says she's deep into editor mode, some article or something. And honestly, I'm relieved. I've been slacking on anything to do with this."

"Sounds as if you've gone into avoidance mode all the way around, Ringan."

He reached for her hand. "To tell you the truth, Pen, I think I just didn't want to have to talk about it, knowing that you weren't here to hear about it. But now you are. I'll come out of my shell tomorrow."

"I wouldn't mind seeing some people who have nothing at all to do with the theatre." She sounded wistful. "In fact, I wouldn't mind hanging out with some people who've never read a play in their lives, or maybe even a book. Seriously, Ringan, why don't we ring up Richard, and Maddy, and my brother and everyone, and maybe have a get-together and a general catching up? I've been holed up in an Italian *pensione* for the past month with nothing but theatre people. And as much as I love my mates, I could use a break."

"Really?" He blinked at her. "Seriously?"

"Absolutely." She grinned at him suddenly—the familiar curve of the lips, sending the vertical dimples that bracketed her mouth into deep grooves. It was a very intimate look, and he felt his breath shorten and catch. "You can't imagine how bored I've got with a month's worth of high-minded drama blather. And that way, we can not only pump our guests for whatever information they've already got, we can also make them feel guilty about not working on it. Two birds with one stone. And we can blare rock and roll for a change, good and loud. Yes?"

"Sounds good to me." He reached out, got her by the hand, and yanked her to her feet. "First, though, madam, I've got other things on our dance-card. Bedroom, first door on the right. I've missed the hell out of you. Anything else gets to wait until tomorrow, at the very earliest."

As it turned out, everyone accepted the invitation to come to Penny's flat. The party was set up for Saturday night; Penny, with no professional obligations on her plate for the next two months, spent that Friday tidying up and Saturday morning going to Harrods Food Halls for cheese, hors d'oeuvres, and wine.

She was in a very good mood. Ringan, it seemed, hadn't been joking about not letting her out of bed, and as a result, she was feeling not only relaxed, but very close to sleek. As an antidote to weeks of costuming and high theatre, she thought, you really couldn't hope for better than a good snog, or two, or three. . . .

Having sent Ringan off in search of cider and a fancy sweet, Penny set out paper napkins and disposable forks, and found herself considering what Ringan had told her. It was an odd story, she thought. She wasn't sure if Ringan had stopped to consider just how odd it was, but of course, he was close to it, in the eye of that particular storm. Whether he knew it or not, that was going to colour his take.

She stacked small disposable plates on the kitchen table, her mind working. Supposing Maggie Laine's information had been right, and Ringan, somehow, was descended from the mother of those two girls. Leaving aside the coincidence factor—which, in and of itself, was nearly too much for Penny to deal with—there was something else going on. Were they supposed to believe that he was also related to the army major who'd apparently chased a ghost into the bomb cavity, and straight into his own death? Because, while he might be sensitive to his ancestor's daughter, he'd heard the bomb-disposal bloke straight off.

Wineglasses, beer in the fridge to get nice and cold, two good-sized bottles of cider. She hoped Ringan would think to buy some bread while he was at the local bakery on Prince's Road; she'd forgotten it, and here was all this lovely cheese. . . .

Then there was the musician. Penny found herself believing, with absolute certainty, that the song contained at least a kernel of truth. That, after all, had been the way every encounter they'd had had gone: every song, as it had come down through the years, had a bit of truth and a twisting of the rest. In the song, the girls had fallen in love with the same bloke, a knight; how did the lyric go? *He courted one with gloves and rings, But he loved the other above all things.*

She rummaged around in one of the kitchen drawers for a corkscrew. So he'd flirted madly with both girls, that knight, and then fallen in love with one, and asked to marry her. If the song was right, the girl he'd loved was Catriona. Margaret, presumably, would have had a slapped ego, a broken heart, and a drawer full of gloves and rings.

But the entire second half of the song—that dealt with a musician. Lying in bed with Ringan in a contented afterglow, she'd talked with him about the song. There was more than one version, apparently, but that, according to Ringan, was quite common for traditional songs. He'd sung a few lines from "Bows of London," the version of the song that was set in the city, rather than on the windy shores of the Isle of Mull. Penny hunted her memory for the lyric: *Oh they laid her out on the bank to die, Hey the gay and the grinding, Fool with a fiddle come riding by, By the bonny bonny bows of London. . . .*

From there, she remembered only snatches of the lyrics. But they'd been nasty in the extreme. Something about using strands of the dead girl's hair for fiddle strings, and bits of bone to make the fiddle: fiddle pegs from finger bones, the actual instrument out of her breastbone.

Penny paused a moment, her hand resting on the bottle of red wine she'd just put out on the table. God, that was gruesome. The Scots version, now, that was a bit less gleefully indulgent towards necrophilia, but it was still pretty macabre. It also had the musician, and the girl's breastbone being used as the base for a musical instrument.

Penny stopped again, this time to savour a pleasurable memory. She'd actually said something about that to Ringan, and suggested they talk about something else. Her mouth curved up. His response to that had been more fun than she'd had in a while, since he'd announced that he didn't want to talk at all.

So, there was likely someone they hadn't heard about yet—that musician. That made two mysterious people they needed to find out about: the musician, and the missing link between Elspeth MacLaine and the second generation that had followed her, but apparently never been noted on the family tree.

And the oddest question, the one Penny found herself really

wondering about, was why on earth Henry Tudor had involved himself in Margaret MacLaine's punishment at all, much less on such a personal level.

Ringan came back with a beautiful pile of petits fours, an extra bottle of cider, and two loaves of hot bread, and shortly after, their guests began to arrive. Liam showed up with a bottle of Irish whisky, but without the girl he'd been rhapsodising over. Ringan, putting the whisky on the table with the rest of the nosh, allowed himself a private grin; the affair had followed Liam's usual pattern. Jane showed up with, of all things, a fresh pineapple, and a bottle of *sambuca* and Matt and Molly Curran in tow. Richard Halligan and Maddy Holt showed up within minutes of each other. Stephen and Tamsin, the last to arrive, brought some mackerel pâté that Penny pounced on, her mouth watering.

It was a nice party. Penny had felt some qualms about the addition of her brother and his wife, but they seemed to hit it off with everyone. Maddy wound up in one corner of the living room with Tamsin; Ringan, passing by on his way to load the sound system up with some classic seventies rock and roll, saw Tamsin looking animated and waving her hands as Maddy listened intently. The Broomfield Hill contingent, who'd known Penny as long as they'd known Ringan, relaxed and ate and talked about music. Richard and Stephen, who might have been thought to have nothing beyond their nationality and gender in common, discovered a joint love for international rugby.

Later in the evening, Penny picked her way through the bulk of her guests—most of whom, she decided, had reached a nice mellow stage of being mildly sozzled—wandered into the kitchen to make sure there was enough food left, and found that Maddy and Tamsin had moved their conversation into the kitchen's relative quiet. She headed over to join them.

"Penny! Lovely party—thanks for having us." Tamsin had a cider in one hand and a cheese straw in the other. "Has Ringan filled you in on what's been happening with my marvellous, if spooky, new house?"

"Yes, he has. In fact, I've been thinking about it all day. Here, let me get a beer—I want to run a few thoughts past both of you, if that's all right. But let's sit."

They settled into Penny's straight-backed kitchen chairs. "Now," Tamsin said. "What's on your mind?"

It took Penny a while to weave and connect the various threads that had been circling through her thoughts all day. The two historians listened to her, absorbing, making their own mental notes. Maddy had a look in her eye, a tautness to her body stance, that reminded Penny of their hunt for the truth behind the two previous hauntings Maddy'd helped them uncover. Tamsin, on the other hand, was birdlike in her attention; there was no way to tell what she was thinking.

When Penny had finished, there was a long moment of silence. Penny reached into the cooler on the table and found a chilled water. Something about that recitation—especially in reliving that moment in Italy, when she'd wakened from a deep sleep and found herself at Ringan's side, staring at the aftermath of a murder, with Ringan himself a pale vagrant ghost—had left her dry-mouthed.

"I'm thinking about the primary male figures in the song." Tamsin, well into her fourth beer of the night, tilted her head. If she was tipsy, it didn't show in her voice; she might have been instructing a student in the best sources for some obscure point of Elizabethan social protocol. The brown eyes were at once distant and focused. "If you don't mind, Penny, I'd like to come back to one point you raised. I've been looking at the song in question— obviously, since it's my house that appears to be going up on a patch of ghost-infested dirt, I've got a personal stake in this. The song mentions two men, yes? A knight who courted both girls, fell in love with one of them, and then got engaged to her. After the murder by the younger sister, we get the first mention of the second male presence in the song: the musician who comes by and mutilates the body, and produces an instrument that plays by itself and that accuses the sister. Is that correct?"

"That's it." Penny's voice was scratchy. She tipped some more of the cold water down her throat. From the lounge, out of nowhere, came Ringan's voice, mellow with cider; he was singing along with Mick Jagger, circa 1969. "And a lot more concise and to the point than I managed, too."

Tamsin looked faintly amused, and hunted up another bottled beer. It began to dawn on Penny that her new sister-in-law might actually be one of those women who got more lucid with every beer.

"What are you thinking, Tamsin?" Maddy asked sharply.

"I'm wondering if you—or Dr. Halligan—might not have been hunting in the wrong bit of bog for the past week." She saw bewilderment on the two faces turned her way, and sighed. "Apparently, I'm not being clear. I'm wondering if your knight and your musician might not be one and the same man."

A few days later, responding to a request from Tamsin, Ringan and Penny drove out to the Isle of Dogs to meet with Marcus Childe.

The ostensible reason for the get-together was to share what Tamsin referred to as an updated time-frame for the work being done; Ringan, however, wasn't sure he believed it. There had been something in Tamsin's voice, a subtle undertone, a sense that something was being held back. But, as he pointed out to Penny, Tamsin had the cheque-book. That meant Tamsin got to assign whatever reason she liked to her wishes.

The truth was, Ringan didn't want to go. The unease he'd felt from his first moment of setting foot on the Wintercraft-Hawkes land had, after the events of his last visit, transmuted into something verging dangerously on phobia. Lunch at the north end of the isle was one thing; that boggy patch to the southeast was another thing entirely. He thought, bitterly, that it was a pity no one had asked for his folklorist's input on renovating a restaurant in the shadow of the Canada Tower, or something.

It was a bright, sunny morning. Under normal circumstances, that would have taken any edge off Ringan's nerves; after all, they were going to be outdoors the entire time, and there were no enclosing walls, no corners or stairways for anything to hide under, no shadows. Yet today, at the wheel of the Alfa, he was as tense as piano wire. He'd been tense since accepting Tamsin's summons last night, but he'd been growing steadily more brittle all morning long.

Penny, in the passenger seat beside him, cast him a considering look. This really was something new. Whatever those voices, those pictures, from a long-dead series of moments on the Isle of Dogs had done to him, it had created something she honestly didn't recognise. This was a new side of Ringan, and she was already quite sure she didn't much like it. . . .

"Penny for them?"

She jumped a bit. "What, my thoughts? I was just thinking that maybe we should tell Tamsin thanks, this is all a bit much, we really don't want to be involved with it any further than this, ta ever so. We can still back out, you know? Yes, I know there's a contract, but my brother's not a monster, and this really isn't making you happy, darling, is it?"

"I've thought all that, believe me." He didn't relax. "But it's too late."

"Why?" She was honestly puzzled. "Stephen wouldn't mind, Ringan—he'd let you tear the damned thing up."

"I'm not talking about the contract."

"What do you mean?" Something in her stomach contracted. "Ringan—what is it? Did something happen?"

"Dream, last night." He hated making the admission, a fact that, by itself, was as dismaying as anything else. "Not even a nightmare, just a dream. Except—damn it. Like that first one, where we both had it? Clear and vivid, the way the first one was—I could feel my lungs working and my heart beating. And I think she could see me."

"What the hell?" She was twisted around in the seat, staring at his bristling beard and mottled cheek. "You had one of those dreams, about Margaret MacLaine?"

"I just said so, didn't I?" He snapped the words out, and immediately sighed. "Sorry, love. I'm probably overreacting, Pen, but I'll tell you what, I'm bloody tired of this. It's not as if I particularly *want* to witness all these nasty little moments in that girl's life, you know? Or in her sister's life, either, considering how impossible it was to tell the pair of them apart. It's not as if—"

"Pull over, will you? Pull the car over."

The words were a command. Ringan, startled, veered into a parking spot, and killed the Alfa's engine.

"Ringan—listen." There was a tight, concentrated look to Penny's face. He could almost see the wheels and gears in her mind clicking over. "Tell me what you saw. I think—no, that can wait. What did you dream? Not broad outlines, please. I want it as you saw it. Okay?"

"Right." Obedient without knowing why, Ringan closed his eyes, wondering if he'd be able, in the brilliant light of a summer's day, to summon up those shades of the previous night's darker hours.

He got his answer at once: the moment he'd blocked out the daylight, the dream was there, clear, drenched in a particular set of colours and feelings and sounds. Dreaming, he'd been an observer only. He'd stood, invisible, watching as one of a huge throng of people. What had he seen?

The centre of attention, not only Ringan's attention but that of everyone watching, had been an enormous man with a russet beard, dressed in a purple velvet doublet so sewn over with jewels that it seemed too stiff to move with its wearer. *Royal purple,* Ringan thought. This was a royal evening. This was a king.

The King had the vast expanse of dance floor to himself and his succession of partners. There were musicians in the gallery. The leader of the band seemed to be a handsome young man with the look of Italy or the south of France, playing an instrument that looked like a sort of fancy ancestor to an oboe. *What are they called?* Ringan wondered, and suddenly remembered: the oboe-relative was a shawm, of course. He'd seen them before, and met a few shawm players in his day, mostly at festivals.

The shawm player, leading the band, blowing into his instrument. Dark bold eyes, fixed on the dancers spread out below him, moving from woman to woman like a collector in a field of brightly coloured butterflies, his fingers flying, music pouring down from the gallery: *Pastime with good company, I love and shall unto I die—Grudge whoso will, but none deny, so God be pleased, this live will I.*

A singer, a sweet tenor voice, standing a bit apart. Ringan, that invisible ghost at the ball, listening and recognising the source of the music. Henry VIII himself, that consummate musician, had written this tune. Up there in the gallery, doing honour to the King in the hall below, the musicians played on.

And the King trod a measure, now with an overdressed woman with no chin, leading her back to the group who watched the King opening the dance, holding out his hand to a round-faced girl in a vivid blue gown, her flaming hair loose down her back, an embroidered French hood above a high brow and a face that was deceptively demure, her dark eyes cast down, then up, roguish and saucy, accepting her sovereign's hand and his invitation to step with him.

It was astonishing, how clear the memory was. This wasn't the memory of a dream; it was the memory of a party. Ringan could smell the place: perfume and must, fabric, candles, roast meat wafting in from somewhere. He could hear the chatter around him, and found much of it hard to place in his Modern English–speaking mind; the language was not the language of now. He saw the scented, powdered flesh of breasts, globes straining above the blackwork embroidery on those tight, flattening bodices, green and blue, scarlet, cloth of gold. He could hear the music. He could hear breath.

*For my pastance hunt, sing, and dance; my heart is set all goodly sport to my comfort. Who shall me let?*

The girl was dancing with the King, and yet she wasn't. Her *doppelgänger* stood beside Ringan, so close he felt his fingers tingle with the sudden urge to reach out and poke at her arm.

Unlike her sister, she wore green. Blackwork danced along the edges of sleeve and bodice, pearls dangled from her neck. Her eyes followed the dancers for a moment, then lifted, as if pulled by an invisible wire, to the musicians in the gallery. There was something on her face, a hunger, a need, a deep raw craving that spoke of carnality, ripeness, all those things that make for a virtuous maid's downfall. As if aware that her face gave too much away, she looked down.

But her gaze had met the eyes of the shawm player. Ringan wondered if the musician hesitated, just for a moment, and pursed his lips to her.

*Youth will have needs dalliance, Of good or ill some pastance. Company me thinketh then best—All thoughts and fantasies to digest.*

And here was King Henry, his jewel-crusted doublet creaking under its own weight, returning the girl to the group, reaching out a hand, laughing, his eyes slitted with amusement and pleasure, leading out the twin, but which was which, which was Margaret and which Catriona?, the girls were identical. . . .

*For idleness is chief mistress of vices all; then who can say but "pass the day" is best of all?*

A sweet, plangent note fell like a fine mist from the gallery to the brilliant throng below: the shawm player, with black-oil eyes and the full, curved lips of a sensualist, played a solo, a dozen bars of haunting lilt, and the King and the second twin stepped lively, a swing, a bow, back to the sidelines, and there went the King, offering his hand and sketching as much of a bow as his ridiculous clothing would permit, leaving the sisters, green gown and blue, standing together, blue looking up towards the gallery, seeing where green's eyes had rested. . . .

". . . and I remember exactly what she said, she said, *Only a fool, Sister, would think to catch and keep such a prize as that.* And she was looking up at the gallery. At the band. And her sister looked up and met her eyes, but she ignored her sister. She saw me, Pen— Margaret did. She looked over her sister's shoulder and met my eye. I swear she saw me."

Ringan heard his own voice, and stopped. He blinked hard, once, twice. The vast ballroom of the night before, with its glittering crowds and its smoky air, had been replaced by warmth, and sunlight. The carved pillar he'd been leaning against was soft and pliant under his touch; he'd taken hold of Penny's arm, not realising, and he was holding on to her, as hard as he could.

He opened his mouth, trying to clear his head. How in heaven's name could he possibly hope to recapture that enough to give Penny the sense of need he'd felt, the urgency, the sheer power of the immediacy of the dream, which had been no dream, but rather a moment out of history?

"Wow," she said. "Just—bloody hell."

He met Penny's eye, and felt a shock wave along his nervous system. He didn't have to find a way to tell her—he already had. He'd been talking all along, telling her what he'd seen even as he relived it. He was suddenly dizzy, swaying in the seat of the Alfa.

And there was more, a sense memory, times coming together, overlapping the vertigo like wavelets covering clean sand: the members of Broomfield Hill, staring at him as he opened his eyes inside an isolation booth, listening to a song in his headphones, singing an entirely different song, one he neither knew nor could name. . . .

"Okay. Right." She was staring at him, very pale. "Ringan, close your eyes. You're a very odd colour right now. Just—take a few long deep breaths, and close your eyes."

"Good idea." The vertigo had suddenly become intolerable, the interior of the car seeming to spin like some sort of homicidal top, a child's toy run amok. He swallowed his gorge, and waited. This, he reflected, was just how he'd felt on the Isle of Dogs itself the day he'd gone alone and heard those voices, the bomb-disposal bloke's and Margaret MacLaine's, one atop the other. After a couple of minutes, the mist began to clear and his stomach began to settle down.

He opened his eyes, and looked at Penny. There was genuine trouble in her face.

"We have a problem," she said quietly. "Don't we? A huge, nasty problem. Because this is what you meant, by saying it was too late to just back out of the gig. Wasn't it?"

He nodded. She had been through something similar to this before, on her own behalf, in her near-possession by Agnés de Belleville. Yet, this was new. What she had dealt with was someone wanting to use her, pure and simple. Agnés had been a woman who had died with a need left unfulfilled; as mad and as desperate in death as she had been in life, she had tried latching on to Penny, the sensitive, in a kind of spiritual hijacking, a way to freedom.

But they had shared nothing else, no touchstone, no meeting place. Margaret, in some way, was blood of Ringan's blood. And there was no threat of possession here. The danger was much deeper: the blood tie, pulling him in, refusing to let him go. And he wasn't safe from it anywhere. Turning his back on the Isle of Dogs was as meaningless a gesture as he could offer.

"Penny, listen." He reached out a hand, suddenly wanting the reassurance of human contact. "You started to say something when I first pulled over—whatever it was, you said you wanted to hear me out first. I'm done, for now, anyway. What was it you wanted to say? Did you have an idea? God, I hope you have an idea. Please say you do. Because right now, lamb, your bonny boy's a wee bit on the wrong side of desperate. Honestly, I'm open to trying anything that might rip the lady loose of my, um, psychic throat."

"I don't know that it's an idea." She spoke slowly; Ringan, watching her face, knew she was trying to tease something out, without knowing where to begin. "Really, it's more of a question. What I want to know is, why Margaret?"

He blinked. She went on, still in that slow, deliberate way; she looked like this when doing acrostics, fancy puzzles he could barely begin, but which she loved doing. "Why is it only Margaret? If you're hearing things, seeing things, feeling things from the time, why not Catriona as well? They were twins, weren't they? Identical twins?"

"Completely. No idea how I would have told them apart, assuming I'd had to."

"Well, then, why are you only getting Margaret? Because you are, aren't you? You said, just now, that you could see what she was doing, where she was looking. From the sound of it, both girls had

a major case of the hots for the horn player, or whatever he was—
what are you laughing at?"

"The twin teens having the hots for the horn player, that's what.
Your phrasing. It makes them sound like some sort of Tudor
groupies, wanting to go home and have a mad bit of belly-bump
with the guy in the band."

Penny grinned, but it faded quickly. "The thing is, you heard
Margaret, didn't you? I mean, *heard* her. And you didn't say anything about thinking Catriona could see you, but you thought
Margaret could. So—why? If the link back is to their mum, why
aren't you picking up both girls? Why is Margaret linked up to
you, and not Catriona?"

"I don't know. But that's a damned good question." He started
the engine. "We should head over there, get it over with. You
know, I think I ought to ring up Maddy Holt, and ask her to check
into some of the trials from that period. See if maybe she can find
something, anything at all, that might give me some sort of weapon
to fight this with."

"Give *us* something, you mean," she corrected him, and the car
pulled out into traffic, heading southeast.


Tamsin was waiting for them at the building site; they spotted the
Mercedes, its wheels pulled safely up into the kerb. Ringan slid in
behind it, killed the engine, and shot a sideways look at Penny's
dropped jaw.

"Amazing, isn't it? I forgot, you've been gone since before the
work started. I've never seen anything come together quite this
fast."

It was almost unnerving. Ringan had been by a week earlier, and
marvelled then at the progress. At that point, there had been
plumbing, foundations, enough of the interior framing to give a
clear look at the eventual footprint of the E-shaped manor to those
who knew how to interpret the architecture. It had been a strong
pencil sketch of a house.

In the space of a week, the sketch had begun to take on dimensional reality. The amount of timbering in place had easily doubled, and the single storey had become two. The entire first floor strut framing was now in place; the door-frame at the top of what would be the grand interior staircase was clearly visible. From his position of relative safety at the edge of Westferry Road, Ringan could see straight through to where the support frames for the vast expanse of Thames-view windows had been set.

"But—but—" Penny was stammering. Ringan couldn't remember the last time he'd seen her confounded. "But it's only been a month! How in hell has it gone up so fast?"

"Maybe your brother's money? Or maybe . . ." He heard his own voice fade, and flatten. "Or maybe the builders want to get this done as fast as they decently can, and get the hell out of here. Maybe I'm not the only one hearing voices."

She jerked her head to look at him, but whatever she was going to say was lost. Tamsin had seen them, and come across from what would be the front of the house, the north façade.

"Ringan! Penny! Thanks for coming, you two—I tried ringing you about twenty minutes ago, but no luck. Marcus can't be here. He's gone off to the dentist with an emergency—a crown came loose, or some such thing. But even though we won't get much house discussion in, I'm glad you came."

"Are you?" She seemed even more birdlike than usual today, Ringan thought. "Why's that?"

"Because I have some information for you, a little tidbit I dug out of a nice extensive internet site devoted to sixteenth-century music." Her plump cheeks suddenly lifted into dimples of satisfaction. "How would you feel about the name of a musician who was arrested in late April 1540 for 'conspiring to bring grief to the King,' and who died under torture? Any good?"

"Oh, hell yes!" Ringan's beard was bristling. "Any details about this bloke?"

"A few." Tamsin really did look smug. "An Italian boy, for one thing, name of Pietro Bendone. From Milan originally—his father was a notary, if I'm remembering properly. Oh, hell, hang on a moment. I have this written down."

She rummaged around in her purse, and finally retrieved a sheet of notebook paper, folded up small.

"Ah, here we are. Pietro Bendone, right, age twenty—poor brat, what a nasty way to die, being tortured. And good heavens, that charge I mentioned was only half—they had him up for treason as well. He wouldn't have stood a chance; I don't think anyone ever got acquitted if they'd displeased the King enough to get charged with that."

"Tamsin." Ringan's breath was a bit short. "Listen—was there anything about what instrument he played?"

"Hang on—ah, yes. I'm not really up on the music of the period, and I've never even heard of this one. But apparently, he played something called a shawm. What on earth is a shawm?"

"A sort of medieval super-ocarina. Or, really, think of it as great-great-grandfather to an oboe." Ringan caught Penny's eye. "A shawm player. Do you know, I was hoping you'd say that. He's our musician, all right—I'd lay good money on it. Let's go up and get some lunch at the Wharf, and I'll tell you all about it."

# Seven

*And out and come the miller's son:*
*"Father dear, here swims a swan!"*
*Two minstrels walked along the strand*
*And saw the maiden float to land.*

"So, where do you suggest we begin?"

Maddy Holt swallowed a mouthful of nan, and looked at Richard Halligan, who'd just finished blotting the crumbs from a samosa from his lips. The area behind her spacious desk had been designed for one chair, not two; as a result, Maddy was feeling a bit crowded. The remnants of Indian take-away, strewn across her desk, added to the problem.

Richard had rung her up earlier in the evening. Ringan had let them both know about the existence of Pietro Bendone, and about the dream, the movement, whatever it was that he'd experienced, that had taken him back to that palace with its dancers and its musicians. He'd told them both about the twins, their reaction to the shawm player in the gallery.

After the call, Maddy had found herself literally twitching with impatience to get started. When Richard had rung her up, within minutes of getting off the phone with Ringan, she'd suggested he grab some comfy slippers and whatever he generally used for note taking, and come over to her office. Her resources, after all, were greater than his, and a lot of them weren't available to anyone outside the library.

Now, after a good meal, they were ready to start. It was likely, she thought, to be a long night's work.

"Well." Maddy began stacking empty cartons together, and pushing them into her waste-basket. "We have a shiny new starting point. Pietro Bendone—the first thing I did after I got off the phone with Ringan was to hunt up anything we had on the subject of his trial."

"Any luck?" Richard took a paper napkin and brushed crumbs off the desk, into a paper sack. The clutter on the desk was diminishing; they were going to need elbow room.

"Nothing. If he actually got to the point of being tried for treason, there's no record of it. But I'm not surprised, because I suspect he died before they could formally try him. Not that it would have mattered, of course. The poor sod never had a chance, not if Henry wanted him dead badly enough to hang a treason charge on him."

"That was my thinking, as well, about Bendone's chances. Ringan said Tamsin told him Bendone died while under torture, in what? April of 1540?"

"April 1540 it is. So I suggest we start there."

For Richard, in his late sixties and without a home computer, watching Maddy use the resources of the internet was an education that bordered on humbling. He, himself, came from a generation of historians who had done the bulk of their professional work in the days before computers, and watching this new breed was enough to leave him regretting that the vast web of information accessible by typing in two words and clicking a button on a keyboard had been denied him.

She seemed, he thought, to have an instinct for what search terms to enter. One thought he'd always harboured was that a historian using computers for research was somehow analogous to children being allowed to use calculators to figure out problems in their math: it had always seemed to Richard to foster a kind of mental laziness. But as he watched Maddy, that suspicion died a fast death. If her first search yielded results, she followed every lead to its conclusion, and took what she needed. If the results led up a blind alley, she swore, shook her head, and tried something else. There was no laziness here.

Her first term was the obvious choice: "Pietro Bendone." She typed it in, clicked, and waited.

"Your search returned one hit."

"Here we go." Maddy slid her own chair slightly to one side. "Can you see the screen from here? Lord, I do love my big-screen monitor."

"Yes, yes, I can." Richard slid his glasses up, and began reading. "I can't quite tell—what is this from?"

"It's from a paper someone's written. Hang on—let me see how much of it I can access."

She moved the mouse, highlighted blue letters that spelled out "cached," and clicked.

*. . . the many musicians at the court of King Henry VIII. It must be remembered that, of course, Bluff King Hal was himself an excellent musician, and was known for several of his freemen's songs. He wrote both lyric and music. One would think, knowing his genuine love and respect for the art of making music, that musicians at his court would have had reason to consider themselves respected, and relatively safe. However, at least two musicians died as a direct result of Henry's personal order.*

*The more famous of these was, of course, Mark Smeaton, who was unfortunate enough to be Anne Boleyn's personal musician, and who was swept up in Henry's mad rush to rid himself of Anne so that he could marry Jane Seymour, already possibly pregnant with the male heir the King so desperately desired. Smeaton's trial for treason and his subsequent beheading are well documented.*

*The second musician who died at Henry's hand is less known: this was a young Milanese shawm player by the name of Pietro Bendone [note: I have seen this alternately spelled as "Bendoni."] who had come to London in early November of 1539, apparently to be part of the resident players at the Palace of Placentia. It is probable that groups of musicians were assembled as part of the preparations of Henry's upcoming nuptials with Anne of Cleves. I have been unable to find any reason for the original arrest and charge of treason against Bendone, and there is no evidence of his ever going to trial. [Note: Papers at the Bodleian show Bendone died while undergoing torture. There was also an arrest made as a result of his confession under torture, of a young woman, but I've been unable to verify either her identity or the reasons behind Henry's ordering any of these charges and actions.]*

"Half a minute—let me print out two copies of this." Maddy's shoulders were taut. *A scent,* she thought, *a spoor, something out there that can be found.* "I think we've just hit the first turn in the maze."

"Appropriate, considering the king in question and the maze at Hampton Court." With Maddy up at her printer, Richard had jerked his chair close, and was rapidly scanning the information on the screen. "Maddy, this is incredible. What do you suppose he—or she—means, 'unable to verify'?"

"Probably just that." She handed Richard a printout. "Damn, what's the date on this paper, or article, or whatever it is? Here, just click the arrow that points down, it'll take you to the bottom of the page—ah. Perfect, thanks. This was written in 1987, by a history student at Merton. Pre-internet, poor bugger. I sympathize, because I had to get kicked into using the internet by a terrifying woman running an exhibit of de Valois artifacts at Cluny. I can't even remember what it's like to not have the resources there online."

"But—I don't understand." Richard had read down the printout, and was blinking at Maddy. "If he wrote this paper years before the internet existed, what's it doing out there?"

"Oh, that's not unusual. People very often upload their work years after they've first done it; if this particular person had wanted to update it with more information that was actually on the net, he or she could simply import the text and use it to update." She was frowning at her printout. "The Bodleian. Hmmmm. Papers at the

Bodleian. Richard, can you slide your chair over a bit? I want to check something."

He moved. Maddy dropped into her own chair, thought for a moment, and opened a new browser window, with a blinking cursor: "Enter search terms." Richard, intent, watched her parameters come up in the box.

"Pietro. Bendone. MacLaine."

A moment, less than a moment. The screen flickered and resolved into words: "Your search returned one hit."

"What is it?" Richard was all the way forward in his chair. "What does it say? Open it!"

"I'm going to, damn it!" She was smiling. "Give me a tenth of a second to do it, all right?"

*. . . from the letters of Alison MacLaine.*

Maddy read it aloud, picking out the salient bits.

*. . . lady-in-waiting and companion, by the King's order, to the Royal Sister Anne of Cleves . . . mentions of a musician, an Italian or Swiss, named Pietro Bendone . . . arrested for high treason and plotting to cause the death of the King . . . was put to the rack near the end of April, and other forms of torture probably used to obtain the names of his co-conspirators . . . carried out by Sir Leonard Skeffinton himself . . . a young girl, Margaret MacLaine, niece of Anne's companion Alison . . . in storage at the Bodleian . . ."*

She stopped, and looked up at Richard. "Damn. Annoying."

"Annoying? Good heavens, Maddy, why? I'd call this a staggering success. We have a name, a location for those letters of Alison MacLaine's, and confirmation of who these people were. If we'd been trying to research this in the old-fashioned way, following the printed records only, it would have taken weeks, not minutes. How on earth can you call this annoying?"

"I was hoping they'd have been uploaded by now. This means a day trip to Oxford." She laughed suddenly. "Yes, I know, I suppose I sound like a spoiled cow. But you have to admit, being able to access damned near anything you want to know just by clicking the button is one hell of a time-saver."

"So, we take a day trip to Oxford." Richard's voice held more than enough enthusiasm to compensate for Maddy's lack of it. "What does your schedule look like? Any chance we can sneak out that way soon?"

"What's tomorrow, Friday? They're on vacation hours right now, I'd imagine, and I haven't used the Bodleian in donkey's years. Damn, which branch of the Bodleian? Probably the Old Library— I can't see a collection of Tudor letters being housed anywhere else, unless they're at the Radcliffe Camera."

Another browser window, another search term, another fast flicker of Maddy's outsized flat-screen monitor, and there was the Bodleian's schedule of hours, up for anyone to see. *Right,* Richard thought, *that's it*—Monday morning, he was going to go off and buy himself a computer.

"Here we go," Maddy said. "I'll just leave word that I'll be doing some research at Oxford tomorrow."

"Lovely. Are you sure we can get in? Should we call them first?"

"Why?" She looked puzzled for a moment. "Honestly, Richard, I don't see them refusing us entry, do you?"

"If the stuff's at the Radcliffe, they might."

"Nonsense. We'll just walk straight up and point out that you're the retired secular archivist for St. Paul's Cathedral and I oversee the King's Collection for the British Library, and Bob's your uncle, we're not only in, but they'll be strewing roses in our path if they're the rose-strewing sort."

He blinked at her. She grinned at him.

"Not to worry, I'll ring them first thing in the morning, and tell them what we need. They'll be able to get us what we need. Seriously, though, bring your credentials, I'll bring mine, and we ought to be settled into any part of the building we choose by licensing hours at the Bird and Baby. I'll come round and pick you up in the morning."

"Ringan?"

Stone walls, a bed hung with draperies, a voice.

He wasn't certain where the voice was coming from. It sounded like Penny, but it was so low, nothing more than a distant whisper, really. There was no way to be sure.

*Hold me, put your hands on me, oh yes, I will not speak of this to any living soul, my sister least of all, nothing, oh hold me, I do beseech thee, oh my love*

"Ringan?"

Breathing, whispering, but it wasn't really whispering, he thought. It was more that the girl was taken up, she was busy and doing, or being done to, and she had no breath to speak.

Breathing, whispering, growing shorter, harsher, the exhale of release, or desperation. Ringan, dizzy and disoriented, realized that the darkness around him was of his own making; his eyes were shut, closed against vision.

*All my heart and body I give to thee, all, oh kiss me beloved, I would be your one true mistress, cast all others aside, I beseech thee, take none but me to be your love, none but me*

"Ringan, what is it? What's wrong?"

Slowly, painfully, Ringan opened his eyes, and saw what, waking or sleeping, he should not have been able to see.

They were naked, both of them, locked together and deep into coupling. The girl, her face visible over the man's shoulder, was flushed as red and as bright as the tangled mass of hair spread out in all directions across the bed. Her small dark eyes were glazed over; her hands clenched and unclenched along the bare flesh of her lover's back, leaving angry red marks. Even as she arched and sucked in her breath, whimpering and mindless, her lips moved, forming words, seemingly unable to stop the pleading, the begging for affirmation.

*Oh my love my friend I put myself in your hands, swear unto me you will take no other mistress, swear it*

Her legs wrapped around him, and she bit back a cry. The man, young and slender, replied, a hushing noise. There was no way to decipher it, no way to tell whether he was trying to soothe her, to give her the words she wanted along with the pleasure she wanted; it was possible, Ringan thought dizzily, that he was simply trying to get her to shut up and let him get on with it, without distraction.

A few words came through, the man arching his back, tightening his hips, pausing a moment to reach out and take up a long strand of that bright hair. *"Morrellotto,"* he said, and brought the hair to his lips, and kissed it. The gesture was surpassingly tender, and Ringan, trying desperately to understand where he was, what he was seeing, how and why he was seeing it, shook his head like a swimmer coming up from deep, dark water.

The girl laughed suddenly, and answered him. *"Non,"* she told him. *"Arrancia rosso."*

He smiled down at her, and moved his hips, sudden and sharp. The girl dug her nails into his back, and bit back a scream; her eyelids dropped suddenly, and she relaxed, and the man went with her, all the strength and tension going out of him with the rest of his breath.

"Ringan, look at me, what is it, what's going on . . . ?"

It sounded like Penny's voice, he thought. His mind was hazy; he felt as languid and as uncoordinated as the couple, their limbs twined, easy and limp. He felt, obscurely, that what he had just witnessed was not for him to see. He felt like a peeping Tom, a voyeur.

*"Bella,"* the man said, soft, quiet. *"Mia donna bella."*

He kissed her, cheek, chin, lips. Her rosy blush had faded, the turmoil of colour ebbing. She looked into his face; Ringan thought he had never seen so adoring a look.

"Ringan!"

He felt a stab of annoyance. What was wrong with Penny, to be making so much noise? If she kept up that racket, the couple would hear her, they would turn to look, see the two interlopers in their perfect silent place, their chamber, their haven. Not that either had shown any awareness of his presence . . .

"Damn it! Damn, damn—sorry, Ringan."

The slap took him across the face. It wasn't a hard slap, just a light sting from the warm palm of a human hand, but it was enough.

He had a moment of blackness, a void of darkness at his feet, threatening the fragile thread that seemed to be holding him between two worlds, wanting to suck him down and into something, somewhere, that was beyond his imagining. He heard himself cry out, his own voice saying something. He felt himself tense against whatever was coming.

For a long, bad moment, he seemed to be hanging there, worlds merging, gears sickeningly refusing to mesh. Then he was staring at his own shoes, down on Penny's kitchen floor, and he doubled over in one of her high-backed kitchen chairs, retching up everything he'd eaten for the last little bit, and stomach bile along with it.

She held him the entire time, supporting his shoulders with strong, steady hands. Ringan, caught without air, unable to clear his head, his stomach in an uproar, was aware of only two concrete facts: she was a rock, and he loved her. It was perhaps fortunate that he couldn't see her face, her mouth slack with horror, her eyes wide with shock.

"Right." His voice was a bare rasp. "It's okay. I'm okay. Better. Back. Christ."

"Good." She got to her feet. "Sit. I'll get you some water. No, don't worry about that—I'll clean it up. Just sit."

He put his arms down across the table, lowered his head, and kept it there. Vertigo danced along the edges, wanting to swamp him, to pull him back in to that incomprehensible place where he stood as a ghost, formless, without substance, seeing and hearing what his senses wanted to deny. His hands were cold, and numb, and his heart didn't seem to know whether it wanted to race or to slow down to almost nothing.

"Here. Sip this." She set a glass of water beside him. "Small sips—don't gulp it down."

"No worries." His voice was a wreck; there was no way he was going to be able to sing for a few days. Hazily, distantly, he wondered why that was a problem, and then remembered he was near the end of recording a new CD. That was with Broomfield Hill. Right. He was Ringan Laine, Rupert Darnley Laine. He had a band. They played traditional music. They were called Broomfield Hill. He was Ringan Laine, he was in London, in Penny's flat.

He thought about straightening up pressing his back against the chair, taking a mouthful of water, and then thought better of it. The dizziness was overwhelming.

"Ringan, you're shaking." She'd pulled a chair up next to him, and was touching him—a fingertip here, one there, light pressure, a kind of human reassurance that comes with contact. "Can you sit up? I'm right here. Right, good, that's it—keep your eyes closed, and sit up slowly. Here. Sip it."

The water was room temperature, blessedly not too cold, and he took a few small sips, waiting between tiny mouthfuls, letting his raw throat absorb what it could.

The scene he'd witnessed, the merging of bodies, the tender touch of the girl's bright hair, was beginning to fade. Eyes closed, he found himself still catching brief, tantalising glimpses. It was odd, he thought, that the visuals should be so nebulous. Clear in his memory were words, her breathless begging, his endearments.

He opened his eyes, and fixed them on Penny. She had taken some cloths to the mess on the floor, and was just straightening up.

"You're just home from Italy," he told her, wincing, as one hand came up to lightly massage the base of his throat. "You speak a bit of Italian. He said something, and she answered, and it was in Italian. What does '*morrellotto*' mean?"

"Wait a bit." She dumped the fouled cloths into the trash, and sat down opposite him. "Back up, Ringan. Who said what?"

"Sorry. Hang on." He took some more water. His voice was coming back, but it was still scratchy. "I was in someone's bedroom—big bed, one of those things you can draw curtains around and shut yourself in. She was there—one of the twins. She was in bed with the Italian musician, the shawm player, Pietro Whatever-it-was. They were making love; it was dead serious, too, something desperate about it. She was begging him to not have any lovers except her. And he touched her hair, and said that word: '*morrellotto.*' What does it mean?"

"No idea, but I can find out. Give me a minute or two."

"Okay. I'll just sit right here, if you don't mind." He closed his eyes again, willing the pictures to come back, hearing the beep of Penny's computer. The pictures obliged, but they were even weaker now, fading out. Oddly, the voices still rang clear in his mind.

He got to his feet, carefully keeping the palm of one hand on the table. His knees were shaky, wanting to wobble, but he'd lost the vertigo. He made his way towards Penny's office alcove.

"Another phrase." He was going to speak as little as he decently could, he decided. "Her answer. She said, '*Non, arrancia rosso.*' But her voice—there was a definite Scots burr to it. She'd picked up phrases. I don't think she could speak Italian, not properly. What's *arrancia rosso*"?

"Wait—ah." Penny straightened up and looked at Ringan; he'd sat down on the edge of the bed, watching her, sipping his water. "They're colours. It's medieval Italian, according to my web search—'*morrellotto*' means ruddy, a kind of basic fiery red. '*Arrancia rosso*' sounds nasty, doesn't it? Rancid red? Oh, here it is. It means orange, a tawny orange. Does that help?"

"It does." He cleared his throat, winced, and took another mouthful of water. "Damn. Need a throat lozenge. He touched her hair—very tender gesture, very loving. Not seductive. They were already well past any need for him to seduce her, or her him. I think he meant it—I think he loved her. And she answered him, with that thing about her hair."

Penny was quiet, watching his face. She could see him remembering the moment, Pietro Bendone touching the girl's hair in wonder, the girl loving him, answering him back, correcting him, No, not red, orange. Ringan's lips had curved into a smile. She wondered if he understood what had happened, or how frightened she was for him.

"Ringan?" He looked up at her. "I don't know if you remember what happened—not what happened that you saw, but what happened before you saw it. Do you? No, don't talk. Rest the throat. Do you remember?"

He shook his head, and watched her fingers clench in her lap. "All right," she told him quietly. "We were sitting at the table, drinking coffee. That's all. You started to say something totally trivial, about Lord Randall needing new strings, and then you disappeared."

His mouth opened. She shook her head at him. Her hands had woven together into a tight knot of knuckles and skin.

"You disappeared. I meant what I said—it's what happened. You were sitting right there, but you were gone. I saw you go. Your shoulders jerked and then they relaxed and your eyes—they emptied. I don't know how else to describe it. They just emptied out, there was nothing in there of you that I could see. You went away. And I was calling you, calling your name—"

"I heard you." He had begun to shake a bit, himself. "I remember. Remember hearing you."

"I had to slap you. You weren't coming back." She raised her eyes, finally, and he saw tears on her face. "I'm scared," she told him. "I'm frightened half out of my mind. It was like quicksand. I could almost feel whatever it was, wherever you were, sucking you down and under. And I'm scared."

Her voice broke. Ringan got up and gathered her in. He offered her no reassurance, because there was none to offer. She'd described it perfectly. And this had been no dream, no wandering of his subconscious during the march of the night hours. He'd been drinking coffee and thinking about restringing his guitar. And he'd been taken away.

"We need this to stop." He swallowed, as lightly as he could. "Need to ring Maddy, Richard. Let them know what happened. Tell them there's—urgency. Danger."

"I'll do it." *Anything,* she thought, *anything at all, oh please let this be stoppable.* She had a cold certainty in the pit of her stomach that, whatever had reached out of history, whatever had travelled down the centuries through the blood that somehow connected Ringan to these people, it had to be stopped. If it wasn't, she was going to lose Ringan.

There would come a time when that grab at his ankles would be permanent. And it was going to happen soon.

She reached for her cell phone, and turned back to the computer, to her electronic address book. As she was punching in Maddy's number, she paused.

"Ringan." She was staring at him. "You said Pietro Bendone, and one of the twins. The twin he loved."

He nodded.

"What do I tell them? Which twin?"

He opened his mouth, and shut it again. Had anything come from the girl in the bed, her rounded legs wrapped around the young musician, her tangled waterfall of hair spilling out across the sheets? Had there been anything to give him the girl's name?

He thought of her tenderness, her response, her need for the boy to love her above all else. He closed his eyes. The pictures had almost gone now, faded into pale mezzotints of memory washed out by the light of today.

"I don't know," he told Penny. "But if I had to lay money on it? I'd say that was Catriona."


"Tell me again why we're doing this. And why we're doing it at this ungodly hour of the morning."

Tamsin glanced over her shoulder and up at her husband. Stephen sounded quite cross, she thought; really, she was going to have to accustom herself to living with a man who couldn't seem to cope properly before eleven at the earliest. She herself was an early-morning person; years of grading papers and writing articles had left her cherishing those few hours of quiet before telephones began ringing, before students began poking their heads around corners and through doorways, before her colleagues began driving her crazy with questions and small talk and chatter and gossip. All of Tamsin's rhythms were at peak functionality between six and eight in the morning.

It had just gone seven, and here they were, husband and wife, standing on a patch of scrub that, in a month or so, was scheduled to be dug up and filled with fertile soil, in which a riot of roses could thrive. The temperature, chilly during the still-short nights that followed midsummer, had begun to warm, and a fine soft mist had left a film of damp on the struts, the supports, the foundations of the house being built. To the south, the river sparkled; to the north, the light atop the Canada Tower blinked valiantly in a battle it couldn't win against the strengthening sunlight of the new day.

"Sorry, Stephen." It was a polite fiction, that apology, a marital sop, no more than that. She wasn't remotely sorry; after all, she thought, there was no point in actually regretting a simple necessity.

And a simple necessity was the only term she could find to define the need that had been building in her. The feeling that she ought to come out, be here, stand on the ground and breathe in the air, see if she could somehow touch whatever it was that had reached out to Ringan, had been growing. It had come to the point where Tamsin, a solid pragmatist, had decided she could no longer ignore it.

She'd told Stephen at bedtime the previous night that she'd be waking him early, because they were going out to the Isle of Dogs. At the edge of sleep, he'd mumbled something she'd missed; at half past five, having been shaken awake, he'd stumbled out of bed, drunk an indecent amount of tea, and driven the Mercedes to their building site.

"No need to be sorry, darling. Not that I believe you are, not for a moment." He had his hands in his pockets, and was regarding her with sardonic affection. "Fair warning, though. You want to do this again, you can damned well learn how to drive an automobile. And I don't want to hear a word about old dogs and new tricks. Ridiculous hour to be up and about."

"I quite like it." She walked up a slab of plywood that had been laid down for the workmen, and through what would be the oversized front door. The room on the other side, with no walls and only the beginnings of a subfloor, would have been nothing at all to a casual observer; to Tamsin, with the blueprint of the house fixed in her mind, the great beams that would span the room overhead were clearly visible, and her imagination placed her feet on the flagstones that would be the floor.

She stood still, her eyes closed. *Questing,* she thought, *that's what I'm doing—very Arthurian, really, echoes of an earlier time. I'm looking for a mythical beast, a mystery.*

She heard nothing, saw nothing. There was only the soughing of the wind as it sighed its way north off the Thames, and the barking of dogs. Really, it was annoying. The damned animals must be very poorly trained to be this noisy so early in the morning. They sounded excited as well. If just the presence of people could set them off like that, Stephen wouldn't last a week, having his lie-ins disturbed. She was going to have to have a word with the neighbours, and speak to them about—

*There are no neighbours. No dogs.*

"Tamsin?"

Her eyes popped open. Nothing; silence. No barking, nothing at all.

"Tamsin, what in hell—?"

"Quiet. Wait a moment, Stephen, please." She reached out a hand, and he took it. "Wait. Listen. Do you hear anything?"

She closed her eyes again.

The snarling rage of the pack, filling her ears and her skull, nearly knocked her over. The barking had transmuted into something to be run from, a crescendo of rage and hunger. Every nerve ending she had was on full alert: *Run you have to run you mustn't stay they'll find you they'll take you down run go.* She could hear them, a dozen at least, hounds in full cry, the pack baying and vicious. She could feel hot breath, flecks of foam at their mouths as they followed the scent, nowhere to go, dogs.

She screamed. It was a tiny sound, never making it past the bottom of her throat. But small as it was, it was answered, a whimper, a human whimper, *oh Christ, the dogs* . . .

The hard jerk on her arm broke the spell, severing her from whatever it was she'd been experiencing. Stephen was larger and stronger than she was, and he was wasting neither his strength nor any time at all in pulling her free.

"That's enough of that." They were down the ramp, back out into the scrubby, barren outdoors. A touch of wind, light and impersonal, lifted her hair from her neck. Tamsin, swallowing a gust of physical nausea, reached out a hand and took hold of her husband. She was clammy with sweat.

"Thanks, darling. My God, that was wretched." She turned suddenly, and knelt. "Sorry. I feel sick."

She stood up a minute or two later, patting her lips, her face pale. If this was what Ringan had been dealing with, she thought, he was officially about to get a whole lot more than her mere sympathy.

"What happened?" Stephen had a supportive hand under her elbow. Neither of them were physically demonstrative by nature or social conditioning, but at the moment, he didn't seem to want to let go of her. As for Tamsin, she was vaguely surprised at how thankful she was for the contact.

"Dogs. I could hear them—I could feel them. They were in full cry, absolutely blood-crazed and vicious. They were at my heels, or at someone's heels. Literally, I could hear someone trying not to make noise, someone swallowing their own fear." She focused her eyes on Stephen's face. "I gather you didn't hear it?"

"Not a damned thing." There was real trouble on his face. "Tamsin, what in hell is happening here? We came out here together, what, a dozen times before we ever broke ground for the house. Nothing like this—"

"I know." *The crater,* she thought, *I haven't been anywhere near the crater.* "I think it's Ringan, Stephen. Somehow he's connected to whatever happened here, or maybe—oh, I don't know. How can I know? But if I'm taking a guess, then I think it's Ringan. And you know, I thought it might have something to do with that bomb-cavity thing over there. Remember what he told us, about the officer getting killed here? But I could hear the dogs, and I wasn't anywhere near the crater."

"I want to know why you could hear it. I heard nothing at all." He turned her head around to face him. His mouth was tight. "Tamsin, talk to me. This is our land, and we're going to live here, but right now, I'd call this place unlivable and unsafe besides. What in sweet hell are we supposed to do about it? You can hardly keep going off into peculiar little trances and hearing dogs that aren't there. I won't allow it."

"No, of course not. I agree. Let's get out of here, go home, have some lunch, and talk. My feeling is that the more we know, the sooner we can put a full stop to whatever is happening here. But there's one more thing I want to do first, all right?"

She patted his arm lightly, a clear signal. He let go of her at once. She turned away from him, and looked at the crater.

Eyes wide open, she saw nothing but a summer morning in London. There were no ghosts, human or otherwise. A few cars moved along Westferry Road; out on the river, an invisible tugboat around the eastern curve of the land tooted its horn in the far distance.

"All right." She spoke aloud, and Stephen, hearing something in her voice that he wasn't familiar with, moved up close to her. "I'm going to walk over, just walk right over, and stand in the middle of that miserable little patch of earth. And I'd be very grateful if you'd come with me, Stephen, because honestly? I think I'm a bit unnerved."

They walked the hundred feet between them and the crater together. Tamsin stopped a few feet from its edges.

"You know, it never looked ominous to me before." She stared at the crater. Stephen had hold of her hand again, and she squeezed it lightly. "It does now, though. How very weird."

"Hang on." Stephen kept his grip on her hand, but the rest of him was moving forward, and suddenly, there he was, with his feet planted inside the perimeter of the bomb site. "Anything?"

"No. No, I don't think—" Her eyes went wide suddenly, and her fingers closed hard and tight. "Yes. Stephen, do you hear—can you—?"

"Nothing. Not a single bloody thing." His voice had gone ragged; her flesh, soft and firm against his palm, was suddenly different, cold and rough. There seemed to be an impossible electricity slapping against him, pinpricks that stabbed wherever his flesh met hers. "Tamsin, talk to me, and do it fast, because we're getting the hell out of here in thirty seconds, and I don't give a damn if I have to carry you. Talk to me, damn it! What?"

*Merciful Mother, I commend my soul to thee, give me sanctuary, sanctuary, take me in, I prithee hold me not out of doors to such a death, shelter, sanctuary*

Dogs, too many dogs, far away, close, there was no way to tell, no way to gauge the distance. It made no difference; in the end, she couldn't hope to hold them off. But surely the chapel, the place consecrated to that most highly noted Lady, she who had borne Our Lord and Saviour, shelter, surely a place to rest, to sleep, redemption, she had only to reach those loving arms and she could rest, sleep, atone. . . .

And then there was nothing, a dull roaring that might have been anything, death, water, wind, a soul departing or just a moment passing. Tamsin began to shake, her entire body transmitting those terrifying shocks the length of her arm to her husband, into his hands.

"That's it." Stephen was moving, out of the patch of deeper earth, both hands wrapped around his wife, moving her, moving them both. "We're out."

And then they were, and she was away from the crater, off the land itself, safe on the paved pedestrian sidewalk of Westferry Road, her back now soaked with sweat as she leaned against the Mercedes, fighting for breath and sanity.

———

In the cool confines of a private reading room at the Bodleian Old Library, Richard Halligan was getting his bearings. He was also experiencing something new to him: a kind of wistful regret that, during his professional life, he had never come to this place to work, or known this atmosphere, this quiet gracious home of knowledge and understanding and history.

The trip to Oxford had been delayed by two days. It was a good thing Maddy had rung the library first; as it happened, she hadn't factored in that, despite her own status at the British Library and Richard's long tenure at St. Paul's, neither of them was actively associated with Oxford in any capacity. The access they wanted fell under a heading that meant they'd needed a signed form, from something called a recommender, a person who could vouch for one or both of them and who was actually connected to the university.

Luckily, Maddy had an old friend from her own London school who fit the bill. While Richard alternated between bemusement and an inexplicable sense of irritation, Maddy had hunted up the friend and obtained the form in question, promising to buy said friend a pint at the Bird and Baby once the research she and Richard had come up to do had been accomplished. Richard, well into his sixties, had long since forgotten the casual scramble, the push and pull, of his university days. And in any case, he reminded himself, he hadn't been an Oxonian.

The email telling Maddy that her materials had been ordered and retrieved came in late enough in the day to push the trip out to the following morning. Richard, by temperament hard to fidget, found himself growing progressively more irritable as time went by. There was a sense of urgency gnawing at him; the stately pace of this particular look into the past had somehow rubbed him the wrong way.

The welcome they received at the Bodleian went a good distance towards soothing his ruffled feathers. Richard, himself deeply respectful towards old papers, the written word, maps, anything that spoke of the past, had even managed to get over being asked to recite a declaration that he wouldn't do anything nasty to the library and its valuables. Considering, he thought, how many hoops the library made you jump through just to get up the shallow steps off Broad Street, through the front doors, and into the Quad, the pledge was a bit of gilding on the lily. But whatever it took . . .

Getting within seeing distance of what they wanted was a masterful exercise in university protocol. They'd been passed through a series of forms. They'd read the declaration, signed it, and been asked to read it aloud. They'd presented their recommender note, their credentials, and their identification. They'd been told they'd be settled in a private room in Duke Humfrey's Library, just above the Divinity School; it seemed that Alison MacLaine's letters, collected but never published, fell under the heading "Rare Manuscript" and had been ordered and retrieved from the stacks. They'd been pleasantly, but firmly, reminded that only pencils were allowed in Duke Humfrey. They'd checked their bags in the Proscholium. They'd even had a quick look in the library's shop, where Richard had bought a short biography of the library's founder and patron, Sir Thomas Bodley. They'd admired his statue, visible in the Quad.

They'd also apparently been assigned their very own minion, or perhaps, Richard thought cynically, she was actually their very own watchdog, ready to bare teeth and rip them apart limb from limb if either he or Maddy did anything to upset the protocol. If so, she didn't look the part; the watchdog in question was a charming, and very young, member of the Bodleian staff.

"Dr. Holt? Dr. Halligan? I'm Elizabeth Jensing, and I'll be helping you with anything you need. I understand you're doing some research on one of the ladies-in-waiting to Anne of Cleves? How fascinating."

"Yes, we are." Maddy offered a hand. "Thank you so much—I'd been tossing out little prayers to the internet gods that the letters we need had been put online, but no such luck. I hope it wasn't too much trouble locating them?"

Ms. Jensing grinned. It was a cheerful, friendly smile, and suddenly Richard felt ashamed of his own cynicism.

"No trouble at all," she told them. "I got the request, filled out one of the green request slips—I know, I know, a very old-school method, but we use it for things we keep out of the catalogue, and honestly, it works beautifully. We've got your letters all ready for you, and we've set you up in one of the private rooms. Have you got a notebook? Pencils? You were told about that, I hope? We only allow pencils into Duke Humfrey—no ink."

"Yes, indeed." Maddy held out her small bound pad. "Not even a metal spiral on this one. I got used to carrying one of these when I was researching during my own student years, and these days I don't leave home without one in my pocket."

Ms. Jensing, leading the way through the Divinity School, threw an appreciative glance over her shoulder. "No more do I," she remarked. "You never know when you're going to need one. One small pencil, one small notebook, and one purse with a zippered pocket inside to hold them both."

"Old habits die hard? I know the feeling. And by the way, I've brought cotton gloves along, just in case." Maddy was clearly distracted; she stopped for a moment, and craned her neck to look around, and up. "Dear heavens, would you look at this? What a beautiful, beautiful library you've got. I love my own office—it overlooks the tower with the King's Collection—but of course it's completely modern, glass and steel and whatnot. This is just gorgeous. I used the Radcliff Camera once or twice, a good fifteen years ago when I came down from Goldsmiths to do some work, but this is my first time in here. Richard? What do you think of it?"

"I think it's staggering." It was, too. Richard found himself wishing that Ringan could be here; that ceiling, he thought, was one of the most beautiful things he'd ever seen, and he had the feeling it would have been right up Ringan's alley. "You know, I spent over twenty years at St. Paul's Cathedral. We have a rather nice view looking straight up, to say the least, but this is stunning. I gather this is one of the older buildings of the university? What's the architectural style called?"

"Actually, I think the Divinity School is the oldest intact. And the style—do you mean the ceiling? I've always been told it's called fan-vaulting, although I've heard a few people say the ribs of the beams protrude too much to be true fan. I've heard the term *lierne-vaulting,* but honestly, I haven't got a clue about architecture." Ms. Jensing paused, and looked around her, and spoke simply. "I just know it takes my breath away every time I walk through the door. I'm incredibly lucky to be able to work here. Shall we head up?"

Ms. Jensing unlocked the door to their reading room, and ushered them in. "Here we are. Let me make sure I've got you everything you requested. My green slip said anything written by Dame Alison MacLaine, with no specific date limitations, but with an emphasis on the years 1540 onward. Is that right?"

"That's it." Maddy's eyes were fixed on the table, a reasonably sized round affair with a few chairs set around it. There was a leather binder on the table, old and rubbed. It wasn't particularly thick, but Maddy felt her fingers tingle. *Right,* she thought, *we're off. It's showtime.* "Thanks again. Do we simply come find someone when we're done for the day? From the looks of it, this may take more than just one day. Having to do this the old-fashioned way means a lot of sorting, unless we want carpal tunnel at the end of the day. And there looks to be a lot of it to sort through and cherry-pick."

"Yes, just let one of the staff know. And I'm sorry about all the wrist exercise, but, well, there's the rule, and as a librarian and an archivist, I'm sure you both understand about the preservation aspect."

"I know, and how can I not agree? Hell, if I found someone using digital imaging on any of the older documents in the King's Collection, I'd batter them with my hard drive, or something. Thank you, Ms. Jensing—we owe you. We'll come find someone when we're done."

"Right. And happy hunting!"

The door closed behind her, and Maddy and Richard settled in to work.

Maddy, herself a librarian, found herself thankful for the lighting system, which seemed to have been designed and installed with the object of providing the least possible strain on the eyes. She had a sudden clear memory of sitting at the abbey in Bernay, France, with Penny at her side, the pair of them squinting at enormous ledgers written in a cramped, tiny hand. The lighting at the abbey had been barely sufficient, but there, at least, she'd been allowed to use her digital camera to take photos of the relevant pages. The Bernay ledgers had been copies, only a hundred or so years old. That wasn't going to be the case with Alison MacLaine's memoirs. These were likely to be the originals, and that meant no exposure to potentially damaging digital imaging. They were going to be reduced to hand-copying anything they needed. . . .

"I like Ms. Jensing, don't you?" Richard had set his own note-book and pencil down, and was exchanging his regular glasses for the more-powerful ones he used for reading. "A charming child. Impossible to miss the pleasure she gets just from being here. She meant what she said. Good heavens, are those actually cotton gloves you've got there? I thought you were joking."

"Definitely not joking." Maddy flexed her fingers; she'd worn them many times before, and knew she could write in them, hold her pencil and turn pages of the kind of paper that couldn't be had for love or money in this age of disposable and recyclable paper, used by the ream rather than the page. She reached for the binder, and slid it gently towards her. "Here, pull your chair a bit closer, will you? We'll need to confab—I'm almost afraid to see what her handwriting looked like. I always seem to find these things that look to have been done with a hummingbird's eyelash dipped in very pale ink."

"Or maybe with the leg off one very small spider. At least you don't need glasses." He watched her carefully open the binder, and took a deep breath. "Oh, my. Nice lady. If I had a time machine, I'd go back and bring her roses."

Alison MacLaine, that spinster of uncertain years, had kept her journal in a careful, beautiful hand. There was none of the finicky playing with style over substance, no one to impress. She had lived her life, and seen a value to keeping a record. Her fist would have rivalled a computer printout for legibility. It was miraculous.

"Oh, *bless!*" It was a phrase Maddy hadn't used in years, and it was perfect and appropriate. Richard, smiling, reached over and, using his fingertips, slid the first page free. He then read it aloud.

*St. Austin's, Canterbury, 27 December, 1539—I have this day from London come, a journey of some two days in poor weather and over poorer roads. My sister Elspeth remains at Greenwich, and my nieces in her care; there will be much merriment come the New Year, when my mistress hath been received as Queen, and those marriages which his Majesty our King hath decreed have been so made.*

*I am bid by no lesser man than His Grace of Canterbury to bide a while, so that the Lady Anne might not lack her rightful complement of attendants. She will be here with all good speed, an God wills it thus. Indeed, I am most willing and right humbly did speak of it to His Grace, to let him know that my heart is set in all obedience to the King's commands to me. His Grace spake most courteously to me, much relieved of his feeling that I might have in some wise been unfairly cumbered with such a task. He saw me comfortably chambered for as long as we might remain here, upon the King's pleasure, and God's.*

"So, the family was in London." Maddy was writing. "It's the day after Boxing Day, and she'd left London on Christmas Day—there's that thing about its being a rotten two days on the road from London, in bad weather."

"Right." Richard looked up. "This is the first one here, Maddy. I wonder how long they'd been in London?"

"Good question." She was nibbling one knuckle. "Actually, there are a couple of things I'm wondering about. First of all, did anything strike you about that 'marriages ordered by the King' bit? Was that plural? Because it sounds as if Henry had more than just his own wedding on his mind."

"It *was* plural—it says marriages. That's a very good point. Ah well—early days yet. I'm sure there's more about that yet to come. What else?"

"The family. The MacLaines." Maddy paused, considering her question, sorting it out in her mind. "There's no mention of a man in there anywhere. She says Elspeth and the twins—but where's the head of the family? It certainly wasn't common for women to travel down from Scotland to London without a male escort. If there was no man to come with them, the King would likely have sent his own escort. And that sounds as if Henry had a very specific reason to go to all that trouble, not to mention spending all that money. No mention of a husband."

"Maybe she was a widow?" Richard suddenly slapped his hand lightly against the table. "Good God, I'm an idiot. Alison's name was MacLaine."

"So?" Maddy was staring at him. "What's your point?"

"If MacLaine was Elspeth's name by marriage, then how on earth does Alison's name come to be MacLaine as well? Whose sister was she?"

"Damn!" Maddy shook her head, dismayed. "Elspeth married a MacLaine. If Alison was also a MacLaine, then either she'd married one and was a widow, or else that 'sister' was a courtesy title, and she was really sister-in-law. Or Elspeth married her own cousin. Or—damn it!"

"Do you suppose it's important? I mean, yes, we'll have to see about tracing it back and finding out for certain, but is there any reason you can see for worrying about it now?"

"I don't know," she told him slowly. "But if I'm being honest, I'm going to say yes, it's important. I don't know why—it's just a feeling."

"Well—why not ask Ringan about it? It's his ancestress, after all. Do you have your cell phone?"

"It's down in the Proscholium. I had to check it in." She got to her feet. "I think you're right, though. Let me go down, get the phone back for a few minutes, and ring him up. You stay here and guard the pretty diary."

The afternoon had turned absolutely beautiful. Maddy, out in the Quad, realized that she had Penny's number programmed into her phone, but not Ringan's. She swore under her breath, sighed, and punched in Penny's number.

Penny picked the phone up on the first ring. "Ringan? Ringan, is that you? Where are you?"

"Penny, no, it's Maddy Holt." Maddy had gone rigid; Penny's voice was all wrong. It was shaking, distraught, out of control. "Penny, what is it? What's happened?"

"He's gone." Penny's voice cracked, splintered, shredded at the edge of complete hysterics. "I can't find him. I woke up this morning, and he was gone."

# Eight

*They made a harp of her breastbone,*
*Whose sound would melt a heart of stone.*
*They took three locks of the maiden's hair,*
*And with them strung the harp so rare.*

Darkness, discomfort, warm breath against his shoulder.

In the small quiet hours of the morning, a few hours before day-break, Ringan opened his eyes and realised he'd awakened into a dream.

At first, this didn't bother him; after all, he thought vaguely, there was no point to getting narked in the middle of a dream. It was annoying that he was still asleep. There was pressure on his bladder, no doubt the result of the glass of cider he'd had before they headed off to bed last night. He made a mental note to himself: *no more booze at bedtime*—he was getting too old to cope with the in-evitable three o'clock loo run. *But of course,* he thought, *I won't re-member this in the morning, because, hell, I'm dreaming.*

It was all a bit weird, he decided. He could hear Penny breathing beside him, evenly and deeply, and the need to oblige his bladder by getting out of bed and coping was getting more urgent with every passing moment.

The problem was, his eyes were wide open, and he could see ab-solutely nothing. There were no familiar outlines, of Penny's room or of anything else, in fact. His subconscious seemed to have made an independent decision to drop him into the middle of outer space, or a chasm at the bottom of the ocean. He made another note to himself: *Have a word with your subconscious.* It seemed to be getting damned high-handed. . . .

"Right." He said the word aloud, but heard nothing. Okay, more proof that he was still asleep, had he wanted any. It was getting beyond weird, and into painful. He suddenly wondered if, in fact, he only had to pee in his dream—if that was the case, he could simply dream himself out of bed and off to the invisible dream loo.

He sat up into the void surrounding him, with his throat dry and scratchy. For a moment, he was aware of just how dizzy he was; even in the absolute blackness surrounding him, he could feel things wanting to spin. He added yet another note to himself: *Even in a dream, sitting up too quickly and making yourself hyperventilate is a bad idea.*

The pressure against his bladder had become a dull roar. It was time either to wake up and go find a real loo, or to somehow define where he was in this particular bit of sleep and find a dream loo. Whether he was awake or sleeping, the issue had become imperative.

"Okay." He heard his own voice, but had he spoken? No matter; if he disturbed Penny while dreaming, she'd never know. The thought was vagrant, fleeting, impossible to catch hold of or parse properly. "Time to move."

He moved his legs, slow and careful, letting his bare feet feel for the throw rug that covered the area around Penny's bed. There was no rug. Instead, there was hard floor, cold, so very cold. Winter came from the floor, shocking him, trying to wake him. And the air in this darkness was icy, as well. . . .

He was shaking with cold, disoriented, but he had to move. Once he emptied his bladder, he thought, he could cope with whatever this nightmare was, whatever it wanted of him. Obviously, he was somewhere between sleep and waking: the need for a loo was real enough, but it was British summertime, and the cold that was raising gooseflesh all over his naked body, that was obviously part of—

*Pietro?*

He hadn't thought he could get any colder, but that name, coming from the invisible bed he'd just left, did it. His breath stopped at the back of his throat.

This was different, entirely different, from those other dreams. This time, he wasn't eavesdropping. This time, he was no mere watcher. This time, the girl spoke to him.

*Return to me, my love, my only one. The night is so cold—tomorrow, the day after, I may never come to you again. Stay.*

Her voice was quiet, the barest exhale. It was soft, drenched with love.

The room around him was still invisible to him. Ringan was beginning to understand that something in him, an interior eye he hadn't known he possessed, was remaining closed, protecting him, keeping him from seeing what he might not be able to deal with. He breathed through his nostrils, opened his mouth, and heard his own voice, but it wasn't his own voice, not this answer, not this language, not these words.

*"In one moment I will come back. Atteso, bella."*

He stopped. Something in his skull was pounding, wanting acknowledgement, wanting to get out.

What in hell? No, this couldn't be happening. He was no longer looking for a loo, because there wasn't one, there was no such thing, not where he was, not when he was—plumbing, that art used by the Romans, had long been forgotten and had not yet been reinvented. So he was looking for a chamber-pot, and it should be close to the bed. He felt his hands, long musician's fingers that would have been right at home on a piano, reaching and fumbling, finding the pot. He heard the long hiss mingling with his own sigh of relief, easing the cramps of a need too long delayed.

Where in hell was he, anyway? The dream was a bit too close, and it seemed to have taken a hard left on him. He'd heard that voice before, the voice that wasn't his but had come from his own throat and lips, heard it when he'd somehow got separated from his own reality back in Penny's kitchen. He'd heard it, replete with wonder and love, touching the bright hair that had fanned out all around the naked girl in his arms. Apparently, the shawm player called Pietro had picked up some English, enough to communicate with his girlfriend.

Ringan was shivering, and somehow the room was defining itself around him. It was neither clear nor complete; he could make out shapes, indistinct and undefined, but little else. This fuzzing of his vision seemed to have sharpened his other senses, in the way deprived senses are said to do; his sense of touch had gone acute to the edge of pain, and his sense of smell, that most ephemeral, yet most evocative, of senses, was threatening to bury him. He could smell the mustiness of fabric, the tang of river water coming from somewhere out of doors, and the girl, the naked girl in his bed, who smelled of something clean and sharp and purely feminine, something his mind wanted to call rosewater. He could smell lavender in the bedding.

*Come back to bed, Pietro. Come back to my arms. Tornare. The night is so cold, and my heart and body wait for you only.*

She was right about one thing—it was beyond cold. Ringan suddenly remembered that long-ago winters in London had seen the Thames freeze solid. Surely, there had been paintings of skaters in the nineteenth century, their Victorian coats up above the blades of their skates, gliding along on the frozen river? How much colder must it have been, then, when Anne of Cleves had sailed from her father's house across the channel to be met by the man who had arranged to marry her, the man who could not wait for fairer weather, the man who, if all the accounts had it right, had gone disguised into his new lady's chamber and come out furious and disgusted, knowing he would never be able to make even a pretence of desire for her?

The bed was warm, the coverlets were heavy, with that faint throat-clutching smell of mustiness under lavender. The girl curled towards him, reaching out for him, her hands on him. She was deliciously warm herself, nestled into the linens. He took her in his arms, his lips to her throat, touching her here and there with the tip of his tongue, resting there.

What had she said? *Tornare.* She had told him, *Come back.* But soon she would be taken from him, married to that widowed lord. It was wrong, obscene; the *nobiluomo* might have been her father; he had a married daughter older than the bride he was being given. Wrong, so very wrong; he could give no part of his mind to that, to the picture of his *camelia,* his perfect flower, in the bed of that old man.

Yet there was nothing to be done, and he knew it. This was the decree of the King, his gift to his god-daughter. And all he wanted, at this moment of her pale legs twining around his, of his lips against that soft salty hollow in her throat, was to weep into that bright hair, and to say to her, not *Tornare,* but rather *Venir via—Come away, come away.*

Her breathing shortened, as did his own. As he went down into pleasure and then into sleep, he allowed himself to admit the one thing he would not regret, the one relief: when she had gone to her new lord, she might never learn of what he had done, what he had been tricked into doing, with her sister.

"Penny, breathe. Take a deep breath. Try to calm down. Then tell me what happened. Please?"

Maddy had found a quiet corner of the Quad. It hadn't been easy; she needed not only privacy from the steady, constant stream of students, but also somewhere that gave her decent reception for her cell phone. Something in her, some obscure instinct, made her want to keep her own voice down.

"He's gone." Penny's voice was still catching and jumping. "I woke up early—still dark early, I mean—because I'd felt him get up. You know the way the mattress moves when they do that, when they get up?"

"Of course I do." Maddy kept her own voice as calm as she could. She'd never heard Penny in this state before, and she wasn't sure how to handle it. "Go on."

"I thought he was getting up to use the loo. We had some cider just before bed, and, well, you know how that goes. I never really woke up all the way—I sort of got halfway there and drowsed and then I suppose I fell all the way back asleep."

She stopped. Maddy, her palms sweating, shifted the phone from hand to hand. "And . . . ?"

"I don't think he ever came back to bed." She was fighting for control; Maddy could hear it, picture it. Penny's fear was infectious. It came through the phone in a wave. "I got up around half past nine and for awhile I thought he'd just headed off to the studio. The band's got a mixing session booked for today. It was supposed to start around eleven. And about a quarter of noon, I got a call from Jane Castle."

"He didn't show up?" *Stupid,* Maddy thought, *stupid stupid question. What other answer could there possibly be but no?* Her own stomach was tight with understanding.

"No. He didn't." Penny's control was beginning to falter. "Jane wanted me to go poke him, tell him to get his lazy bum out of bed, everyone was waiting for him, they couldn't get started until he got there. I told her I didn't understand, I'd been up for a couple of hours already and he was gone by the time I'd got up."

"Can you ring his cell?" *Bad,* Maddy thought, *this is bad, this feels wrong, all wrong.* Penny's fear had become her own.

"He hasn't got it." There was a break in Penny's voice now. "Maddy—I went and looked. Wherever he went, he's in his pyjamas. And I think he's barefoot."

"What in hell . . . ?"

"He doesn't live here, remember? He lives in Somerset. He's just staying with me so that he can be in London for the CD and Isle of bloody Dogs. And I know what he's got with him in the way of clothes and shoes. He's got two pairs with him. Maddy—they're both here. And his pyjamas aren't anywhere. And, and . . ."

Her voice broke entirely. Maddy heard a strangled plea for her to wait, just please wait a bit, and then listened, sick with helplessness, as Penny put the phone down and succumbed to complete hysterics.

The plea was unnecessary. There was nothing Maddy could do

but wait; she couldn't offer solace, she couldn't offer advice. Penny, in her Muswell Hill kitchen, was sobbing, and there was nothing to be done. Maddy heard herself muttering under her breath, words no one could hear, useless, pointless words of comfort. The soft warmth of the English summer falling on her skin, the students moving busily from place to place talking as they went, none of it seemed real. . . .

"Maddy?" Penny had stopped sobbing, but she'd got the hiccups and simply wasn't breathing properly. "Are you still there? Please say something."

"I'm here. Penny, stop breathing, hold your breath a moment, you'll cramp up if you can't get rid of those hiccups."

"They'll stop in a bit. Maddy—his car's gone. The Alfa was parked halfway up the street and it's gone, and his car keys are gone as well."

"But—" Maddy swallowed hard. The picture that had come up in her mind was vivid and bizarre. "You think Ringan walked out of your flat while it was still dark, barefoot, in his pyjamas, and drove somewhere?"

"Of course he did. There's no other explanation."

"Damn. Penny, listen—what are you going to do?"

"What can I do?" Her voice went up, dangerously near to cracking. "He hasn't got a cell phone. I can't leave to go look for him—suppose he comes home and he can't get in? His house keys, the ring that's got all his house keys on it, including mine? Right here on the kitchen table. I don't want to ring the police—that could be a complete disaster, and he'd never forgive me. What can I do?"

"The Isle of Dogs." Maddy's own voice had gone up; a few passing students shot her curious looks, and she took a deep breath, trying to speak more quietly. "Penny, listen. This is all about whatever's happening at the construction site. Call your brother. Tell them to go look for him, if you can't leave. Will that work? You can trust your brother, surely?"

"Oh God. Yes. Yes, I can, and I think I'm losing my mind, because why in hell didn't I think of that?" Something came distantly through the phone line, the squeak of chair legs settling under human weight. Maddy realized suddenly that Penny, under the spur of impossible anxiety, had been pacing for the entire conversation. "Okay. I'm ringing off and then I'm getting Stephen and Tamsin on the phone. Maddy, look—I hate to be a nag, or push, or anything like that, but honestly, this has to stop. We have to figure this out. This isn't the first time something's happened to Ringan. And it's getting worse."

"Hang on a minute." Something moved down Maddy's spine. "What do you mean, this isn't the first time? Penny, what's been going on?"

"He faded out." She sounded disjointed. "Sitting at breakfast and saying the guitar needed new strings and then he was gone, eyes empty, cold, unresponsive. Just—gone. I yelled and shook him and nothing happened, and finally I slapped him and he came back. He'd been there—the musician and one of the sisters, making love. He said he could hear me calling him, but he was there. He couldn't get back—he couldn't get back."

"Christ. Okay. Penny, here's the problem: We're in Duke Humfrey's at Oxford right now, that's Richard and me, with the full file of Alison MacLaine's journals. And I'm not allowed to have the cell phone with me in the library. They made me check it. I think we need to stay with these journals, to find out what in hell happened, but if you want me to stay by the phone, I can tell Richard to— Penny? Are you there?"

Something, a distant ringing somewhere. "Maddy, wait. Please? There's someone at the door."

Silence, too long a silence. Maddy listened, sick with apprehension. A minute went by, two minutes, three, a confused murmur of voices, Penny's sounding sharply, male voices, a door closing somewhere. . . .

"Maddy—are you still there?"

"Dear God, yes. What's going on?"

"He's back." Penny sounded limp. "I've just put him in bed and put the kettle on. My sister-in-law and a nice architect bloke named Marcus Something-or-other just brought him home. They met up at the building site to confab about something, and he was there, sitting in his car. Tamsin says he was very confused, he was rambling and not himself. I was right. He's in pyjamas, he's barefoot. The car's still out on the Isle of Dogs." She stopped abruptly. "Tamsin says he was muttering to himself, and he wasn't speaking English."

"What?"

"Italian. She says he was speaking Italian, little bits, just words and phrases." Her voice shook. "Maddy, Ringan doesn't speak a word of Italian. Not one word."

She began to cry, slow wrenching sobs that she was too obviously trying to muffle, not wanting Ringan, confused and cold and disoriented in the next room, to hear her. "Sorry," she managed. "Look, I need to go."

"Wait a moment. Listen to me." Maddy's nervous system had gone into high alert; every instinct she possessed was trying to send her back upstairs, to where Richard and her notebook and those journals waited. "Penny, listen to me. I want to go read Alison MacLaine's journals. I want to see what happened. I want you to do something for me, all right? When he wakes up, if he's coherent at all, find out what happened and ring my cell phone. I haven't got a limit on message length—tell me everything."

"I will." Penny was sniffling a bit. Her hiccups seemed to be gone. "Maddy, you've got something. Don't you?"

"I have a suspicion, is what I've got. Just find out what happened, and tell me. I'll take breaks off and on while we're working, and come down and check my messages. And Penny—I won't stop with those journals until I have answers."

She rang off, and brought the cell phone back inside and checked it in again. The sense of urgency was thumping against her temples like an incipient migraine.

Richard glanced up as she let herself back into the reading room. He'd obviously been hard at it while she'd been on the phone; his once virginally clean notebook was now open nearly to the halfway point, and she could see the neat backstrokes of his small, careful handwriting.

"So did you talk to——?" He saw her face, and broke off. "Oh, lord. Something's wrong. What happened?"

She told him, sinking back into her own chair. Richard listened until she stopped, then he opened his mouth and closed it again. There was trouble in his face, and Maddy knew he'd reached the same conclusion she had.

"I don't like this," he said slowly. "This is bad, and it's dangerous. It sounds as if he somehow got himself stuck in this musician. What Penny said about his fading out at the breakfast table, and now this thing about him mumbling in Italian . . ."

His voice died away, and he swallowed. Maddy suddenly found herself wishing desperately for a big bottle of something, anything at all, that was cold and wet. Her throat was dry.

"Exactly. Your mind's gone down the same road as mine." The thumping in her head had become a rhythm of necessity: *Find it out get it done find it out get it done.* "Richard, I'm very much afraid we're about to be out of time here. Because if he gets stuck and can't get out——"

"Oh, Christ. Maddy, that musician was put to the rack and died while he was being tortured at the King's pleasure, by Henry's pet executioner." He swallowed, hard. "If Ringan's stuck there, caught in him, when that happens . . ."

"I know." She pulled her chair up beside Richard's. "Believe me, I know. And that means we're going to have to kick this up a gear or two."

"It may not help." There was trouble in Richard's face. "It may not do a damned bit of good. Suppose we find out everything there is to find out—how do we know it will do any good?"

"We don't." Maddy met his eye. "Hell, we don't even know that Ringan's actually in any danger—this may just be some sort of bizarre psychic special effects. But I don't think knowledge, any knowledge at all, could hurt our chances of figuring this out. Now tell me where you got to while I was on the phone."

In a straight-backed kitchen chair, Penny sat at the side of her own bed, and watched Ringan sleep.

She sat there for close to three hours. For the first hour or so, his sleep was so deep that he seemed inanimate; Penny found herself looking at the duvet, fighting the urge to touch him, to make certain he was still breathing. Once she actually managed to convince herself that he'd stopped breathing, that she had lost him, that he'd gone to that shadowy place between himself and someone else, that he'd never get back. She'd reached over to touch his cheek, and he'd given a small sigh and resettled himself under the covers, his shoulders moving. Then the slow breathing had resumed, and she'd sat back in her chair, her palms damp, her own breath forcing its way out from lungs that had held the air in them too long.

Over the last ninety minutes or so, he seemed to get closer to waking. Penny, who badly needed a trip to the loo, stayed where she was. She wasn't leaving him alone until he was awake, and himself. Even then, she was going to find it difficult to leave him. She could no longer trust the real world, their world, to hold him in his proper place.

Finally, as she watched, one hand slid out from where he'd had it tucked beneath his pillow, and he flexed his fingers. It was a purely Ringan movement; she'd noticed, over their years together, that the bending and cracking of finger-joints, a musician's motion, always preceded his opening his eyes.

*But Pietro Bendone was a musician, as well. Suppose that was the shawm player, not Ringan at all.*

The thought was cold, and heartbreaking, and beyond her capacity to deal with. Before it could come back, Ringan rolled over, muttered something, and opened his eyes. He focused them on Penny.

"Penny—oh God." He blinked. "Thank Christ. I'm back where I'm supposed to be. What is it? What did I say? Lamb, don't cry. I'm right here."

"I know. I'll stop. Ringan, give me a minute, please. I've been sitting here a good long time, and the loo's calling."

She went to the bathroom, washing her face and splashing cold water on her swollen eyes. As she dried her hands, she was appalled to find herself offering up an inchoate prayer to whatever might be listening: *Please let him still be Ringan.*

"All done in the loo? Pen, come over here, and curl up with me." He was still in bed, but sitting up. She climbed in next to him, and he got one arm around her, pulling her close. She wondered if it was possible for a human being to die under the weight of unadulterated relief.

"Jane rang me up, to see where you were." She heard herself babbling; she couldn't stop and didn't bother trying. "I didn't know. I found both pairs of your shoes. You went out in your pyjamas, and you were barefoot."

She started to cry. *Damn,* she thought, *damn it, damn, stop that, crying is simply no damned good, it doesn't fix anything, and you've never been much for easy tears anyway, stop it.*

His arm tightened around her momentarily, and she sniffed back tears. "You left your house keys," she told him. "I couldn't go look for you. I couldn't leave, in case you came back and you couldn't get in. I had to sit here, waiting. I was totally helpless, and I don't like being helpless, I hate it. I just hate it. Maddy told me to ring up Tamsin and Richard, she said you were probably on the Isle of Dogs. I was going to, but they got here with you just as I was about to ring. Ringan, oh God, Ringan, what in hell happened?"

"I'm not sure, lamb, but calm down, and I'll try to put it together for you." He stroked her arm. "Right. Okay. The last thing I remember about being here was getting up in the small hours—and remind me, by the way, next time I decide I want a nip of cider that close to bedtime, not to do it if I plan on sleeping through the night."

"I'll remind you." She snuggled up close. He was warm; remembering how cold he'd been to the touch when she'd first pulled the duvet over him, she was insensibly reassured. "What do you mean, the last thing you remember about being here? You're making it sound as if there was some sort of, I don't know, actual stop between places, or something. Damn it, that's not right—that sounds like a stop-off at a roadside café for sausage and tea. I know what I'm getting at, but it's very hard to describe."

"I know just what you mean, lamb, believe me. But I'll give it a pop." He closed his eyes for a moment, not wanting to. He was aware of a deep reluctance to take any chance at all that the simple act of lowering his lids might let the familiar room, the warm bed, the woman he loved, his sense of himself as a unique human being, slip away from him again. "Give me a minute here. And Penny—if I start sliding away and you see it, hit me. No, don't look at me as if I was a nutter. I'm serious. That first time, I knew you'd slapped me—I could hear your voice, and the two things together pulled me back. So do it again, if you need to."

"Right. I will." She settled back, rubbing her cheek against the soft cotton of his sleeve. "Take your time—but be warned, if the cell phone rings, I'm going to answer it. Because Maddy and Richard are up at the Bodleian with the collected Dear Diary of Alison MacLaine, and she's supposed to sneak out of Duke Humfrey's and ring me every few hours, with updates. She was very worried about you."

"So was I—worried about me, I mean." He took a deep breath, and opened his eyes. *Good,* he thought, *so far, so good.* He was himself. He was here, he was now. This was Penny's bedroom, and that was Penny relaxing in the circle of his arm, her dark hair its nice normal dark and not red. "Okay. Here's what happened: I got up, or started to get up. And at first, there wasn't anything that struck me as different—I mean, I just needed the loo, from all that cider. But I waited for my eyes to adjust, and they didn't. The room stayed black around me. I couldn't see a damned thing, Pen—nothing, not an outline or a shape or a shadow. But I could hear you next to me in bed. I could hear you breathing."

"So, it didn't feel like a dream, then?" She forced herself to remain as relaxed as possible. Her entire body wanted to tense against the situation. *Relax,* she told herself, and tried to remember anything she could use from the few long-ago yoga classes she'd taken.

"It did, and it didn't. I got up, and by that time I'd sort of decided I was actually still asleep. But that didn't do anything about the need to pee, so I started for the loo, or rather towards where your loo is, because I couldn't see anything. And the floor—it was unbelievably cold. I could smell cold water, river water, in the air, and it felt like I was walking on blocks of ice. And then you called me from the bed, telling me to come back. But the voice was wrong. The girl in the bed—it wasn't you."

Penny's hand had been resting lightly on Ringan's thigh. The hand clenched, suddenly and painfully, digging into flesh and muscle.

He jumped. "Oi! Careful, you, I need those blood vessels."

"Sorry." She loosened her grip, but her hands were shaking. "Who was it—one of the sisters? Do you know which?"

"No, I don't. But she called me Pietro, she was speaking that weird Tudor English, very formal, with the occasional Italian word thrown in. And dear God, Penny, whichever twin that was? He loved her."

She blinked at him. "You felt it, that strongly?"

"Hell, yes. He loved her so much, it was nearly unbearable, Pen. There were things he was thinking, feeling. A lot of it was just, I don't know, stuff, things that basically had to do with who he was. The point is, I got all of it, because—well. I'll tell you about that in a minute. But this is important. There were two things I remember. One is that the sister, whichever one she was, was being married off to some older bloke, some widowed nobleman crony of the King, and at the King's order. No, wait, let me finish—the other thing I got . . ." He stopped, and bit his lip.

"Ringan?"

"Sorry. It makes me feel as if I'd cheated on you, but it wasn't me, it was Bendone. That doesn't make it any easier to tell you, though." He took a deep breath. "I—he—made love to her. That's the last thing I remember, the girl in my, our, arms. But he had a moment of relief—it hit him hard, really hard, and that was because he felt guilty about it. Penny, he'd spent a night with the other sister. And I got a really strong sense from him that he'd somehow been tricked into it."

She was quiet, watching his profile. He turned his head and gave her a straight, steady look.

"Listen to me, lamb. I want to be really clear about this, because I don't think I've seen the end of whatever's happening here, not by a long shot. And I'm betting it's important, vital, in fact—if it happens again, and I need you to get me out."

She nodded. Her eyes were enormous.

"I was in him, Penny. More than that, I *was* him." He saw the question forming, and shook his head at her. "No. I know what you're going to ask, and the answer is no. It wasn't possession. How could it be? Every time we've come across possession—when bloody Andrew Leight got to me at Callowen, for instance—that's been all about something dead taking over something living. And this was different. It was backwards. He didn't take me over at all, Penny; the boot's on the other leg. He didn't inhabit me. I inhabited him."

# Nine

At ten minutes of seven, Elizabeth Jensing tapped on the door and let Maddy and Richard know that the library was about to close for the day.

"Damn." Maddy stretched, and then winced. She'd been working steadily for a few hours, barely stopping long enough to raise her eyes. Unlike Richard, who had made a point of getting up and shaking the pins and needles out of his limbs, she'd stayed in her chair. "Ouch. My entire body hurts. Elizabeth, can we leave this here, locked up? Because we're going to need to come back in tomorrow bright and early, and pick up where we left off. I'm sorry to be a nuisance, but there's a time factor involved, and I just found out today, it's gone critical on us."

"Deadline?" Ms. Jensing sounded sympathetic. "I know, they're absolute horrors. Let's see—normally, these would go back where they belong. But since you're coming straight back here in the morning, I can lock them up for the night, and have them ready for you when you get here. Tomorrow's Friday, right? Same hours as today; we open at nine."

"Perfect. And oh, lord, I've only just realised—we need to find a hotel for the night." Dismayed, Maddy stared at Richard. "I never even thought about it. But driving back to London and coming back here in the morning? Damn!"

"Not to worry—the Victoria House is only a few minutes away in George Street, and it's reasonable and comfortable." Ms. Jensing turned off the lights and, having led them out, locked the door behind her. "My parents stay there when they come down to visit—I've got the hotel's number in my office. Let's stop off there, and get you two booked."

It was past ten by the time Maddy and Richard were able to sit down at a small table in Richard's room and compare notes on what they'd got done that day. They'd gone for a drink, and found an open restaurant serving Greek food. Other than Maddy taking a few minutes to check on Ringan and Penny, the conversation during both the pub stop and the dinner break had been general. Neither had wanted to begin a discussion that each knew was likely to take all their concentration.

"All right, then." Richard had cleared the table of everything except notebooks, pencils, and a carafe of cold water. "I did a good bit on the earlier journals while you were off talking to Penny. Shall I begin with those? They're fairly basic, but they give the tone of what was going on, and a couple of pertinent details as well. And before we start, you haven't told me what you got from Penny. Was Ringan able to remember what had happened?"

"He certainly was," she said grimly. "Penny put him on the phone. He doesn't remember anything about how he got from Penny's flat to the Isle of Dogs, but what was going on inside Pietro Bendone's head? That, he remembers."

"And . . . ?"

"And, leaving out the smaller stuff, here's the gen that matters: Bendone was in love with one of the two sisters, but Ringan doesn't know which. Whichever sister it was, she was about to be married off to some older bloke, a friend of Henry's. And Ringan said Bendone had somehow been tricked into spending a night with the other sister, and he was scared to death the sister he loved

would find out. Did I say something right, Richard? You're looking very pleased all of a sudden."

"I don't know that 'pleased' is the word. 'Satisfied' might be
better. This dovetails perfectly with what I found out. I've got my
notes right here. Shall I?"

"Yes, please." Maddy settled back. "What have you got?"

"Right. The first entry after that one she wrote, about waiting at
Henry's digs at St. Austin's just after Christmas? That one was basically
nothing at all. There was a bit about her morning prayers—I find that
sixteenth-century documents tend to be a tad obsessive about prayer.
There's a bit about having stained the sleeve of her gown with something at breakfast, and she wonders if the weather would allow Anne
to travel in any comfort. So I let those be. But it begins to get interesting again a couple of days later. I wrote out the entry. Listen."

*Sittingbourne, 29 December 1539—I am in much perturbation of
spirit, and find myself sore vexed in heart and mind. The Lady
Anne, having by God's grace come safe to harbour, was escorted with
much ceremony to our lodging. The King having sent ahead of his
person a sumptuous bed, as a show of his esteem, the Lady is most
comfortably settled.*

*With the advance of the King's own party came Lord Kesleigh. I
had not, before this day, known of him beyond his name and estate; he
was most kind and I found that I must needs keep my composure, for he
is to be my niece Catriona's new-wedded lord, come the new year. I had
given no thought to his countenance or person, and therefore was hard
put to hide my dismay, for tho I knew of his widowed state, I had spared
no consideration for his age, and was most discomposed to find him a
man of greater age than the King. I can in no way think this a suitable
husband for my niece, so tender in years.*

Richard stopped. Maddy's eyebrows were up around her hairline.

"So it was Catriona who was being married off." She was chewing her lower lip. "Nothing in there about Margaret?"

"Not a word. There's a bit I found in a later entry; apparently Margaret was named for Henry's sister, who was married to the King of Scotland. Bizarre, isn't it? I'd have expected the namesake to be his god-daughter. But no—as it happens, the god-daughter was the older twin, Catriona. And from what we know, this confirms it: Catriona was madly in love elsewhere, and the sister that Bendone had been tricked into bed with was Margaret." There was a sudden regret in his face. "That poor child Catriona. What a mess."

"God, yes. An older man, obsessive love, a clandestine affair, a jealous sister. All the ingredients for tragedy, present and accounted for. What is it, Richard? What did I say?"

"I'm not sure," he told her slowly. "But something pinged me a bit—wait, I've got it. What you said about the jealous sister. Jealous of what?"

"What do you—oh!" She'd caught up, finally. "Damn it, of course! The song lyric says the evil sister drowned the younger sister because she was jealous of her marrying the knight they both loved. But Catriona wasn't, was she? She was being married off to a doddery widower who was probably fifty to her sixteen. What are you wincing at?"

"That doddery widower comment." He sounded rueful. "He was probably younger than I am. But back to the meat of this, you're exactly right. Catriona was being married off to a much-older man whom she likely had never even seen. And are we supposed to believe Margaret was jealous of that? Because personally, I doubt it."

"Doubt?" Maddy snorted. "Sorry, Richard, but I'm past being delicate. I'm in full disbelief mode over here. No, the murder—if it came from jealousy—was jealousy over something else entirely, and my money's on the cute shawm player with the Italian accent."

"That certainly makes the most sense," he agreed. "But let's get on, yes? I'd personally like to get as much of this covered tonight as possible, and we're both going to want some sleep. It's going to be a hard day slaving over the rare books tomorrow."

"Good point," she grinned. "Carry on. What's next?"

"Next is the second of January, and we've had Anne finally meeting the King. And from the sound of it, our sensible spinster wasn't nearly sentimental enough to think there was anything to come but trouble. Also, there's a confirmation of something you and I had both wondered about. Here we go."

*Rochester, 2 January 1540—Today hath the King come to Rochester, travelling with neither pomp nor notice, and with five of his Privy Council as retinue, that he might meet with his bride in secret, and see her before she might guess at his glory and rank. I know not of what passed between them, but of what followed, it is meet that I have it writ down, tho it be for naught by mine own comfort, and easiness of mind.*

*I did espy the King, as he came from the Lady Anne's apartments, where she had been watching the bull-baiting, set out for her pleasure in the courtyard below. Tho he went most heavily disguised, I knew him at once, and did make obeisance to him. At this, His Most Gracious Majesty did raise me up, and hold one finger to his lips, to enjoin my silence. He then bade me come with him to a quiet embrasure, saying that he wished to have speech with me where none might overhear.*

*I did accompany him at his will, noting with some worry that his brow was creased with displeasure. He gave vent to grave dismay and disappointment, saying he had been deep misled and sore misinformed as to the Lady's charms; indeed, he did compare her in most unflattering wise to one of her own horses, saying that she hath neither wit nor charm, nor grace of person either. I was sore shocked to hear him speak thus, but held my tongue, for he is my King, and worthy of all respect.*

*After this release of ill feeling, he did collect himself, and spake to me of my niece's wedding; he asked how I liked the match, and I was deep discomposed, not knowing how to say truth, for I could not tell my King that I thought so young and tender a maid as my dead brother's child could find anything to like in a man of Lord*

*Kesleigh's years, since he hath more years than the King himself. Yet even this was not the least of what passed between us, nor yet the font of my gravest care.*

"Hang on a minute." Richard paused for a mouthful of water. "I did warn you it was a long one. And by the way, I don't know about you, but the historian in me is looking at this little lot and doing the dance of joy. I've seen accounts of that sneak peek at Anne—the Lisle letters and the accounts of the French ambassador, for instance—but this?"

"Treasure trove," she agreed. "But I'll lick my lips over the historical significance later. She referred to Catriona as being her dead brother's child, yes? So, when she uses 'my dear sister' or whatnot, it's a general term only—she was actually related to the twins' father."

"That's it," he agreed. "Which explains how she comes to be a spinster and a MacLaine at the same time."

"Right." Maddy was arranging the pieces in her mind, turning them around, seeing what fit. "You know, I'm damned curious about that last bit, about there being something even more upsetting. Does she elaborate?"

"She certainly does." Richard sipped his water, and turned the page.

*Fortunate was I that the King did not press me as to Catriona's marriage. His mind was clear set on his own wedding, and it was sore obvious to me that he cannot like the Lady, nor does he wish to wed her. He laid commands upon me, to do my duty to God and to my King, saying that I must watch the Lady Anne close, so that I might inform him if she in any wise behaved in such fashion as might allow him to disavow her. I am sore cumbered by this, and can see no safe road to refusal.*

"He asked Alison to spy on Anne?" Maddy's jaw had dropped. "He asked the nice middle-aged spinster lady with the conscience made of granite to spy on the woman she was supposed to be a companion to? He must have been out of his mind."

"Either that, or desperate," Richard agreed. "At the very least, ill-advised. One thing that occurs to me is that he seems to have trusted Alison in a way I would never have expected. And there's that implication that he specifically brought her down from Scotland to be with the new Queen. It makes me wonder just how well he knew her, to go to that much trouble."

"True. Hang on, I need to stretch." Maddy rolled her wrists and ankles, cracking joints that had settled in place. "There, that's done. Did you get anything else?"

"Yes, but nothing major. I've got her eyewitness account of the wedding; it's a nice bit of history, but for what we need, it's not really relevant, except for one small bit about the music—she seems to have noticed the musicians, the shawm player especially. But our personal librarian lady came in to turf us out just as I was getting to the return to London."

"Then if you don't mind, I'm off for some kip. It's been a long day, and tomorrow looks to be longer. Good grief, make that today, it's past midnight! Tell you what, I'll come get you around eight, and we can go get some breakfast before the Bodleian opens. Sleep well."

Music, music. All the world was music.

She was down there, in a gown of bright yellow. Her hair was bound behind her, the bright copper smooth beneath a jewelled French hood. She wasn't dancing; she was waiting only, standing alone, with none to compare to her.

Ringan played his shawm, hearing the other musicians around him, caring for nothing at all but the girl, his perfect flower, bright as a daffodil capped in rosy gold by the sun. She seemed to stand apart from all the others; once, she looked upward, catching his eye. His fingers worked the shawm, drenching her with sound, meaning it for her alone. He thought he saw a vagrant dimple, but then she cast her eyes down once more, and he saw the crowd around her eddy and part, and an older man came and spoke with her. *Play, Ringan thought, you must play, you must not falter, or let any see what you feel.*

She kept her gaze turned down, her shoulders stiff and unyielding. But the old man reached out and took her hand, leading her out to the lines of dancers. The King, at his high table, gestured upward with one hand, signifying his desire for a merry tune, something to set the feet flying. He himself was not dancing, and Ringan, who had heard the rumours, wondered if this bluff, powerful man was dreading his own wedding night as much as his goddaughter, condemned to wed a man older by many years than her own dead father, was dreading hers.

*Play,* he thought, *you must play. It matters nothing that your heart breaks within you. No one must know. Play.*

And so the musicians, above the throng of nobles and diplomats celebrating the wedding of the King to a woman he found repellent, fingered and blew and sang. At Ringan's left was François, a viol player, a skinny Frenchman from the south, always hungry, looking as if something devoured him from within; to his right was an Englishman, playing a citole with verve and panache. And the singer, the conceited Breton Corentin, sang with his heart throbbing falsely in his voice, meaning nothing, hearing only himself.

Ringan scanned the crowd, watching Catriona. She was dancing with the old man, this was true, but she was stiff and somehow apart, letting nothing of her feelings show. He froze a moment, seeing a lilac skirt moving up the dance. He knew that dress; there had been a night, a very long night, when he had mistaken the girl who wore it for his own *camelia,* and had taken the girl, kept her with him all through the night. He had called her by the name he thought was hers, whimpering it, crying it out loud, muffling it in her bright hair: *Catriona, mia tesoro, mia amore!*

And she had let him believe it. She had said not a word until the morning, until those first rays of day had crept into the chilly chamber, and she had risen from his bed, gathering herself, ready to leave. She had spoken, then.

Ringan looked down at her, hate in his eyes and in his heart. She had tricked him, stolen his seed and his attention and his fidelity, and all through trickery. He remembered the moment when he had known what had been done; he had called to her at the chamber door, and she had turned, a smile on her face, all of darkness, no love, no joy. He had seen the triumph, and he had known then. His own voice, calling her what she was—*baldracca,* whore, liar, cheat, false in every way.

And she had stared at him, that same dark smile on the face that was the mirror of his darling's, and yet so different. One hand had crept down, to cup her belly.

"I've a name," she told him, and her voice was a thing to cut him, to cut his sleep to ribbons in the nights to come: amused, contemptuous, a voice knowing it had won some dark trophy. "A good name, sir. I was named Margaret, for the King's own sister. 'Tis a good name, I swear. Take care you use it not by inattention when next you love my sister."

They were both dancing now, and the King had left his chair, joining the dancers. He had a hand out to the girl in the lilac gown; she took it, glancing up boldly under her lashes, letting the dance swing her around, flirting with her smile and her eyes and the very rhythm of her—

"Ringan. Ringan, wake up."

The voice was a distant echo, not real, something to be ignored. He knew it, that was true, but there was nothing, no reason, to pay it any mind. He played on, a sprightly tune, and below him the dancers wheeled and circled on each others' arms, changing partners.

"Ringan! Come on, wake up, damn it, you're scaring me."

The song was coming to an end, and the dancers had moved up and down the length of the line, and there was his love, his life, his beautiful *agnello,* yes, she was a lamb, but she would be a sacrificial lamb before the new year had seen the turn of one month's passage, that old man would have her, it was not to be borne, not to be accepted, yet he must and there was nothing he could do. . . .

The slap, with the full force of a strong arm behind, rocked him backwards. For a horrible moment, Ringan hovered; there was the sense that he was falling, but was he falling through time or through space, was that the edge of the gallery, the balustrade, was he going to crash to the stones below, spilling his blood and his brains, ruining this travesty of a wedding, horrifying the new queen . . . ?

And then he was gagging, his chest on fire, trying to swallow, but there was something in his throat and he was choking. There were hands on his shoulders, strong hands but soft, competent, and caring, holding on to him as the burn in chest and throat resolved into bile, acid from the depths of his stomach as he retched violently.

"You're okay." The voice was Penny's; it was under as hard a control as he had ever heard in his life. "You're all right. It's all right. Just take your time. I'm right here, darling. I won't let go, I won't go anywhere. It's okay."

It seemed to take forever. Every time he thought it was over, and tried to raise his eyes from the porcelain of the toilet, it would start again. Vertigo washed over him, battering him like storm waves, keeping him from opening his eyes. And behind his eyes were two faces, identical and yet so different, and a voice, a voice in the night. . . .

"What?" Penny's voice was stronger now, clearer; she sounded somehow real, and present, slipping from the shadowy hinterland he'd been inhabiting and into his heart and mind, back into the world at his shoulder. "What did you say?"

"I've a name." He heard his own voice, rasping over a throat left raw. "A good name, sir. I was named Margaret, for the King's own sister. 'Tis a good name, I swear."

He heard her indrawn breath. It was important that she should hear this, in case he was somewhere, in some place, where he himself couldn't tell her. *Important,* he thought, and another wave of vertigo swamped him, forcing his eyes closed. He breathed through his nose for a moment, and willed the dizziness away. His own voice came again, the barest thread. "Take care you use it not by inattention when next you love my sister. Oh God. So sick. Penny? Are you here?"

"Yes. Right here." Her voice was shaking, out of her control. "Can you open your eyes? Please try."

"Right. Okay." *Slowly,* he thought, *take it very slowly, let a bit of light in, it's all right, good, progress, keep it going, get on with it. . . .*

The room came into focus around him. He blinked.

The first thing he knew as being really there, the first thing actually recognisable, was her touch. She had a firm hold on him; when she'd told him she wasn't letting go, she'd been telling the simple truth.

He leaned back against her, unabashedly letting her support his weight. One of his own hands moved, and it covered one of hers. She leaned her cheek against his, and he saw tears, three huge tears, splash one after another on the tile floor.

"Don't cry," he managed. "I was playing shawm at Henry Tudor's wedding a few minutes ago, a few centuries ago. Some time, anyway. Back now. Don't cry."

"I'm not." She squeezed his shoulders gently, her hands warm under his. "You are. Those are your tears, not mine. Can you stand?"

"Don't know. Let's try."

He managed it, Penny supporting him. She led him out of the bathroom and over to the sofa.

"Here." She handed him a glass, and watched him wrap both hands around it, ready to support him if needed. "Apple juice, not too cold. Drink. Very small sips—don't gulp it, or you'll be sick again."

"Thanks." He got a mouthful down, and felt his stomach move in ominous protest. "Wow. Right, okay, I needed this. Steadier—I can cope again."

"Do you remember what happened?" She was watching him. There was something new in her eyes, the muscles of her mouth, the way she was holding herself, that spoke of a hard-earned control. "Think back. Do you remember? Not what you saw from— wherever you were, not yet, anyway. Do you remember—?"

"We were tidying up." He spoke immediately. This time, it was clear in his mind. "I was doing the washing up, and you were hoovering the carpets. I remember I was holding that pan with the very long handle, and then I got dizzy and I felt a tug, a yank, almost as if something had got hold of my hair, or my collar, and then it wasn't a pan any more. It was a shawm, and I was playing it."

"Christ. Back in Pietro Bendone?" She blew air out through her nostrils. "Okay. Tell me what happened. Tell me all of it. And Ringan—do something for me, please? I want you to keep your eyes on my face the whole time. Try not to break eye contact." She saw him raise an eyebrow. "I have a reason," she said quietly. "Just try."

He gave her the full story. The details, this time, were clear, showing no sign of fading. Obedient to her request, he kept his eyes locked to hers. As he spoke, he began to understand why she'd wanted him to watch her. There were a few moments—seeing Margaret dancing with the King; Pietro's surge of hatred for the older man, presumably Catriona's betrothed; the shared memory of the night Pietro had spent with the wrong sister—when Ringan could feel the pull backward, the need that seemed to have found a chink in the curtain of time or reality, the understanding of how easy it would be to sink backward, to leave the here and now, to be there. . . .

"So that's what you meant, about his not using her name by accident." She had hold of his free hand. "Margaret spent the night with Catriona's shawm player, and let him think she was her sister. And he didn't twig until morning?"

"Apparently not." He was fully back within himself, and his mind was working. He looked up and saw that Penny's face was taut with concentration. "Penny for them?"

"My thoughts?" She managed a small grin, but it faded at once. "Easy. I'm scared to death. Ringan, whatever it is that's happening here—it's chronological. Do you realize that? Every time this has happened, it's been a little bit farther along." She bit her lower lip, hard enough to leave an imprint against the skin. "It's moving along in time, and it's getting stronger with every hit you take. And I'm so damned scared, Ringan. I'm out of my mind with it."

He sat in appalled silence. She was right. He hadn't thought about it, but every incident had been a little farther along in the progression of events that had surrounded the royal wedding, and the death of—

*death of death of death of*

Ringan's mind stopped for a moment, and so did his heart.

Catriona had died; he'd seen it, watched that murder happen in real time. From what he'd heard of the fragment from Alison MacLaine's journal, found and read by Maddy Holt, Margaret had died as well, although he still had no clue as to how or when.

But they were not the only deaths. Clear and vivid, Tamsin's voice came into his head, reciting facts, reciting a death knell.

*Pietro Bendone, right, age twenty—poor brat, what a nasty way to die, being tortured. And good heavens, that charge I mentioned was only half—they had him up for treason as well. He wouldn't have stood a chance.*


"Tamsin? It's Penny. Sorry you're not there—I hope to hell you get this message, and soon. Look, something is happening to Ringan, and I want to confab with anyone who might be concerned at all. If you can ring me the minute you get this, that would be good. Ta, bye."

"Not home, I gather." Ringan, with a hot meal under his belt, was looking more like himself. "And Richard and Maddy are both up in Oxford. I like the idea, but you know, it's beginning to look as if it simply isn't going to happen."

"It will if I have anything to say about it." Penny sounded grim. "We need to do something, damn it!"

"Yes, love, I couldn't agree more. But you can't yank family and researchers out of the ether by pure strength of will." He yawned suddenly. "Christ, I'm exhausted. If the weather wasn't so warm, I'd run a hot bath and take a soak, maybe doze off for a bit."

She opened her mouth, thought better of what she'd wanted to say, and shut it again. But he'd seen the movement.

"I know," he said quietly. "But I can't not sleep, Pen, can I? I mean, at some point, it's all systems shutting down and a bit of kip, what with the whole being-human-in-a-human-body bit. And anyway . . ."

She bit her lip. His own unspoken words hung in the air between them: sleep, as a state, was apparently not a requirement for whatever was happening to him. Neither was distance. If he could fade back four-and-a-half centuries while he was rinsing off the breakfast dishes in Penny's kitchen, he wasn't safe anywhere, or under any circumstances.

"I'm going to call Maddy." The need to do something, anything at all, was verging on intolerable. Penny had been increasingly miserable all afternoon, pacing, unwilling to let Ringan out of her sight.

Ringan, with a mixture of amusement and sympathy, found himself thinking that passivity, the willingness to simply sit and let events take their course and trust they'd turn out right, was simply not in her make-up. If it had been, she'd have made a very bad theatrical producer. "I'll leave her a message," she announced. "Another message, I mean."

"Penny, for heaven's sake! Didn't you already—?" he began, but was interrupted by the electronic jangling of Penny's cell phone. She nearly dropped it in her haste to answer it.

"Hello? Tamsin! Oh, thank goodness—what? No, Ringan's fine at the moment, but he wasn't a few hours ago, and I don't think he's going to be fine much longer at this rate. Yes, of course something happened. Listen, I know this is short notice, and honestly, I wouldn't ask under normal circs, but there's nothing normal about—what? Oh. About seven?"

Ringan watched her face. She was quiet for a few moments, listening to the muffled voice at the other end of the line. Even at this distance, it was clear to Ringan that Tamsin was asking a question. "Can you bring who? Who is Marcus Childe? Why would you want to bring—oh! Oh, the bloke who was with you when you brought Ringan back here? Yes, I suppose so. Unless Ringan minds? Half a tick, I'll ask him."

She covered the phone with the palm of her free hand, but the gesture was unnecessary; Ringan was already nodding and giving her a thumbs up. She returned her attention to the phone.

"Ringan says it's fine. Bring him along. And Stephen. I don't know who else. I think we need to do some sorting out, and it needs to happen fast." She heard her own voice waver, and steadied it. "I'm going to call Maddy Holt, our friend from the British Library—she's up at Oxford, burning the midnight oil at the Bodleian with Richard Halligan, used to be the secular archivist at St. Paul's. They've got their hands on some interesting stuff, but right now? I wish they were both here in London, instead of hours off. Anyway, see you sevenish."

She rang off, and stood with the silent phone in her hand, looking undecided. It was time, Ringan thought, that he got a hand in on this particular party.

"If I can make a suggestion? I think we ought to get the band over here if we can. I mean, I know they aren't directly involved in it, but it's a song, and anyway, it's me. Even if they aren't involved, they're certainly affected, right? Because if anything happens to me," he said, with a misplaced attempt at humour, "there goes the mortgage."

She looked at him, very steadily, for a long moment. He was shocked at what he saw in her face.

"Sorry." He meant it; she looked as though he'd told her he was leaving her, or something. "Bad joke. Trying to lighten it, love, that's all. I didn't mean to make it worse."

"Well, you did make it worse." Her face was tight with what might have been pain, and her voice seemed somehow muffled. "And honestly, Ringan. I'd appreciate it if you'd not do that again.

I don't have any of the Broomfields' numbers, you'll have to ring them. Here, use my cell." Her face suddenly began working. "I need to—I'm going to the loo."

She walked out. Ringan, silently calling himself a wide variety of rude names, began punching in telephone numbers.

When she came back, she was surprised—and relieved—to find him on his feet. He met her in the kitchen doorway with a strong hug.

"They'll all be along between seven and half-past. Liam sounded fierce about it—okay, right, I know, he generally sounds fierce, but really, this was something extra." He kissed her. "I'm really sorry," he told her, and she wondered whether the apology was meant for the poor joke, for the situation in general, or for those actions shared with Pietro Bendone that had left him feeling somehow as if he'd been faithless. At some point, she thought, she was going to have to reassure him about that.

"Boot's on the other leg." She rested her cheek against his for a moment. "I'm sorry I ever put you on the phone with my brother. Ringan, fair warning: I have every intention of getting as deep into what we actually know as I can tonight. I want to really sort out as much as possible—what we know, or what we think we know. I can't just sit back and wait. Right, I'm a bossy cow and a hideous control freak, but damn it—"

"Did you think I was likely to argue with you, Pen? Not such a fool. After all, brutal fact is, it looks to be my head on the block. And no, I wasn't being funny. Not that time." He met her look. "I think it may be coming down to that. Now, what do we need to do to tidy up the place for company, and what shall we do about nosh?"

The invited guests—Tamsin, with Stephen and Marcus Childe in tow, as well as the rest of Broomfield Hill—showed up within minutes of each other. Stephen, first through the door, gave his sister a fast once-over and then surprised her mightily by offering a hard, fast hug.

"You look like hell," he grunted. "Not at all surprised, either. How's Ringan holding up?"

"He's all right," she told him. "For now, anyway."

"Good. Because after Tamsin rang off earlier, we realised we had an experience out there ourselves, and you haven't heard about it yet. It might be a help." He glanced over Penny's shoulder, to where Ringan was talking to Marcus Childe; he seemed to be reassuring Childe that he hadn't caught cold during his trance-fuelled drive out to Westferry Road. "Ringan looks a bit tired. Has anything else happened?"

"Yes." The energy that had been driving Penny all day suddenly deserted her, in a huge rushing ebb. She glanced around and sank into the nearest chair. "Sorry, I just realised how drained I am. Totally played out. I need a nice sit-down and maybe an enormous bottle of booze. Anyway, yes, something else happened, but I want to tell it once, not three or four times. There's stuff in the fridge, if you want anything. I think we should get started."

Long after that evening was over, Penny would look back on it with the sense that it had been one of the oddest gatherings she'd ever been party to, much less hostess for. On any other evening, the source of the discomfort might easily have been traceable to the presence of Marcus Childe, a relative stranger. But that hadn't been why, and Penny knew it, even at the time.

It was simply that no one knew how to deal with what had been happening to Ringan. Even Liam, who liked to say that the Tact Fairy had been left off the guest list for his christening party, confessed later that he hadn't felt comfortable meeting his old mate's eye. Penny, trying through her exhaustion to put a name to what the undercurrents in her flat reminded her of, was horrified when she made the connection: this was the way people looked around someone with an incurable disease, someone who'd been given six months to live. Either that, she thought, or it was a kind of social ineptitude, not knowing how much eye contact was permissible.

She was aware of a sudden helpless spurt of outrage on Ringan's behalf. She pushed it away, and with it the desire to scream at her guests. If he was aware of what she was finding so upsetting, he wasn't showing it, and surely, she reasoned, he had a far-greater right to mind and react than she did. She gave herself a moment to make sure her voice was steady. Then she looked around the crowded room and, from her place on the sofa at Ringan's side, spoke up.

"Here's the thing," she told. "We're in trouble. We're in very deep trouble, and we need a way out of it."

Startled, everyone turned to stare. She raised her voice, pitching it to carry.

"I'm sorry if everyone expected me to act like a party hostess, but this isn't a party. We're in trouble. We need help, and we need it fast; and right now, the only thing I can think of that might be of any use at all is information."

She stopped, hearing her voice edging towards the higher registers of hysteria. Jane's voice, even and calm, broke the appalled silence.

"Information is generally useful, yes. But remember, we haven't been told what's been happening, and I, for one, haven't got a clue what you're talking about. What on earth has been going on, Ringan?"

He told them. He omitted nothing, not his sense of being caught, not his own inability to either completely blend into or completely separate himself from Pietro Bendone. He spoke slowly, clearly, letting them all hear and see and understand the shawm player's love for Catriona, his hatred for her sister, and the seduction she'd tricked him into. He gave them every detail he could remember; when he came to those moments of Bendone and his lovemaking, of Catriona in his arms, he kept his voice as flat and detached as he could manage, and avoided Penny's eye. It had to hurt her, he thought, whether or not she showed it. There was no reason to make it worse by lingering on it, or dramatising it. He remembered, at the last, to tell the Broomfields about the snippet of Henry Tudor's song.

When he finished, he looked down at his own hands. Without his realising it, they'd come together and clenched hard in his lap. There was a fine mist of sweat along his hairline.

"Jesus." Stephen looked at his wife. "Tamsin, tell them about the dogs. Tell them what you heard."

"Yes, Stephen, I was about to do just that. Ringan, dear, I think I heard your murderess being chased by a bunch of dogs—that was a few days ago, out on the Isle of Dogs." Tamsin's tone, conversational and free of emotional undertones, seemed to put everyone at ease. There had been a sense that everyone in the room had been holding his or her breath; listening to Tamsin, they were able to exhale. "It was really very peculiar. I closed my eyes, and I could hear the cars, the boats on the river, and the dogs. But of course, there weren't any dogs."

"Where were you?" Something, the seed of realisation, was beginning to take root in Ringan's mind. "Physically, I mean? Were you in the crater, that bomb cavity?"

"Not at first, no." She'd followed Ringan's train of thought easily. "I was standing inside the frame of the house, and I heard the dogs, and thought I'd really have to have a word with the neighbours about it—so noisy, you know? And Stephen does like to lie in at the weekends. But of course, we don't have any immediate neighbours. And there weren't any dogs."

"Just the dogs." Ringan was nodding. "No human voices?"

"No, not there—that came later, once I was out of our house. And really, hearing a snarling pack of hunting dogs coming closer and closer was quite upsetting enough for me. But when I went near the bomb cavity, I heard her. Stephen went and stood in the cavity, and held my hand, and that was when I heard her, asking for—"

She broke off suddenly, remembering. "Sanctuary. She was asking the Virgin Mary for sanctuary. I heard—she said—"

Her face had gone pale, and her brow clammy. Ringan reached out and got hold of her hand. Words, unspoken, imprinted, remembered, jumped silently between them.

*Merciful Mother, I commend my soul to thee, give me sanctuary, sanctuary, take me in, I prithee hold me not out of doors to such a death, shelter, sanctuary*

Tamsin screamed. It was low, all the way at the back of her throat, but Ringan's eyes had widened as he heard it, heard beyond it, his hand tightening around her own, hearing the dogs, snarling and vicious, smelling blood, her blood, she was bleeding, the dogs had been given her scent, they were at her heels, if she could get indoors she would be—

"Let go." Stephen pulled Ringan's hand free. "Ringan, for Christ's sake, let go of her!"

"It's all right. I'm fine." Tamsin was staring at Ringan. He was the colour of old linen, his pupils enormous. "You heard it. Didn't you?"

"She wanted to be let in." Ringan was shaking. *Her voice* he thought, *it had to be Margaret, surely.* "She was out of doors, and she was begging the Virgin Mary for sanctuary, for shelter. What did she say, Tamsin? *Sanctuary, take me in,* wasn't it? Something like that, anyway." He put a hand to his mouth. "Bloody hell."

"She said, *I prithee hold me not out of doors to such a death.*" There was nothing remote in Tamsin's eye now, nothing detached. "And I can't shake the image of her locked out of somewhere, desperate to get in."

"But there was no building there." Penny had got hold of Ringan's hand and was holding hard. "Didn't you say there was no record of any building on your site? If there was nothing there, where in hell was she?"

"Maybe she was right there, where you felt her to be." It was Marcus Childe, speaking up for the first time. He looked from Tamsin to Ringan. "You're quite right—the official records show nothing on the site. But has it occurred to anyone that there might have been something long gone, a ruin, perhaps? Even just a few stones of the foundation left? It wouldn't need to have been right there—just somewhere on the Isle of Dogs. I could check the records for that if anyone wanted me to."

They all stared at him. Marcus turned a bit pink.

"I'm not really a part of this." He sounded apologetic. "I came along to make certain Ringan was all right. And honestly, I don't believe in ghosts. But if you don't mind my being a complete sceptic, I'd be happy to check the records, at least the ones for the time period you think is in question."

"The man's right, I'd say." Liam, who'd watched the unnatural interplay of information between Ringan and Tamsin with narrowed eyes, took a long pull at his beer. He alone among the guests had taken Penny's suggestion and helped himself from the fridge. "If your murderess was begging the Virgin for sanctuary, I'd lay good money on there being someplace that might have offered it. Might help if the records were complete, but just because they're not, it doesn't mean there was never something there. Because really, it seems obvious there must have been."

He turned his head suddenly, and regarded Marcus Childe with curiosity. "If you don't mind my asking you, what's your interest in this? Have you bumped into anything yourself, out there in East London? Bumped into any bogles?"

Marcus turned a bit pink. Ringan, watching him along with the others, thought it was a damned good question, and very odd that no one had thought to ask him before.

"No. As I said, I don't think I believe in ghosts, or any of that." Marcus looked at Tamsin. "But—the first time I visited the site, there was nothing odd about it. And every time after that, I've been feeling as though I were standing in quicksand. It just feels shaky, and wet, as if the river was seeping its way up straight through the foundations. I did wonder if perhaps I wasn't just being suggestible. And I probably was." He shrugged, looking a bit embarrassed. "But I'd be happy to check the council records for the entire Isle of Dogs, as far back as we can. There may have been a chapel somewhere. I can check for Millwall, see if there's anything about it in the parish registers. Would that be useful to you?"

"I think you're right about there having been a chapel." Jane was leaning forward, concentrated and intent. "She was asking for sanctuary. I doubt she'd have thought that some medieval outhouse was blessed by the Virgin Mary, or some old stables or even dog kennels, because she—is that someone's cell?"

It was Penny's, shrilling beside her. She snatched it up and got it open.

"Maddy? Thank God, finally! Listen, we're having a thing here, everyone except you two who might be involved at all, or even just useful, and we've got some new information. Can you do me a favour and have a look into Alison MacLaine's journals, and see if there's any mention of a chapel anywhere on the Isle of Dogs one that might be nearby to my brother's property? Preferably one dedicated to the Virgin, but any chapel would—what?"

She listened a moment. They all heard her swallow hard.

"Right. Maddy, hang on—let me get this on the speaker phone. One second—okay, here we go. Can you repeat that?"

There was a pause. Madeleine Holt's voice came through the tiny speaker, far-away and mechanical, but audible.

"I said, we've found a journal entry about Pietro Bendone being arrested. It's dated 22 April, 1540. He was arrested for treason, plotting to cause harm to the King. Penny—it wasn't only him. He was arrested along with Margaret MacLaine—at the same time, I mean. They were arrested together, as part of the same writ, for conspiring against the King. It was a treason charge. From what we're able to get from Alison MacLaine, Margaret was also charged—this was a bit later on—with killing her sister. And get this: Margaret was pregnant."

# Ten

*The first string sang a doleful sound:*
*"The bride her younger sister drowned."*

That Saturday morning, driving too quickly for safety in a weeping downpour, Maddy and Richard got back into London.

On the rear seat of Maddy's car was an overstuffed manila envelope containing handwritten copies of every word of Alison MacLaine's that either of them considered even vaguely pertinent to what was happening to Ringan. They'd given up on the idea of getting it all into their individual notebooks, and begged several dozen sheets of paper from Elizabeth Jensing, and had begun copying in earnest.

As a result, both were nursing aching wrists; Maddy, in particular, found herself snarling under her breath. She was so used to being able to make electronic images of what she needed that she'd forgotten just how exhausting hand-copying could be. Thirty years her senior but accustomed to that particular necessity, Richard was in far better shape after it, and less resentful at having had to do it in the first place.

"Have we got a course of action?" Richard, settling back in his seat, watched Maddy navigate the car off the North Circular Road, and down into Hendon and Finchley. "I'm sorry if you've already told me, but I'm afraid my mind has been thoroughly locked up on Alison MacLaine's letters."

"Don't apologize for that, for heaven's sake—you're a historian. Of course you've been focusing. Anyway, no, you didn't ask. Penny's expecting us at her place after lunch; she said she had a meeting she couldn't get out of, something about having to sign off on some repairs to her theatre, but that was supposed to only take a bit, and she'd be home between one and two, sometime. And Ringan's off in the studio with his band—Penny said he was a few days behind on mixing down their new CD." Her stomach grumbled audibly. "Damn! Richard, are you hungry? Because that bit of pastry I had before we hit the road has pretty much faded out, and since we've got time for lunch, I wouldn't mind eating."

"No more would I." He was suddenly acutely aware of how tired, how under-fuelled, he actually felt. He thought, ruefully, that his days of poring over old manuscripts, of taking copious hand-written notes, of getting neither enough sleep nor enough food in the process, were decidedly on the wane. "Do you know, I think I'm getting old? Let's track down some food, and go from there."

They found a serviceable local café near Muswell Hill. Having parked the car at the end of Penny's street, Maddy and Richard went off for a leisurely lunch. There was no hurry.

It was just after two when they pushed back their chairs, left a small pile of money on a table littered with empty plates and the dregs of two pots of tea, and made their way to Penny's flat. Richard, who had been here before, led the way.

Maddy's first reaction when Penny opened the door to let them in was to forcibly bite back an exclamation. Penny looked terrible. The light shadows under her eyes had become deep chasms, bruised looking with exhaustion. Her usual easy grace seemed sluggish and slow. Her mouth seemed to have developed a tremor at one corner.

Maddy began to speak, then stopped. Richard was not nearly so tactful. "Penny, for heaven's sake, are you all right? I hate to say it, but you look as if you haven't slept in a week."

"No, just the last couple of days, actually. I've been afraid to sleep." Penny managed a brief smile, and stepped back from the door. "Very perceptive of you, Richard—not tactful, but perceptive. And honestly, you both look a bit like I feel. Totally exhausted, I mean. Maddy, love, how are you? You can't imagine how thankful I am to see you both, or how grateful I am for all the work. How was the drive back? Come in, come in. Why are we standing about? I want to sit."

"The drive back was fine, but never mind the chatter. We've got information for you. Into the front room?"

"Yes, I think so. If I doze off, wake me—kip sounds brilliant right now, but I really shouldn't." Penny led the way into her front room, and waved them towards chairs. "Do we need to wait for Ringan to get back? Does he need to hear the actual letters? Or can I get it now, and recap the important bits later? And excuse me a moment—I've got an espresso in the kitchen, and I need my caffeine right now, rather badly."

She retrieved her coffee, and sank into her sofa. "Right. Now, what have we got? Talk to me."

"We've got a lot, is what we've got. Some things are missing, of course; they always are. That's research for you." Maddy opened the manila envelope, and slid the contents out into her lap. "First of all, the basic gen: Margaret MacLaine, the younger twin? Our red-haired murderess? Was apparently visibly pregnant when she was arrested and shoved into prison, at the same time Henry had Pietro Bendone pulled in."

"Visibly?" Penny swallowed a mouthful of coffee. "I'm going to have the jitters for weeks, I've drunk so much of this stuff the past few days. Sorry. When you say visibly—"

"She was showing it." Richard had his notebook in his lap. "Here, no need to dig out the full copy on this one, Maddy—I have it, and don't look so cross, please—this isn't a competition."

She glared at him. He cleared his throat, and read.

*Greenwich, Palace of Placentia, 22 April 1540—Deep thanks I must in my devotions offer in the name of the Lady Anne, who found me in deepest distress, and offered me both comfort and ale. For my dearest sister, Elspeth, deprived of her firstborn after so gruesome a fashion, there can be nothing offered to comfort. Today all the palace was rife with whispering in corners, full of the news that one of the King's own musicians hath been ta'en for treason, and my younger niece, Margaret, as well, and on the same charge.*

*If there be shame to match this that hath befallen the good name of MacLaine, I wouldst most easily marvel at it. My niece goes with child, and no father to bear its name. Tho she hath dressed herself most modestly in recent days, she could not hide the swelling of belly, the fullness of face. Shame, deepest shame, and my sister would hear none of this. We stand together under Our Lord, however, with no means to hide from Him.*

*The Lady Anne, finding me weeping and in travail most sore, of-fered me what comfort she was able. I believe she understands little of the events that had so overset me, yet her kindness to me was such that I was overset worse, and could put neither stop nor control o'er my grief.*

"Wow." Penny's eyes were wide. The picture drawn by this moment of pain out of history was uncomfortably clear; in her mind's eye, she was suddenly back on the Isle of Dogs, standing for the first time on her brother's property, gazing out enraptured at Richmond and Deptford across the Thames, watching the *Cutty Sark* sway in the light wind off the river. "So they knew by then that Catriona had been murdered? And for whatever reason, Margaret and Bendone were somehow bracketed in Henry's head, and he had them busted together?"

"Oh, yes." Maddy was thumbing through her handwritten papers. "Catriona disappeared the day before she was due to be married off to an elderly widower called Lord Kesleigh; he was a protégé of Henry's. Henry seemed to think he was doing his goddaughter a good turn, but I doubt she thought so."

"No, she didn't." The shadows under Penny's eyes suddenly pinched up as she remembered. "Ringan saw her. He heard her.

She was completely in love with Pietro Bendone—hell, she was obsessed with him. Anyway—she disappeared?"

"Disappeared, yes. They didn't find her straight off—no one knew she'd been drowned, not for nearly a week. It's all here." Maddy cleared her throat, and read.

*Greenwich, Palace of Placentia, 31 January 1540—All the palace is in an uproar, and my sister, Elspeth, most of all, is distraught. My older niece, who tomorrow should be joined to Lord Kesleigh, is nowhere to be found. All is rumour and speculation, and my sister hath begged the King, most piteously in her extremity, that nothing might be left undone to find her.*

She stopped. "Very terse, for Alison, isn't it?"

"They thought she'd run off." Penny was upright now, a bit of energy restored between caffeine and interest. "Not that anything had happened to her—they thought she'd decided she simply couldn't bear to marry this Kesleigh bloke and had run off."

"I wonder if Margaret dropped some hints, trying to keep them thinking that? After all, it would certainly have been in her interest to delay them finding the body for as long as possible." Richard got up. "Penny, that coffee smells wonderful. Would you mind if I made myself one?"

Penny waved him towards the kitchen. Her mind, which had been feeling sluggish and overweighed, was beginning to work once more.

What did they know, know for a fact, know enough to work from? Catriona had been murdered by her jealous sister. Said jealous sister was pregnant at the time. The murder had happened the day before Catriona, in love with Pietro Bendone, was due to be married off to someone else.

*All right,* Penny thought, and emptied her cup. But there were other things they knew, things that didn't make sense. Margaret had somehow got her sister across the river, away from prying eyes and

189

possible witnesses, to the Isle of Dogs. How had she convinced her to do that? The only thing on that part of the isle was, presumably, a kennel full of Henry's hunting dogs. And the biggest question was maddeningly unanswered: why had Margaret killed her sister in the first place?

"I don't know."

Startled, Penny jerked her head. Richard, back on the sofa, had spoken, and he and Maddy were both watching her.

"Oh, lord. I was talking out loud? Sorry. Or, no, I'm not sorry—it saves some time. Is there anything in those journals to answer a few basic questions? Such as, how Margaret got Catriona over the river, and why Margaret felt the need to kill her sister in the first place? And, oh yes, do we know for sure that it was Bendone who knocked Margaret up?"

"I don't think Alison talks about any of that, no." Both of Maddy's eyebrows were raised high. "Penny, what you just said, about who got Margaret pregnant—what made you ask that? Wouldn't that have been Bendone? We know she spent a long naughty night with him, tricked him into it. Unless you think she was just generally sleeping around."

"Unlikely." There was a note of authority in Richard's voice. "It's true that Henry's court was noted for bad behaviour—it certainly started at the top. But even if they weren't big on pursed lips and shocked looks, a sixteen-year-old girl from a good family who was caught being sexually promiscuous? No. She'd have risked more than her family's name—she'd have risked her neck."

"I know, but . . ." Penny's cell phone, sitting on the kitchen table, rang in the next room. "Hang on, be right back."

She was gone less than thirty seconds. They barely had time to register individual words: "Liam? What? Oh God—on my way. No, stay there. Just—what? Slap him—yes, I said slap—no—oh God, God—coming. On my way."

Maddy was already on her feet, fumbling for her car keys. Richard was stuffing their notes back into the envelope.

They turned towards Penny as she came back. Her face was ashy.

"He had another episode. Right there in the damned studio, another episode. Liam says he's not responding." Her breathing began to clutch up. "They can't wake him. I have to get there. I have to go."


Night, but almost gone now.

Today, he thought, there would be no sun. It was wrong, a wrong thing about this country, this England, that the winter held no colour, no light. In Milan, even in winter, the sun touched the distance, kissed it with colour, with the promise of hope and a softer touch on the skin. In England, there was only grey and cold. No beauty, no seed of it, to this English winter.

*Pietro, mio marito, come to me. Stay with me a while longer.*

"*Non posso, cara.* I must be away." Pietro's voice, Ringan's own voice, whose was this, dulled and muffled against the heavy stone of the chamber walls? And had she called him her husband? The poor child, to be wishing so for what must never happen, what could never come to pass. He looked down at himself, a slender body, hair on his chest, the same black as Ringan's own, but the chest was thinner, more wiry, and the ribs were narrower. "I will come back, *cara,* when everyone sleeps."

*Then kiss me before you go. Baciami, marito, piacere.*

He wondered if she had learned his language better than he had thought, to use that word, *piacere;* she had asked him to give her pleasure. And he had no will to deny her. Her hair was a pool of glory, the only colour in this dark cold place, the flame of the sun against the ice of this chilly country. He came back to the bedside, listening to her murmur, feeling her hands on him, trying to get him to stay, feeling himself rise to her, pulling back. . . .

He kissed her, deep and long; that much he could do for her. She stayed quiescent against him, and finally let him go, offering no resistance as he lowered her back down to the warmth of her bed, and got his shoes on, and left.

He had stayed longer than he'd meant to; the dawn had come,

and there was too much light, too much. He felt exposed, too visible, easily seen by eyes whose owners might be spying, reporting, hoarding the secrets and information that, at the court of Henry Tudor, meant power.

Down the corridors, the endless passageways, safe away from his beloved's apartment, beyond where anyone might guess his business. He let himself breathe deep; the risk was averted for yet another night. He had gone unseen to Catriona's bed, and come away free with no harm.

He moved cautiously now. Ringan, somehow knowing the turns of the palace as his host knew the turns, understood the sense of danger this last set of corridors posed: here were only the King's own chambers, where Henry lay in state.

A turn, staying close to the wall, but not too close. A chancy business, this balance of overt and secretive. It would be dangerous to court remark. . . .

Bright red hair, a swirl of it, turning the corner. She looked dishevelled, replete, a cat who had spent the night in the courtyard with a tom who would not let her leave. Drowsy, and sated, her dress thrown on, her shoes in her hand, her feet bare. *Catriona, oh no, no,* he thought, and then he realised and understood his mistake.

They saw her at the same time, the shawm player and the guitar player. They nearly ran into each other, the girl and her sister's lover, coming so close that she bit back a startled noise, her hand flying to cover her plump chest, and then her mouth. In silence, they stared at each other.

For a moment, Ringan felt himself in his own body, his knees going weak. But what he felt in his chest, a stab of pain, a warning like a clarion call, an alert of something amiss—that was Pietro and Pietro alone. It was the Italian's heart seizing up dangerously, not his own.

Then she moved her hand from her face, and smiled at him. It was as dark a look as any Pietro had ever seen, as dark as Ringan had ever seen.

"A fine morning and God in His majesty be with you, good sir."

The curtsy she gave him was mocking, a travesty. "You go early abroad for one who stays wakeful so late. And hath this night been kind to you?"

*Whore,* he thought, and hated her. *Whore, and cheat, and liar.* He had no way of understanding what she wanted of him; he knew only that she was the mirror of his darling, but as dark as God had ever seen fit to make a maid, rotten as bad sloes.

Yet she was no maid, either in body or in heart. There was no virtue in her, and no warmth; there was only hunger, and need, and the raging desire to control, a slow burn that could be fed only by some sort of power. And Ringan, suddenly understanding whose room lay at the end of this corridor, what she must have been doing and in whose bed she must have spent the night just gone, caught his breath.

For the first time, with that intake of air, Ringan felt the Italian recognising that he was not alone in his body. No mistake was possible; the precise moment was as clear as the smell of the river in these halls.

Ringan took in breath, using the borrowed lungs. A bare second later, there came a second inhale: Pietro, using his own lungs, feeling those vital organs already full, coming to his own conclusion. He knew he was sharing this space, this use of his most intimate self. Ringan felt him stop, felt him question, felt the muscles around Pietro's eyes contract, felt the pupils in Pietro's eyes follow suit.

And there was Pietro's heart, slamming, stuttering, frightening Ringan. There was something wrong here, something badly wrong. It was arrhythmia, an irregular beat, a valve broken, something; it sent Ringan's hands, invisible and present only as his own thought, grabbing wildly at a chest he could neither claim nor touch. They had no medicine for this, not for Pietro; no way to treat his disease, no way to diagnose it, certainly no way to cure or rescue him. It would be centuries before ways were found to crack the fragile shell of humanity and fix the vital engine within. There was nothing to be done for him, nothing at all. . . .

A harsh, horrible sound: the sound of a guitar falling to the floor, its strings jangling in cacophony. And then a voice.

"Ringan? What the hell is going on—Liam! Jane! Someone do something, he's falling!"

He knew that voice. Surely, he knew it? Through the sudden increase in the race of that damaged heart against the Italian boy's ribs, Ringan heard it and knew it. Matt Curran, of course. A member of his own band. But where was Matt, and why was he calling? There was panic in his voice, and Bendone was aware of it, and it was making it worse. As surely as he, Ringan Laine, could hear Margaret MacLaine's voice, so too could Bendone hear that other spectral human in a time not yet come, that distant voice being impossibly filtered through the ghost in his machine, Ringan the intruder.

There was a moment of violent noise, a painful echo. Bendone's hands, with their long beautiful fingers, had come up hard, clapping against the sides of his head. He was trying to cover his ears, to shut out the demon resident inside his skull, the strange presence who was, in turn, being called by other voices, other times.

Bendone was moving now, stumbling down the long stone halls, terrified and uncomprehending, talking aloud in a torrent of Italian, pleas and prayers, pictures of devils and demons flooding his head and Ringan's, too. Margaret had fled in the other direction for the safety of her own rooms, lest some early courtier or lady-in-waiting chance to cross her path and guess what she'd been up to.

"Shake him. No, not too hard, damn it, he's gone as limp as laundry." He knew that voice, surely, a woman's voice. "God, he feels peculiar, I just hate touching him like this. Liam, ring Penny. Tell her he's not responding, I'm not even sure he's breathing, just ring her, get her here, tell her to hurry up and get here. Ask her what we ought to do in the meantime."

He was being buffeted, pulled back and forth between impossible places, impossible situations, arms wanting to go towards the voices he knew, legs pinned in place by the silently screaming terror of the man in whose body he'd been caught.

An image came up, clear as if it had been acid-etched into metal, a horrifying picture: four horses, a man between them, arms and legs bound. *Quartering,* he thought, *the penalty given for crimes against royalty and nobility.* Someone screamed, possibly himself or possibly Pietro Bendone, sharing the vision, knowing it.

It was dark, it was light, he could hear his friends, and he knew that name, *Penny;* it meant safety, and sanity, and love, and home. He felt his own heart trying to match Bendone's abnormal stammer, and he cried out, called out something in the frowned-upon Lallans Scots of his childhood.

The words were interrupted by a light hand slapping across his cheek. A female voice, light and high and clear, called his name: "Ringan? Ringan, come back, you're scaring us. Come on, mate, come back. Ringan?"

"Did you get her? Is she coming? Oh, Jesus. Ringan?"

"She's coming, she's on her way. Matt, is he breathing? Someone get a mirror, a bit of paper, anything, check his breathing—oh God, I'm so scared, Ringan, please wake up, please come back, for God's sake don't die on us. . . ."

A door opening, heavy, swinging shut behind him. And then he was done, gone, unable to sustain his working mind, his awareness, his sense of self in any place at all, pulled and pushed until the only option remaining was the silence of the void of unconsciousness.

Quiet, a soft hand on his cheek, a sense of light coming through his closed lids.

Ringan opened his eyes.

There was no dislocation this time, no vertigo, no violent wrenching nausea, no pain. He was awake, aware. He knew who he was, and where he was. He also knew precisely where he'd been.

He looked around, not lifting his head. They'd laid him on the beat-up old sofa just outside the sound booth; last thing he remembered, Jane had been inside the glass box, headphones on, listening to a playback of her vocal on the new CD version of "Reynardine." He wondered, rather lazily, just how long he'd been gone, caught, trapped in some ridiculous fold in the fabric of time.

He focused his eyes. The first thing he saw was Jane, looking somehow smaller and bleached in her worry. Christ, he must have given them a fright—she looked like she'd been left out in the rain. To her left, Liam and Matt stood, looking as stiff and helpless as something out of Madame Tussaud's.

He turned his head slightly the other way, and found himself blinking. There was Richard Halligan, with Madeleine Holt at his elbow. And at Ringan's own head, her hand against his cheek, the biggest and best reason in all the world to not get himself stuck somewhere else.

"Hello, lamb." His voice surprised him; it was as fluttery as a butterfly in a high wind. "Penny for them?"

"Ringan." She kept stroking his cheek. It was very bizarre, he thought; her hand never wavered, just kept touching him with the same light, even cadence. Yet her own voice was cracked; had it been flesh, she'd have been bleeding. "Never mind paying for my thoughts—give me a minute and I'll share them for free. Just rest for a bit. Where's that water, Liam?"

Liam broke out of his stillness, and hurried over with a half litre of still water. Penny took a mouthful, and looked down at Ringan. "Can you sit up?"

"Sure, no problem." It was true. He felt lazy, and limp, but he was as fully alert, as aware, as he'd ever been. Every time he came back from one of these little sorties into Pietro Bendone's head or heart or wherever he actually was, it seemed he was a bit more de- fined in his reactions. . . .

"Here. Drink." Matt had come over to his other elbow, and be- tween them he and Penny helped Ringan up. Ringan took the bottle, tilted it back, and drained it.

"Wow. Better." He regarded the empty bottle for a moment, and set it down. "Um—what's everyone doing here? Everyone who isn't a musician, that is? It *is* still Saturday, right?"

"Yes, it's still Saturday." Penny sat beside him. She'd got hold of his hand, and Ringan suddenly understood that she was unwilling to not be touching him just at this particular moment. Her voice seemed a bit steadier. "You've been out for close to ninety minutes. I'm here because Liam rang me up on Jane's phone, saying that you'd gone down, just out, that you were unresponsive, they couldn't wake you." The even tone suddenly disintegrated entirely. "I thought you were dying. When I got here, you weren't breathing—then you started breathing, but it was wrong, all wrong, you were trying to inhale, but you couldn't. You looked like you were fighting your own lungs. I have never been so frightened in my bloody life. This can't keep happening. Ringan, what actually did happen? Can you remember?"

"Oh, yes. All of it." He looked around the room, at the instruments, the sound booth, the recording console, all the paraphernalia of the modern world. Something moved in the pit of his stomach, reacting to the incongruity; the picture of the vast stone palace, with its endless corridors and its whispering and its intrigue, was as clear in his mind's eye as the room he sat in. The first touch of understanding settled on him, and with it, the first touch of panic.

"It's okay." Penny had sensed it, or seen it in his eye; everyone else was completely silent. "Right here, love. Can you talk about it? Because if you can, if there's anything we can add to what we've got, I want to hear it. It's a weapon. I want every weapon we can get our hands on."

"It was morning." Ringan spoke immediately; there was no need to consider, to think, to try and bring it up. This wasn't only Pietro Bendone's memory, it was his own; the memories were more and more his own each time it happened. His hands and voice both wanted to shake. "I—he'd spent the night with Catriona. It was first light, and he was getting dressed and getting out of there, before they were caught. She said something about how she was about to be married off. He left her there—told her he'd come back later."

Richard had found a folding chair, and was straddling it. "Where was this, Ringan? I mean—the setting? Location?"

"Across the river, in the big stone palace. Pleasaunce? Placentia? Whatever it was called." The memory was right there, catching at the back of his throat, tickling at his sinuses. "I—we—the river smell was really strong. Anyway, he slipped out. The place is—was lousy with hallways, long stone things, tapestries for warmth, but it never seems—seemed to get warm. Major winter chill, in every room. There was a spot where a few corridors crossed—and I, we, knew that down one of them was the King's chambers. Nothing else, just the King. And Margaret was there, looking like she'd spent the night on the tiles."

"Margaret was there?" Maddy spoke up for the first time. "Ringan, are you saying she was coming from the King's rooms?"

Ringan nodded. There was a long silence. Jane broke it.

"Dear God." She shook her head. There was disgust in her voice and on her face. "You know, no offence meant to anyone, but Henry Tudor was a dirty old man. How old was that girl? Sixteen? And he was—what, fifty?"

"Not to mention, his god-daughter's twin. Ringan, are you sure?" Maddy asked. "I mean, is there any doubt in your mind that Margaret MacLaine had slept with the King? How sure are you? Because this is important."

The members of Ringan's band all looked bewildered. Penny, still holding Ringan's hand, suddenly sucked in her breath, and tightened her grip; she had just caught up to Maddy.

"Oh, dear God." Richard had also understood. "Ringan, listen. We found Alison MacLaine's journals, Maddy and I—they're at the Bodleian, at Oxford. Margaret and Pietro were arrested together—not hand in hand together, but as part of the same treason charge, conspiracy against the King. And she was pregnant, visibly pregnant, when they arrested her." He sounded very grim. "Bendone, the King—how many others, I wonder? I wouldn't have thought she'd have got away with being promiscuous, not under those circumstances, but now I'm not so sure. This was not your typical sixteen-year-old of the period, apparently."

"What, she was shagging the king?" The question was startled out of Matt Curran. "And then he arrested her?"

"When?" Ringan had straightened up. His heart was thumping, and for a moment he felt the disturbance under his ribcage and paused to listen to it. *No,* he thought, *there's nothing wrong with it— the rhythm's fine, regular, just as it should be. This is my heart. It's healthy. I'm not Pietro Bendone.* "When was the arrest?"

"Late April." Maddy was calculating rapidly in her mind. "If she was showing, it had to have been at least four months, yes? That would put it middle-to-late December."

"If she'd had it off with the King, as well . . ." Penny stopped, appalled at her own thoughts. She felt Ringan's hand against her own, a reassuringly solid pressure.

"She'd done her bait-and-switch with Bendone at that point," Ringan said slowly. He was remembering Bendone's loathing, his disgust at his own gullibility, at the girl he'd called a whore. "Tricked him into spending the night with her—she pretended to be Catriona. I don't know exactly when. But the King . . ."

His voice trailed off, and he sighed. He was suddenly tired, with a bone-deep exhaustion he could neither explain nor hide. "Bloody pervert. Hard to believe he'd stoop that low, though, even him. Girl was hardly more than a kid. He was about to be married. What was he thinking? What did I say—why are you staring at me like that?"

Maddy had made a noise in her throat. Her eyes were wide. "Wait a minute. What you just said, the question you just asked, about what he was thinking—"

She jerked her head to face Richard Halligan. The two researchers might have been alone in the room. "Even money on its being the same thing he never stopped thinking: that he wanted a male heir. A legitimate son. And he was still free, still single. And that girl was pregnant."

———

"Penny for them?"

Penny, watching the road with perhaps less attention than she usually brought to bear, turned her head briefly, and then brought her eyes back to the always-tricky job of navigating the London traffic. She said nothing.

Ringan was becoming aware of a very unwelcome sensation, one made more unpleasant by his complete unfamiliarity with it. He was feeling guilty, as if he'd done something that would give her a reason to be upset with him or, even worse, unhappy. The feeling was beyond logic, or sense, but it was there, and the problem was, he had no clue how to cope with it.

"Penny?" Her silence was unnerving; it fed into his discomfort. "Look, I'm sorry—"

"For what?" Her eyes were straight ahead. He had a splendid view of her left profile, the one she always said she preferred to show an audience. That view, while very nice to look at, was as un-revealing as her voice.

He opened his mouth, and shut it again, frustrated. She was watching the road, which offered a splendid excuse if she happened to not want to make eye contact with him. He was aware of a tiny spurt of temper. Damn it, he was trying to apologise, and she seemed to be going out of her way to make him sweat over it, and really, it wasn't even his fault. He hadn't asked to be sucked into the body of a Milanese shawm player who couldn't keep his trousers zipped or his pantaloons knotted or whatever the hell blokes wore and did, back in old Henry's day. . . .

"I said, 'Apologise for what?' Ringan?"

The sudden worry in her voice left him feeling obscurely ashamed of himself. "Yes, still Ringan, no worries. Penny, I'm sorry about being in that boy while he was having it off with Catriona. That's all. I didn't want to be there, and I felt like a voyeur, but . . ." He stopped.

"But . . . ?" She turned the Jag off Priory Road and up Muswell Hill. "We should stop at the shops and get dinner—something tells me we're not going to want to go out again once we're indoors. But what, Ringan? Come on, whatever it is, get it off your chest."

"It was—damn." He swallowed. "This sounds worse than it is, but the fact is, even though I couldn't help it—"

"Ringan, for heaven's sake!" They'd crested the hill, and Penny had spotted a parking space. She nudged the car to the curb, checking her mirrors. He thought she sounded blessedly normal, if a bit exasperated. "Are you seriously apologising to me for being stuck in that poor boy while he happened to be making love to Juliet?"

"Juliet?" He blinked at her. "Who in hell is Juliet? Her name was Catriona."

"Yes, dear, I'm aware of that. I just think it ought to have been Juliet—they were all about doomed love, from the sound of it." She killed the Jag's engine and sat for a moment. She looked regretful, suddenly. "Poor brats. But seriously, if that's what you're apologising for, you're being absurd. Don't worry about that— there's no need. I don't feel cheated on. I'm worried about the entire package, not that bit of it. Any idea what you want for supper? Maybe a couple of chops and a veg?"

He was silent, following her into the market. *Juliet,* he thought, *Juliet.* Penny was right; they couldn't have known they were doomed, of course, but he and Penny knew at least some of what those two didn't know, and it was pure Shakespearean tragedy. And hadn't Romeo Montague been Italian?

"Ringan?"

He stopped, suddenly dizzy. Theatre was Penny's thing, not his, but no one spent more than a week at school in the modern world without picking up a bit of Shakespeare. That particular play hadn't done much for him, personally; he doubted it was high up on most schoolboys' lists, especially since Romeo had been such an ineffectual git.

Yet, somehow, bits of it that must have been lodged at the back of his memory all these years were popping up. What was it Romeo had said to his love, his wife, his death, his secret, that first morning when he knew he had to go, and she'd been half-asleep begging him to stay? *Night's candles are burnt out, and jocund day Stands tip-toe on the misty mountain tops. . . .*

"Ringan . . . ?"

*Non posso, cara. I must be away.*

"Jesus." He reached a hand out, groping, trying to find something to steady himself against. The market was liquid, it was an ocean, a tide, washing up and ebbing just out of reach; there were tins of beans and peas and loaves of bread, and they were stacked, not on sensible mass-produced shelves, but against high stone walls, walls behind which were chambers where young lovers stole a night together, and where ageing, desperate kings tried to plant their seed in fertile young ground.

"Oh, hell!" Penny's voice was quiet and edged with desperation. "Ringan, hang on to me, we're heading out."

What had the girl called him? *Marito,* wasn't it? And Ringan, with no Italian, had known it meant husband. . . .

" 'Night's candles,' " he said, and felt a huge disturbance under his ribcage, his heart too loud in his own ears.

"Right, that's it. Sod the lamb chops—we'll send out. We're off." Penny's voice was a lifeline, firm and calm. He felt her get an arm around him and lead him back out into the warmth of the afternoon, and back to the car.

He sat there a while, drenched and shivering, keeping his hands on the leather seat, holding himself steady. After a few minutes, the shivering had stopped, and so had the mad thump of his heartbeat. He turned to stare at her.

"Bloody hell." Cars went by, people wearing jeans and listening to music on portable electronic devices. "I'll tell you what, lamb, this is getting old. It can stop, any time now."

"You were quoting Shakespeare." She was watching his face, her own deeply troubled. "Act III, I think; I haven't read it in forever. Their conversation, the morning after the secret marriage; he spends the night with her. I wouldn't have thought that particular bit of Shakespeare would be your cup of tea. Do you know the speech?"

He shook his head. She folded her hands in her lap and quoted, her voice beautiful, redolent of pain and an assumed youth, a trained actor perfectly interpreting what she felt the words to mean. " 'Wilt thou be gone? It is not yet near day. It was the nightingale, and not the lark, That pierc'd the fearful hollow of thine ear; Nightly she sings on yon pomegranate tree—Believe me love, it was the nightingale.' "

He was quiet. The sense of Pietro Bendone was tangible; something in him yearned towards the musician, knowing him, understanding him. He looked at Penny, feeling a sting behind his eyes.

"Right. And he tells her it's a lark, the morning bird, it's morning, and he has to get the hell out before they find him there. And Penny—that's exactly what happened. She begged him to stay, but she didn't go on about birds. She just told him she might not ever have the chance again, because they were marrying her off to someone else."

"This thing you have, with Bendone." She was chewing her lower lip, trying to phrase it carefully, choosing her words. "It seems fairly obvious that there's a link."

"You think he was my ancestor? That makes two of us."

"Oh, good. I was afraid you'd hate the idea." Her relief was tangible. Had he fought the suggestion, she thought, it would have made the follow-on very hard to broach. She took a long breath. "Ringan—"

"Yes, Penny, I know. Margaret is the missing link, isn't she? Well, not the Missing Link, but the mother of Bendone's child." It had to be that, he thought; even Henry wouldn't have put a pregnant woman to death. And that would explain why the family records his own mother had rattled off at him hadn't included Margaret's name. Arrested for murder and treason, unmarried, pregnant, nothing but a source of grief and shame . . .

"We've got to find out what happened."

Ringan, his own thoughts wandering down the possibilities of what had happened to Margaret MacLaine and her bastard, brought his attention back to Penny, fast. There was something going on at the back of her voice, something hard and sharp and compelling. He blinked at her, and realised she'd got her cell phone out and was punching in a number.

"Maddy? Yes, it's me. I wanted to ask you something today, you and Richard both, but, well, yes—anyway. Interrupted, distracted, right. Look, I want to know, were you able to read everything of Alison MacLaine's? Because we still need to know a few things, and we've reached a few conclusions on our own, and—what?"

Outside, the light had begun to fade, the subtle shift in the patterns left by all those hurrying pedestrians going about their business, heading home towards their own supper, cars sliding past with their radios going, everything casting a shadow, but the clarity of those shadows growing softer and less distinct as the light changed around them. Ringan was aware of none of it. He was entirely concentrated on Penny, and he would have been surprised had he known he was holding his breath.

"Right. Okay. That's a good idea—I'll ring Richard up and ask if he wants to come round later tonight. Can you come by, or will your husband get stroppy about us dragging you away from him again? Not that I'd blame him—you're always pulling us out of trouble. Oh, Gary's in Liverpool on business? Perfect. Bless you, Maddy. We'll see you around nine."

She disconnected, scrolled back through her dialled numbers, and found what she wanted. Ringan forced himself to sit still and breathe evenly. There was a familiar tingle running along his nerves, a kind of electric jolt he remembered from earlier encounters, from knowing that they were close, that maybe something was about to break their way.

"Richard? Listen, we're having a confab—Maddy's coming over tonight, to finish telling us about Alison MacLaine. Can you come round, with your bit of gen? Yes, nineish. Ta."

"Right. We're on. Nine tonight." She put the phone back in her purse, and started the car. "They've got more. They're coming round. We should send out for something, or scramble some eggs and maybe heat up a tin of soup, or something. I've gone ravenous suddenly."

She got the car into traffic and headed for her own quiet side street, off the main road. "Ringan?"

"What?" He had his eyes closed. *Soon,* he thought, *soon.* They would find out what in hell happened and find out how in hell to get him free of it, and then maybe he'd be able to stop this fading out, this moving back and forth, this sense of getting stuck in someone who was going to fetch up on the rack, his bones and joints stretched beyond endurance, his life ending there with his beautiful Catriona already gone. . . .

"How do you suppose Margaret managed to dupe her sister into crossing the Thames to the Isle of Dogs? What do you suppose she told her? And why?"

"I don't know, lamb." They'd turned down Penny's street; she was searching for a place to park. "Just one more thing we're going to want to find out."

# Eleven

*The second string, as that they tried:*
*"In terror sits the dark-haired bride."*
*The third string sang beneath his bow,*
*"And surely, now, her tears will flow."*

"They didn't believe it. The women in the family, I mean—Elspeth and Alison. They didn't believe Catriona had run off."

Richard Halligan was sounding tired. Penny, who had offered beer and cider and been asked for strong tea instead, felt a moment of remorse; he was not a young man, not by any stretch, and he'd been slogging through Alison's journals on their behalf for days. If the situation had been less critical, and had it been for anyone but Ringan, she thought, she'd have felt a lot guiltier than she did; after all, they'd put Albert Wychsale through just this much trouble, and put him in danger as well, and he was much the same age as Richard. Yet not only had neither Ringan nor Penny felt guilty, they'd offered Albert the chance to participate as if they'd been offering him a lovely surprise. And he'd not only taken them up on it, he'd flatly refused to be left out.

She was aware of a sudden wish to ring Albert up, and tell him all about it. At the same time, she was devoutly glad that he was safely away from this mess. Involving him in four hauntings, one after another, was really a bit much. . . .

As if he'd guessed what she'd been thinking, Richard caught her eye and gave her a reassuring smile. She forced herself to focus and concentrate. Her thoughts wanted to wander, and that wouldn't do, not tonight.

"Are you sure?" she asked. He looked exhausted, she thought. He looked every minute of his sixty plus years, and more. This situation was draining everyone who came near it.

"Oh, yes, quite certain. Here:

*Greenwich, Palace of Placentia, 1 February, 1540—Today I keep myself fast, to my own apartments. This place has become all that is hateful to me, those echoes and speculations, those whispers in every corner of this great Palace. For those who would so much as hint, by raising of eyebrow, that my niece hath set all the court into uproar by fleeing her marriage bed know naught of this child. There is no place for such thought, nor does knowledge of Catriona permit such an idea to fester in darkness or in malice. To this, I with my sister can do naught but agree: Catriona would not bring such grave shame upon her family or her name.*

*We have both of us by God's mercy been given the King's own ear, beseeching him that he might not listen to those who would poison his godchild's virtue and fair name by such insinuations. The King, in his wisdom and trusting Catriona's own blood to know more of her than any others, hath sent men out, to search the marshes and the stream beds.*

"So they guessed right away that something bad must have happened to her." Ringan was working it through in his mind. "Or maybe it was just intuition, refusal to believe it? Either way, they were right; she hadn't run off."

"No," Maddy agreed. Where Richard looked tired and played out, she looked somehow thinner, as if the tension behind what she wanted to discover was eating away at the edges. "She hadn't. But that doesn't make them right about the rest of it, Ringan, does it? Because she was having a hot-and-heavy affair with Bendone, and she and her sister apparently both had a thing for him. I'm not saying they were both in love with him—I don't know that Margaret's feelings were that uncomplicated. Everything you've told us about Margaret makes me think she hated Bendone as much as she wanted him. Who knows? Maybe she had some outraged ego going as well, resenting his loving her sister instead of her."

"There's no maybe about it, Maddy. She resented it, all right." Ringan thought back, closing his eyes, bringing up a dance, the King leading the women out singly, Catriona gazing with naked adoration in her eyes at the musicians in the gallery, the vicious sniping of her twin's reaction. "More than resentment. I'd have called it hate, myself."

"Good to know. But my point is, that stuff Alison wrote about Catriona being a good girl? All wrong. She was shacked up with Bendone, and desperate to get out of that marriage to Henry's pal Lord Kesleigh. Elspeth and Alison didn't know those girls half as well as they thought they did."

"That's how it usually is in families." Richard turned a page in his notebook. "They found Catriona six days later, washed up a little way east of where we know she was drowned." His voice changed subtly. "I'll read it—but be warned, I don't think this is easy listening."

*Greenwich, Palace of Placentia, 6 February 1540—Today is grief, and naught but darkness. My sister's child is found, her drowned body brought hither by a miller and his son, against whose mill dam her river-soaked gown did catch. Upon her ruined and bloated face I could not make my eyes to look, and to see her hair in such state, its bright fires filthy with Thames weed, was more than I might bear. Clear upon her throat are marks of violence, and murder done.*

*As for my sister, Elspeth is in care of the Lady Anne's own women, for she hath fallen insensible; she had but heard the word come in that Catriona was found before she came in great haste to the King's presence. She was too quick for me, and therefore saw what will colour her sleep most horridly for all her days yet to come.*

*In deep grief, too, is the King, for to have lost his god-daughter on the eve of her wedding has sore distressed his heart and temper, and his eyes filled with tears of woe. He has within our hearing commanded that any who might any light throw upon how my niece came to the river's edge come forth. He spoke in most ominous manner, promising reward for honesty and grave punishment for untruths or secrets withheld.*

"Wow." The scene had suddenly been too graphic, too vivid, in Ringan's mind; he remembered a dream, alone in Penny's bed, a dream in which he was observer and ghost, in which he saw Catriona die at her sister's hand, in which he listened to the girl plead for her life, listened to—

"Ringan!"

He jerked his head, startled; Penny's eyes had gone wide, and her voice was urgent. "What? What's wrong?"

"That dream, the one we both had at the same time, when you were here and I was in Italy. Ringan, Catriona was promising—she was begging Margaret to let her live, and she swore, she said she'd *give him up.* That was what she said, wasn't it?"

*No Margaret please please I'll stand away I'll give him up he'll be as nothing to me no sister please oh please. . . .*

"That's what she said, yes. She said, *I'll stand away—he'll be as nothing to me.*" The choked words, the rattle of lungs full of water, had come back to him with dreadful clarity. "She was half-dead by then. And we know now, she was talking about Bendone. And Margaret was pregnant with Bendone's child."

Richard and Maddy exchanged a glance. "Are you sure of that?"

"Of course I am." Ringan met Maddy's eye. "Do the math—it's a simple-enough sum, really. I've got this bizarre link with Bendone. We know one of those women was an ancestress of mine. Well, it couldn't have been Catriona—she was murdered. Margaret, on the other hand, was visibly pregnant. Link to Margaret, link to Bendone—I'd say that one solves itself. Were you thinking I might be the illegitimate spawn of Henry Tudor, eighteen generations or whatever removed? Sorry to disappoint you, but if that's the case, then nothing that's been happening makes any sense at all."

"It had occurred to me. But you're right—the sum of the other story just doesn't come out right." Maddy grinned suddenly. "And honestly, in your boots, I'd take Bendone. Henry? Not one of my favourite kings."

"Nor mine." Penny got up and stretched. She'd been sitting too long in one place; it was amazing, she thought, to not realise that half your joints had locked up and gone to sleep until you actually got off your bottom and tried to move. "Ouch. I still want to know how Margaret lured her sister over the river. It must have been something hugely important to Catriona. Hell, she was due to get married the next day, to a dirty old man who was a chum of the even-dirtier old man her nasty sister was apparently shagging. Catriona was desperate not to marry the bloke. How in hell did she get suckered into getting into a boat and risking a Thames crossing? What possible inducement could Margaret have waved under her nose to get her to agree to that? Why would she have trusted Margaret as far as she could throw her? From everything Ringan's told us about the sisters, they couldn't stand each other. So I can't figure it out, and I have the feeling it may be the key to what's happening to Ringan."

There was a moment of quiet. Richard sighed—a long, tired inhale of breath.

"I don't want to sound like the Voice of Doom." His voice held an undercurrent of regret. "But the truth is, if that knowledge is critical to putting a stop to what's been happening to Ringan, we may be out of luck. Suppose Margaret was put to torture, as well as Bendone. Suppose she broke and confessed and told them the truth. The only record we have is Alison MacLaine. Does anyone honestly think the spinster aunt and lady-in-waiting would have been told the details her niece had spilled under the persuasion of thumbscrews or the rack?"

"Damn." Penny sat back down. "Damn, damn, damn. No, you're right. Alison and Elspeth were just about the last people on earth who'd be told any details. So Alison wouldn't know, and now what the hell are we supposed to do?"

"Our jobs, that's what." Maddy set her teacup down. "I go back to the library, and I use every inch of our database, every word, every link. If I don't find it there, I try hard paper. Richard? Any ideas?"

"Just one," he told her. There was the hint of a smile lifting one corner of his mouth. "And that would be, don't be so hasty. Just because Alison didn't write down details she didn't know, that doesn't mean I'm done with her information. There's more here." He lifted his notebook, pinching off a small stack of pages. "Every entry I copied has something I thought might be relevant. For instance, I know I've read you her entry about the arrest for treason, and her shock at Margaret's pregnancy, but there's one a few days later that ought to interest everyone. Listen."

He cleared his throat.

*Greenwich, Palace of Placentia, 25 April 1540—In all the darkness of that place where dwell souls abhorred by God, there can be no greater horror than this. My niece Margaret, already kept fast at the King's pleasure at that grim fortress upriver, is today accused of murder, the charge being that she drowned her poor sister. I shall speak no more of this, lest I say too much.*

Richard looked up. "You'll notice it's three days after the arrest. Presumably, they'd racked Bendone by then. He must have said something that incriminated Margaret, told them something under torture, before he died."

"Three days." Ringan was up and moving restlessly, picking up small things, setting them back down. "That's bizarre—the time differential, I mean. Just look at the time line: Catriona went missing New Year's Eve. They found her about a week later. There were bruises around her throat—remember that bit Alison wrote about there being marks of violence? Henry's furious and grief-stricken and vows to find out the truth. And then? Three-and-

a-half months of sod-all, followed by those two arrests, a fast torture, and the additional charge laid against Margaret. Why so long
a gap before all that flurry? What happened?"

"God only knows." Maddy sounded cranky and frustrated.
"What I want to know is why Bendone was arrested at all, much
less on treason charges. Maybe someone had seen him coming
from Catriona's rooms, and took a while deciding to play copper's
nark? Whatever it was, we're going to have to speculate and then
go from there, and we'll have to hope like mad that we're on the
right track. Because we don't really have the time to research it, do
we? Not with—with what's been happening."

Chilled, remembering, the others looked at her. She twitched
her shoulders. "Sorry. But I want to know. And we *need* to know.
By the way, did anyone else notice that 'grim fortress upriver' thing
Alison mentioned? Only building she could have been talking
about is the Tower."

"But—" Penny's jaw had slackened. "Maddy, that can't be right,
can it?"

"It's the only grim fortress upriver in existence at that point.
Maddy's right." Richard's hands lay lightly across his notebook.
"So, Henry had Margaret locked up at the Tower of London?
Good grief, murderess or not, she was sixteen, and she was pregnant, and for all he knew, it was his child. The man meant serious
business. And that tells me we're missing something here. Ringan,
why are you staring at me that way?"

"Back up a bit." *Disappearance,* he thought, *a week to find the body,
nearly four months . . .* "What you said about its possibly being
Henry's child. It wasn't—but he didn't know that. We're ignoring
the obvious: What took four months to become obvious? Margaret's pregnancy. And once it became noticeable, if the King
thought it was his . . ."

His voice trailed away. Penny, who'd been listening, spoke up.

"She'd have wanted him to think it was his. What's more, she'd
have wanted to make damned sure he had not even a whiff of a
reason to think it could be anyone else's; they didn't treat harlots

kindly back then. But she didn't give a damn about Henry, did she? We know she was obsessed with Bendone. That's why she killed Catriona. So if we jump past all the stuff we don't know yet—the timing of the murder, how she got Catriona across the river, why that spot—what have we got?"

"Someone spilling the beans." Ringan's beard was at full jut. "Someone telling the King, or someone who had the King's ear, that Margaret had been to bed with a handsome shawm player from Milan. Someone giving Henry a reason to have one of his patented meltdowns, and arrest them both."

"I think Ringan's right." Maddy looked at Richard, and saw the agreement on his face. "The timing, the long lull when nothing happened, the King already looking to annul a marriage he couldn't bring himself to consummate, sleeping with Margaret, and then wham, she and the cutie from Milan are both grabbed. It's the only thing that adds up."

"But who?" There was something they weren't seeing, Penny thought, something they were missing, something that mattered. "Who would have? Alison was shocked half out of her skin. Elspeth was a weeping wreck. Bendone wouldn't have, nor would Margaret; that would have been suicide, and they'd have both known it. So who . . . ?"


Wind, cool and dark, a soothing, beautiful wind. Wind sent by God, slipping through the slits high up in the stone walls that marked the boundaries of this place of horror and pain, wind sent to brush gently against all hurts.

Ringan felt the wind before he felt anything else. A few moments later, when the rest of his borrowed senses kicked in, he found himself hoping that the wind would be what would inform his dreams in the future. It was a spring breeze, light, aromatic with the first of the seasonal foliage. He kept his eyes closed, focusing on the scent; something told him that doing anything else would be a poor idea indeed.

The voices came next, a low muttering, an exchange between two men. The words were incomprehensible to Ringan. And who were they, anyway? Last he'd looked, he'd been curled up beside Penny in her comfortable bed in Muswell Hill. But these were men talking, strangers, and he couldn't move his arms or legs, or ask them what they wanted, why they were here, why he was—

"He speaks no words I understand. I have no Italian." One voice, chilly and detached. Something moved in Ringan—it was familiar, that voice, known to him. He'd heard it before. "How are we to discern a truth for the King, much less a name?"

The answering laugh lifted the flesh on Ringan's bones. It was cold, merciless, redolent of something dark. Here was a sadist, given an outlet for his delights. . . .

"Small reason to worry, whether the poor fool speaks or no, Sir Leonard. The girl may deny all—betwixt them, they go to make a fool of the King. His Majesty will weep o'er his Scots whore to-morrow, and forget them both by the next new moon. We know what the King most desires to hear. It is but our duty to get it."

There were tiny shafts of light in Ringan's interior darkness now, but they were not the light of vision. Something was happening, an awareness, an understanding that he, himself, was being seen, regarded. . . .

*I can see you. My eyes can see you, and my heart. Who are you?*

The words came to him in no language, or perhaps in every language. In the strictest sense, they weren't language at all; they were a series of a thousand pictures, a million, beyond counting, pictures of recognition, puzzlement, and feeling. They came from the mind, or perhaps the spirit, of Pietro Bendone, travelling through something Ringan had no name for, implanting themselves whole and complete as thought and feeling in Ringan's own mind.

The pictures were jagged, fluttering, moving. It took a moment for Ringan, caught like an oyster in someone else's net, to register the picture that meant pain, and the pain was there because one of the two men, either the smooth-voiced man called Skeffinton or his companion, had turned something, a heavy wooden lever, making ropes creak somewhere, sending something down the length of Bendone's body, down Ringan's own spine, something that was hot and cold: pain.

Bendone screamed. It was a horrifying sound, a full-bodied howl of physical torment. Ringan heard him, felt him, and a fraction of a second later the pain hit Ringan as well.

It was monstrous, unbearable. With a kind of disbelief—*not happening not happening not*—he felt both his shoulders separate slightly from their nest of socket and muscle, nerve endings disintegrating and screaming.

There was a soft creak, unspeakably ominous. A moment later, the pain—excruciating, agonising, intolerable—registered as raw fire, from ankle to knee. He felt the ankle joint separate; had he had his own body to hand, his gorge would have risen.

Someone had cranked a rope. The rope was attached to something that was attached to Pietro Bendone.

*The rack,* Ringan thought, and he was sick inside. They were destroying that boy, stretching him, pulling joints free, mutilating him. It was impossible, unacceptable. His fear—and it was enormous, all-consuming—suddenly transmuted into something akin to outrage. What was happening to this boy, who had done nothing but fall in love, should never have happened to anyone.

And Bendone was a musician. To do that to a musician's body, to make it impossible for him to play—no. No, it had to stop.

*What do you do here, are you angel or devil, were you sent here by God?*

The voice, the images in his head, brought Ringan up short. With an act that was pure will, he turned his attention away from the screaming hell in his shoulders and ankles, and managed to concentrate. Think; all he had to do was think, to send a thought, in this shared space. Send the boy something to comfort him, something to ease him on his way. And find out, find out . . .

*I'm the blood of your blood.* He had no idea where the phrase, the image, had come from. It came to him, whole and complete, with the knowledge that Bendone would understand it. *I'm the seed of your seed. I'm a child of the child you made.*

"What said he?" It was the colder voice, that of the man who had been called Sir Leonard. Why was that voice so familiar? Ringan wondered, and suddenly thought that he had his own interior vision blocked from seeing what Bendone could see. He tried to open himself up, to see what Bendone saw. Something, perhaps his own sense of self-preservation, kept him in this wind-shot darkness. "His tongue is nothing I understand."

"I could not say, but only that he mutters like a man possessed of a poor conscience, belike." The second voice held an undertone of amusement. "Best to break him."

*I have no child. How can you be of my seed?*

A turn of the lever, a small, hard ratchet.

Bendone blacked out. It was short-lived, that relief, and Ringan, writhing and bereft of any semblance of breath, suddenly understood what day this must be, Bendone's last day, and knew his own danger. *Penny,* he thought, *real life, the real world, no bloody way.* He was going to get out of here.

*Listen to me.* He could feel his own urgency slicing through Bendone's pain-shattered awareness. *You made a child, with Margaret. She was arrested—she killed her sister, your Catriona. Margaret was put to death for it, but the child survived her somehow. Show me. How did she come to be arrested?*

Something was intruding on that hard clear line running between them. It was a rhythm, a beat, irregular, dancing, first sharp and then stuttering. Bendone's breathing was torn, ragged.

His heartbeat. *Oh, Christ,* Ringan thought clearly, *he died under torture. Bad heart, probably a prolapsed valve, or something. That's what I'm hearing. He could go any second.* If they tightened the pull of the rack again . . .

*Talk to me. Why were you arrested? Why was she? Tell me quickly, Grandfather. I must know, or we both die here, and your line is snuffed out like a candle. Hurry. How did it come about?*

Something, perhaps his own driving urgency, seemed to be getting through. Four-and-a-half centuries behind Ringan, Pietro Bendone understood, and responded.

*She killed my darling, my beloved. Catriona was to be married to an old lord, the King's friend, and we could not bear that. We were to go together to my father in Italy. He would see her, my Catriona, and understand. But her sister drowned her. I could prove nothing. She wanted me, witch and whore, and I would have none of her. I waited, and she showed with child, the child I planted. She would have told the King the child was his; he would divorce the Lady Anne for a healthy son. Better to die than to allow her that. She took my reason for life from me; I take her life from her. I want to tell them, these men—why can they not understand me? I have said it, two times, three times, and still they hurt me, and understand nothing. Why?*

Ringan, suspended in nothing and nowhere, heard and understood. He could have wept at the pointlessness of it all. Margaret, pregnant from her night of trickery in the arms of her sister's lover, had killed her sister and tried to convince the King of his own paternity. And Bendone, with the one thing he desired taken from him, had turned her in to the King, and signed his own death warrant. It was insane; it was ridiculous.

*They speak no Italian,* he thought, and felt a sudden despair in Bendone. *And you have not enough English to tell them what you want them to know.*

"That this boy is a traitor is known to the King." It was the man called Sir Leonard. "Yet he must confess it."

"Margaret." The word was out, fully formed, a dark flower of a thought, knowledge, before Ringan had time to think. It was Bendone's voice, broken, torn, a fragment of itself, but it was Ringan who spoke, condemning the woman who would bear the child that connected them. This was no thought, no line of dancing pictures; this was a voice, Bendone's voice, Ringan's voice. "Margaret MacLaine. My child. She meant to trick the King, to make a fool of the King. And she murdered her sister. She murdered her sister, for love of me."

There was silence, stretching out. The wind was stronger now, lifting the hair off Ringan's brow, or was it Bendone's brow? he couldn't tell, it didn't matter. Words came suddenly into Ringan's mind, a frantic girl's voice, tactile in its clarity: *Help me someone help me Go-damercy the dogs no don't leave me please you cannae be so cruel please give him back to me give him back I must have him please oh please sir . . .*

He knew what had happened, now. He knew, too, where he had heard that cold detached voice before, and who Sir Leonard must be. There was no time left; Bendone's heartbeat was soaring, slamming with its own mad illness, his breath catching, his light beginning to fade. There was no time left, Ringan thought, no time at all. He was going to die here, wherever here actually was.

He spared a moment to aim a warm, loving thought out towards Penny, who he hoped was comfortably asleep in her London bed, something that might slip through the cracks at night and be there in her dreams to remind her—

Bendone's heart paused, glitched, and stopped. As his eyes glazed, Ringan thought he felt something, a push, a hand, more than one hand, there was something pushing at him and something pulling at him, as well. There were voices, too, voices he knew, a confusion of tone and tears and the wind that had transmuted into a different texture, a different scent. Above all else, there was a voice, Bendone's voice, saying one word only.

*Vivere.*

Wind, a light breeze, carrying with it the mild chill of night air. Voices, male and female. They were known; so was the language they spoke.

"He's breathing again." A male voice, clipped, concern in the undertone.

"Good steady pulse." Someone was touching him—there were small warm fingers against his wrist, a light pressure, incredibly welcome. "It stopped there for a few seconds. I think we've got him back. Dear heavens, that was a near thing."

"Are you sure?" The voice he knew best, under as hard a control as anything she'd ever put across on-stage. "His heart stopped. I can't believe—"

Ringan opened his eyes.

The first thing he saw was the night sky, shot with distant lights from buildings in the West End, from something that might have been the busy blinking pyramid atop the Canada Tower. As he focused, understanding and allowing himself to believe that he was, in fact, in the here and now, a jet split the clouds and moved towards a landing at Heathrow.

"Ringan—"

But the sky was broken, only visible in patches, scored and segmented with struts and beams and uprights. He was indoors, at least partly; he turned his head, feeling a sudden phantom spasm of agony in his shoulders. Stretched out on his back, with his head slightly raised, he stiffened against the remembered pain, drew in air that tasted like the Thames, and then the pain was gone, as insubstantial as the wake of the airport-bound jet, leaving nothing of itself behind.

Tamsin sat beside him on the right. It was her fingers against his wrist, keeping a weather eye on his pulse. Since moving his head was apparently an option, he decided to risk another jolt to his shoulders, and moved his head slightly the other way. Stephen was watching him; his face was as impassive as ever, but Ringan thought he heard a tiny exhale of relief.

"Jesus," Stephen said simply. "You scared us."

"Sorry." Soft, capable hands rested on his upper arms, and his head seemed to be raised because it was cradled in a lap. The lap seemed to be wearing terrycloth.

He tilted his head backward, and found himself smiling up into Penny's face.

"Oi," she said. There wasn't enough light to be certain, but her face looked streaky. "Are you all right?"

"I am now." Beams, supports, partial sky—he had it now. They were inside Tamsin's burgeoning E-shaped manor, on the Isle of Dogs. He had no memory of how he might have come to be here. Speech, true speech, seemed a bit beyond him yet. "What . . . ?"

"You got out of bed and walked out the front door." She seemed to know what he wanted to hear. "Barefoot, pyjamas, just like last time. I was awake—I got a robe on, and slippers, and ran after you. You weren't waking, and you were mumbling, eyes wide open. You took your car keys off the table and walked out and got into your car. This time, I had enough brains to take my cell phone along. I got in on the passenger side—I was going to grab the wheel if I had to. You drove straight here." She swallowed hard. "You had no idea I was there. I don't think you even blinked the entire way here."

He said nothing. She bent suddenly and kissed him, full on the mouth. It was an unusual move from Penny; she was rarely physically demonstrative in the presence of others.

"Anyway—you parked the car. It was bizarre; your body seemed to be right here and now, knowing what it had to be doing, but the rest of you was elsewhere. I followed you. I was scared to death you'd fall in the Thames, but you went straight indoors, where we are now. You were staring off across the river, where the hospital is. I watched you, and you said something, and then you screamed and you went down in a heap. Your shoulders were rigid—I couldn't move them."

Suddenly, shockingly, her voice fractured, and with it her façade of calm. "So I got under you, got your head supported, and I rang Tamsin and Stephen, and they came out, and your heart stopped. I have never been so damned scared in my entire life. What in hell happened, Ringan?"

"Bendone. They had him on the rack. He died—I felt him die. And he turfed me out. Wouldn't take me along with him." Her hands were warm, and real, and he was awake, with no pain anywhere. "Here, help me up. Why are you all staring at me as if I were a nutter?"

"What do you mean, he turfed you out?" Tamsin asked.

"Just what I said. By the way, I don't know what *vivere* means, but he said it to me when his heart stopped. He had a bad heart— I felt it. Thumping all over the place. These days, he'd have been on a transplant list somewhere. Does anyone know what *vivere* means?"

"It means, live, live on." Tamsin's fine hair, lifted by the breeze coming through the uprights, stood away from her head, giving her the look of a friendly witch. "He was telling you to survive."

"Was he? Nice bloke, really, my however-many-times-removed grandfather." Ringan bit his lip; he seemed to be compulsively babbling. "Anyway—it was Bendone who turned Margaret in. He knew the baby had a good chance of being his—and Margaret, who'd been spending nights with the King, was trying to convince Henry it was his. She knew Bendone was a lost cause, she wasn't getting him, and she knew, everyone knew, that Henry was looking to divorce Anne and get himself a healthy son."

"Are you saying she was making a run at the crown?" Penny was holding his hand. The night air was growing steadily cooler; it occurred to Ringan that it must be not far off from sunrise. "That she was seriously trying to convince the King of England to marry her?"

"That's what Bendone thought. That's what he felt. And believed. God, he hated her." He had a sudden moment of hearing the voice in his head, the twist of the ropes, the blinding scream of agony running down every muscle. For a moment, his voice deserted him.

"But that would have been suicide." Tamsin sounded bewildered. "Are you sure, Ringan? Henry would have had him arrested, tortured, executed. Bendone must have known that. And Margaret—good heavens, there's your treason charge. It would have allowed Henry to do whatever he chose to those two."

"It *was* suicide." Ringan slipped an arm around Penny's waist and leaned against her. "Once Margaret murdered Catriona, Bendone had no reason to live. All he wanted was revenge on Margaret, and he got it. He didn't give a damn about the cost. But the King had apparently demanded a full confession and Bendone, on the rack, couldn't give them one—he'd reverted to his own language. And neither of the torturers spoke Italian."

"Oh, lord." Penny bit her lip. "So he was willing to tell them anything they wanted, and they didn't understand?"

"That's it." He heard the two men in his head for a moment, the unknown torturer, the chilly detached voice of judgement. "There was someone called Sir Leonard, seemed to be in charge of the rack. We—he—it was at the Tower of London. And I'd heard the bloke's voice before. It was the same voice I'd heard, sentencing Margaret—what, Tamsin?"

"That would be Sir Leonard Skeffinton." She suddenly wrapped her arms around herself, and Ringan saw she was shivering. He had a fleeting, vagrant thought: *So much for that detachment of hers.* "Master of Ordinance at the Tower of London. The man was an absolute horror. He invented a few extremely nasty torture devices. Bendone and Margaret must really have got under Henry's skin, to rate the attentions of the top bloke."

"Horrible," Ringan said, remembering. "Can we get out of here, please? My feet are cold. Penny, love, I'm curious—what made you go screaming off to Stephen and Tamsin for help? Not that I'm sorry you did, mind you, but why? I mean, why not one of our pet historians, or maybe emergency services?"

"They're family." She blinked at him. "Who else would I ring for help but my family?"

Ringan pressed her hand, but said nothing. They walked towards the cars, skirting the bomb cavity. In a few months, Ringan thought, it would be covered in perennials. . . .

"Damn!" Stephen stopped. "I nearly forgot—I got a phone message from Marcus Childe earlier today, and I'd meant to pass it on in the morning, but of course, it's morning now. He's been digging in the council and parish records for the entire area. Turns out there was a chapel somewhere on the isle, consecrated to the Virgin, but not for the time period we're looking at. He said it was built around the seventh century and was in ruins, nothing but a few stones and part of a retaining wall or something, by the fifteenth century. He couldn't pinpoint an exact location for it—the river reclaimed a lot of land, and things shifted around, so precise records simply don't exist. But surely the girl couldn't have been mad enough to think a few scattered stones would provide sanctuary against the dogs?"

They had reached their cars. Around them, the sky was lightening, soft pale streaks of lilac and rose showing the promise of a beautiful day in London.

"I don't know." *Help me someone help me Godamercy the dogs no don't leave me please you cannae be so cruel please give him back to me give him back I must have him please oh please sir. . . .*

He shuddered, and swung his feet into the Alfa. The voice of judgement, the executioner who must have been Sir Leonard Skeffinton himself, was suddenly in his ears like an incipient nightmare. . . . *writ by the King's own hand, this sentence, carried out in the sight of God Almighty, and no more shall you see the world . . .* "I don't think she was sane, do you? She'd have been post-partum, hormones raging, the child taken away, her hands bound behind her—"

He stopped, hands closing hard on the wheel. Something was coming, a picture, a voice, a sense memory of something left over in the blood, something come down to him from Margaret. . . .

*Facing the palace. Facing the river. Skeffinton behind her, at her shoulder, her hands behind her in irons. Something cold and sharp, precise cuts, deep enough to bleed. A scent of her, a scent of her blood, something to give the dogs, Henry's pack of trained hunting hounds. She'd have heard them, weak with loss of her own blood dripping behind her, no way to save herself, the dogs baying, closer, no place to go, sanctuary . . .*

"Ringan?"

"God," he whispered. Bendone had been lucky; an hour or two of terror and a fast death from the heart that had been so truly broken, in so many ways. Margaret, who had killed her twin and tried to make a fool of Henry Tudor, had not been so fortunate. And he, himself, as much a child of her blood as he was of Pietro Bendone's, had given Skeffinton and his unknown assistant the information that had sent her to that death. . . .

"Maybe she drowned."

Ringan jerked his head up, and met Tamsin's eye; she was remembering a line of shared thought, the terrified prisoner begging for shelter. "It's what I'd have chosen, in her place—just jump into the river. Justice for Catriona, rough justice, but still preferable to being torn apart by a dog pack."

"Maybe." She hadn't drowned, and Ringan knew it; he was remembering what Peter Cawling had seen, the girl running straight for the bomb cavity. Whatever had happened to Margaret MacLaine, newly delivered of a baby boy, it had not happened in the river. But there was no point in harrowing Tamsin with it. After all, Margaret and Bendone had been *his* ancestors, not hers. Pietro Bendone had told Ringan to live on, and no one else. "We'll probably never know for sure. And just for a change? I'm happy to not know."

# Epilogue: January 1948

"Did you hear something?"

Mick Caslow, twenty-four years old and the senior member of the Royal Engineers Bomb Disposal Unit's Company 33, had been digging steadily and carefully. He had good reason to take care; a few feet away, lit by portable lamps, was the ominous outline of a fifty-kilogram bomb, dropped years earlier by the Luftwaffe.

The disposal effort, despite darkness and the thick unbreathable smog that characterised London winters, had gone quickly and efficiently. They'd got a support scaffold set up, and begun steaming out the explosive. The timer and fuse would follow. They'd created a protective enclosure, using heavy canvas sheets.

For now, the pit in which the bomb sat needed to be wider, and deeper. Mick Caslow, in charge of the operation until the commanding officer could get across London to the Isle of Dogs, was digging.

"Heard what?" He straightened up and wiped a filthy hand across his brow. Jimmy Walsh, the newest member of Company 33, had been wielding his own spade. He'd set it aside, and was resting his hand on one of the larger stones they'd dug out. Caslow himself had sworn under his breath a few times, coming across one of those larger blocks. There were quite a few of them: pale and worn, with an indefinable air of antiquity to them, they seemed to be a remnant of some long-ago construction project. They were heavy, and too cumbersome to move easily, and they were very much in the way at the moment. "What do you mean?"

"I thought—I don't know. A girl's voice." There was a puzzled look on Jimmy's face, a far-away look, as if he was straining towards something only he could hear. "Crying, yelling, something like that. You didn't hear it?"

"All I hear is us, mate. Let's get back to it—this pit needs to be wider and deeper, and it needs to be both damned quick, too. Look lively, Jimmy—I don't want the major tearing a strip off me for not getting on with it. What, another of those stones? Blimey, I hate these big ones. Not going to mess about with moving them out. Just pile them to one side."

They kept digging. A third member of the squad, his job of erecting a safe perimeter done, joined them, throwing the piles of clay-laced earth out of the pit. Eight feet, nine, the cavity grew deeper. The diggers kept one eye on the two experts, steadily steaming out explosive; no one was happy being in this close proximity, but there was no way around it. This was their job; and their pride, and duty, were in getting it done.

The pile of those pale squared-off stones they'd kept hitting had become a good-sized pyramid when Major Windle and Peter Cawling arrived with the news that the Millwall police were nowhere in sight, and that no diversion of the local traffic away from the bomb site had been established. Mick and his two mates, leaving the experts behind, went up the ladders to meet them. Mick shooed the others up first, stopping for a moment to stare at the stones heaped beside the foot of the ladder farthest from the bomb. He was aware of a momentary unease, a disturbance under his ribs he couldn't identify.

*Help me someone help me Godamercy the dogs no don't leave me please*
"Mick?"

He jumped. Major Windle was calling him from up above, and he sounded very cross. . . .

*Merciful Mother, I commend my soul to thee, give me sanctuary, sanctuary, take me in, I prithee hold me not out of doors to such a death, shelter, sanctuary*

Mick Caslow shook his head, a short sharp jerk, the motion of a man trying to clear water or dust from his ears. He had a job to do. His commanding officer required his presence. Whatever he was hearing, he couldn't stay to listen. His legs and arms felt like jelly bags, flabby, useless.

He got both hands on the ladder, and forced himself up and out. As he crested the rim and got himself clear of the bomb cavity, he looked back down, over his shoulder. The stones sat there, lighter than the newer stuff they'd dug out, at the ladder's base.

Less than two minutes later, a large lorry came rumbling by, swaying in the darkness. All hell broke loose around them, the experts shouting to take cover, everyone out of the pit, the bomb was live and the fuse timer ticking. Mick, along with Peter Cawling and the rest of the company, ran for the perimeter. He saw Major Windle shooing, counting, checking that everyone was safe. . . .

Darkness, a swirl of soot and filthy air, parting for just a moment like a look into the other side of hell. There was a girl there, running, stumbling, heading straight for the bomb enclosure. And Major Windle, what was he doing, what in hell was the girl doing?, the major was chasing her, oh, no . . .

*sanctuary, take me in, I prithee hold me not out of doors to such a death*

There were dogs barking, snarling, the sharp excited sound of a pack in full cry. Mick Caslow, without even realising it, had both hands on Peter Cawling, keeping him safe, even as the timer ticked down and the fuse ignited and the major, the girl, the barking dogs that no one could see, became a volcanic eruption of dust, a dust lightened with streaks of powder that was all that remained of that pile of pale ancient stones.